Table of Co

Dedication

To the woman who was " Always There. "

This book is dedicated to my mother, my best friend, and my role model, Geraldine Ann (DiNapoli) Albright. You were my inspiration to make this dream a reality. Writing this novel brought you back to me, keeping you even closer to my heart. You will always remain with me. No matter how much time, distance, and "lifetimes" we're apart, you will forever be a part of me, the best part of me.

Chapter 1

Here

"Nana, Nana! We're getting a new one!"

"Adam honey, calm down. They already told us," Virginia, my sister, responded, ruffling his already messy hair.

"Do ya know who it's gonna be, Nana?"

Poor Adam. They never tell us who it's going to be. "Adam dear, all we ever hear is it's someone we know," my sister, Virginia said, stroking his hair. "It hasn't been anyone we've known in seven years." Yes, seven. Seven long years, I thought.

"I hope it's somebody my age," Adam shrieked with hope and innocence. "Seems like it's never anyone my age," he added, momentarily disappointed. He was such an eager, fun-loving little guy. Watching him, I felt badly for all that he missed, all that he never experienced.

Quickly forgetting his disappointment, "I'm gonna go wait," he said, regaining his enthusiasm. Watching Adam walk away, I still longed for his wonder and excitement. Oh, to be that naïve and hopeful.

"Virginia, are ya ever going to tell the boy to stop hoping for people we know and especially to stop hoping for people his own age? It's just wrong." Virgie's husband always picked on her, but she always gave it right back to him.

"Raymond, are you ever gonna stop asking me that? Gin!" She threw her cards down triumphantly.

"Gin? You hate cards. You hate games. How d'ya always win?" He whined, throwing his cards in a haphazard pile on the table.

"Ray dear, you never pay attention to what you're doing. You're insanely easy to beat—even if I don't like what I'm playing." She shot back at him, scolding him like a child, despite the many years they've been together as a happy, loving, and bickering couple.

"Would you two stop arguing?" I yelled, feeling the tension of the day's upcoming events already wearing on me. "I get so sick of you two bickering every day! I'm not sticking around to lose every hand of Gin either." I complained as I stalked away.

My sister Virginia and her husband, Raymond, constantly fought over how to raise their grandson, Adam. If you asked me, (which nobody ever did) they did the best they could, considering the circumstances. Children here weren't necessarily getting raised anyway. They just are.

I always get a little anxious when I find out someone new is coming. Adam was right. We hadn't had anyone new around here in a while. Well, someone that we all knew. For a while, it seemed like everyone we knew started showing up. I always have mixed feelings when deciding if I want someone new here or not. Of course, I would love the gossip and details that a new person brought with them, news we all wanted to hear and know. I just didn't know if I could handle it if it were someone that I really wasn't ready to have here. There were days that I prayed to not know anyone. Just keep them there, where they really belong. For instance, I adore my sister, Lila, but she needs to stay right where she is. Unfortunately, I do in fact believe she'll be here soon enough. Lila is quite the jealous type; she's probably so sick with envy that we're all here together without her. She hates being out of the loop.

I remember a time when we were kids and my sisters, Rosemary and Anna, got into a crazy fight over something insignificant, probably one of them wore another's sweater. I don't remember the details. It was a long time ago, so long ago, a lifetime ago. Anna, my oldest and most feisty sister, actually threw a paring knife at my sister Rosemary's back. It stuck in her back, and they had to rush her to the hospital to get it removed.

Being the youngest of the family, I just cried, because I didn't want my sisters fighting. There's a fifteen-year age gap between my oldest sister, Anna, and me. Lila was not home to witness the "knifing" battle, but she did request a reenactment when she got home. Rosemary, with stitches in her back, was so mad that she didn't talk to any of us for days. Lila sulked and didn't speak to us for even longer, because she'd missed out on it. Like I said, she's the jealous one of the bunch.

It's probably important to know that I have five sisters: Anna, Virginia, Patricia, Rosemary, and Lila. We've always been very close. Honestly, people have often said that if one of us gets a cut, then all of us bleed. Being so close also means that we do a lot of fighting—more fighting than most families. My sisters and I are very old school Italian. We love our manicotti, our deck of cards, and spending all day together making the perfect sauce, which usually ends in a battle over whose sauce tastes the best. (Mine's irrefutably the best.) And we especially love our profanity. If an evening together doesn't end in some argument, complete with tears, brutal profanity, and a threat of casting the Malocchio (Maloik/evil eye) on someone, then we don't really consider it a good evening. We are so old school Italian that there have even been rumors about my uncles having mafia connections, but we've all learned and perfected the standard "I ya gotta no idea what you're fucking talking about" response with our most stereotypical Italian accent. Oddly enough, that quickly silences the accuser.

My husband, Carl, he loved my uncles, but he always steered pretty clear of them. I never knew if it was his fear of them or his disgust of cigar smoke that used to keep him away, but it was and still is something. They do talk and laugh with one another, but Carl is visibly uncomfortable in their presence. Even here where they can't do anything to him, he gets unnerved. I married a lover, not a fighter, which has always pleased me.

"Aunt Betheny, Aunt Betheny, the new person will be here within the next few hours. Aren't ya excited, huh?" Adam came running toward me with his face beaming with excitement. I'm still so baffled by how people can run so fast without panting and keeling over. It's amazing to watch. Maybe since it was so easy here that I'd actually consider taking up running. Consider.

"Adam, go tell your other aunts, your nana, and grandpa that they'd better get ready for our new arrival." Watching Adam walk away, I wondered if any of us were doing the right thing not telling him the truth. But they could be right. To an eight-year-old, did the truth really matter?

There

"Aunt Lila, hold on. Please be strong." As I sat and held her hand, I couldn't imagine that this was happening to us again. "How can we just let her go?" I asked my brother.

"Shelby Lynn," my sister, Darby, started, "You've got to understand she's been suffering for a long time." My sister could barely get the words out.

Was I supposed to believe that we should truly just sit back and let those doctors who really had no clue what they're talking about convince us that there was no hope? If my Aunt Lila died, then I would have nobody left. That was it. There was nobody else in this world that tied me to my mother and father. Granted, I'd have my brother and sister, but I needed, I wanted, someone who could tell me, tell us, about our backgrounds, our past, our histories. Was I being selfish by just wanting someone—anyone?

"Darby, you need to tell her that it's okay to let go, and we're all going to be okay," my brother said to my sister. "She worries about you the most; tell her that you and Becca are going to be fine." My brother was a smart guy, but was he serious?

Were any of us going to be fine without her? I thought that Darby and her daughter, Becca, needed Aunt Lila just as much or even more than my brother and I did, more than anyone did. I don't think that my sister will be okay. How could my sister say goodbye to my Aunt Lila when they've always had the closest bond? I used to wonder if they were even closer than a mother and daughter. Their bond had always been strong even before our parents died. I envied their relationship. Now, my sister was supposed to look at her and tell my aunt that it was okay to die. It wasn't. It's never okay. Why do people ever think that? Maybe if they didn't tell my mother that it was okay to die, then she'd still be here too. Why do we have to look at our loved ones and tell them that it's time to let go? We never really want to let them go. What we want is a freaking miracle to swoop in and save the day, but instead we look them in the eyes and say, "It's fine, I'm done with you now." I know, I'd feel hurt and betrayed if the people I loved the most in life looked at me and said, "Alright, go ahead and die now."

My brother took me by the arms and forced me to look at my aunt. "Shelb, you're being childish and selfish. Her pain and suffering has gone on long enough," he said, shoving me toward the cold, hospital bed. "For Christ's sake, nearly every time she moves, she breaks a bone," he emphasized. "The cancer is destroying every bone in her body."

Aunt Lila started with breast cancer years ago, and we'd thought it was gone. Cancer's never gone. Damn shattered hope! Anyway, it came back and metastasized to the bone. My brother, Vaughn, continued, "Her breathing is labored and shallow. Look at her eyes, they've lost their shine. Shelby, look, they're becoming cloudy and dark. Death is setting in."

I knew he was right. Death was setting in. I'd seen this before. Darkness clouds the eyes. Soon, all her eyes would see is blackness, the blackness of death as life leaves them forever.

"No, I can't do this. I can't be here. I have to go," I started to walk away, crying.

6

My brother grabbed my arm, pulled me close to him again, and said, "No way Shelby, this time, you aren't leaving. You're gonna stand here with us until the end, no regrets," he said hugging me. Then he whispered, "I won't let you do that to yourself again."

Years ago, when my mother died; her suffering was unbearable—for me. I couldn't stand to witness her agonizing pain. I hated to look at the ghost of a woman who used to be my mother—the most beautiful, lively, and vibrant person I'd ever known—wither away in front of me. When it was evident that she was minutes, maybe hours from death, I left her room, secluding myself in my bedroom, away from the abhorrent picture being painted in my mom's bedroom. The hospital bed, the oxygen machine, and countless vials of medicines and medical paraphernalia was turning her bedroom, the place where I spent many of my "afraid of the dark nights," into my own personal Hell on earth. Alone in my room, I hid from the realities and evils that lurked on the other side of the wall. It was a sanctuary from heartbreaking torture, until the doorknob turned, and I was greeted with the pained, crying faces of Vaughn and Darby.

My mother died while I was in my bedroom. She looked at Vaughn, and Darby, and the faces of her five sisters. She smiled, aware that she was with those who loved her, and took one final gasp of breath. Vaughn knew that I regretted not being a face she could focus on and mentally say "goodbye" to, but I was twenty years old. Being so young, so immature and so supremely selfish, it was too hard for me to face.

So now, my sister, brother, and I stood with my aunt, telling her stories and saying "goodbye" to our last living aunt. All of my aunts died the same way, the same way that our mom died, with an incurable cancer taking them away slowly, painfully, and certainly, leaving us to pick up the crumbled pieces of life that only death left lying around.

Watching five aunts and a mother die from cancer seemed like cruel and inhumane punishment, which made me often wonder what I did to deserve such an unjust sentence. I guess that I'd call my father the lucky one. His death was quick and painless, in the comforts of his old, tattered La-Z boy. If we get to choose, then I am picking the grim-reaping, fast-acting heart attack, instead of the cruel, calculating cancer. Although, something tells me that we don't get to choose. Death chooses us.

I know it seems crazy that I've seen, experienced so much death. I often feel like an expert on the matter. Both of my parents died before I turned 21-years-old. I was 10 when my father's heart stopped, 20 when my mom lost her battle to cancer. Battle? It never really seemed like she stood a chance of winning that war. Then, four of my aunts died after that, taking turns, prolonging their lives with agony and despair. The family death total before today: 1 mom, 1 dad, and 4 aunts, which is way too much death for a twenty-nine-year-old woman to endure within a 20-year span, if you asked me. (Nobody ever asked me.) And now, it looked like my aunt, my beloved Aunt Lila was going to join her sisters, once again proving that cancer was always the victor. Cancer was a son of a bitch winner, making all of us losers another horrific time around.

My aunt's eyes began to fill with tears. I watched the tears flow out of the corners of her eyes and down the sides of her face, into her hair. I'd seen those tears and that tearing path before, ten years earlier on my mom's face, hours before she died. Those tears trailing down my mother's face always haunted me. I'd spent the last decade wondering what she'd been thinking about to cause those tears to ooze out of her eyes. What were her final thoughts as she watched, but couldn't respond to the people already mourning her death when she was still alive?

Looking at my aunt, I stroked her coarse, gray, matted hair. I felt badly for her; she hated to be seen without a hair cut and style. (She always claimed to need a trip to the beauty shop.) She opened her eyes wide, looked directly at me, and mumbled something that I thought was "I love you."

I leaned down, kissed her tear-stained cheek, and said, "I love you too."

She shook her head ever so slightly and said, "Not love, forgive, I forgive you," falling soundly asleep—a sleep that she never woke from.

Chapter 2

Here

My husband, my sisters, and I joined hands nervously awaiting our new arrival. I said a silent little prayer that it was not Lila or any of my three kids. Carl, my husband, looked over at me with a knowing nod, probably saying the same little prayer. I always find it rather odd that we still pray when we know how it really does work here. I knew that my sisters and I were all thinking the same thoughts, thoughts that would deem us selfish and uncaring. We would never say it aloud, but we would rather our new visitor be hers or hers or his, not ours. On cue, the brightness increased, the hues became vivid and magnificent—all colors were magnified and brilliant and in a split second, my sister, Lila, was standing before me.

My sisters gasped as they saw their final remaining sister standing before them. Lila was overtly confused and out of sorts. She stood gaping at us, unsure of how to react to this unknown, unexpected reunion.

Ten years ago, my arrival was very similar. I couldn't believe that I was standing before my husband; I'd dreamed of seeing him again, holding him again, and inhaling his familiar and calming scent. Suddenly, there he was, arms open and welcoming. Looking at him, I saw the man I loved; the decade apart from him vanished.

It was as if it were yesterday that he was returning from work, smelling of paint and turpentine. Now, he was beaming with love and adoration. I felt giddy, like a new bride approaching her welcoming and unsure groom. I realized that this was our anniversary day. We were reunited on the day that we were united in matrimony. My husband. My anniversary. My love. My dream.

Immediately, I allowed him to envelope me, feeling the familiar protection of the man who could erase my worries with a slight touch of my arm. My worries faded, but only for a few moments, only until reality set in. This man, the love of my life, could not be holding me, should not be holding me—unless...

I panicked and couldn't get my bearings. The gravity of the situation overwhelmed me. I had young children; we had young children. Okay, excuse the hyperbole, twenty years of age did not deem "young children," but to me, they were still my babies. My oldest, Darby, was only twenty-seven, and she'd selflessly put her entire life on hold to be there to help ease my pain as my caregiver. Day and night, she was there to monitor my medicine, take care of my pain, and listen to my worries and concerns.

My son, Vaughn, only twenty-six at the time, was carrying the financial burden of the entire family; my debt and my girls' debt had become his crosses to bear. I'd left him with so much responsibility, too much responsibility for such a young, single man. Being so attractive, ambitious, and intelligent, he should've been out meeting women, having fun, and making memories. Instead, he was dealing with the deed on the house, life insurance policies, talking to doctors about second opinions, and handling all the household bills and financial responsibilities.

My baby girl, my Shelby Lynn, was in college, callow and new to adulthood. How could Carl and I leave them all alone to fend for themselves when they were mere babies? Understanding, Carl assured me that eventually I would find peace, and my parental worries would soon fade, leaving me with only serene and peaceful memories, memories that would fill me with tranquility and pride. I couldn't imagine ever feeling comfortable being away from my children. (Honestly, I'm still not comfortable being away from them.) Back then on that day, I calmed slightly as my husband's arms soothed me, and as I held on to the thought that my children, my not-so-babies, had five aunts to cling to in their time of terrible loneliness. Their aunts would protect them, be there for them, and hold them when they were too frightened to face the world alone. But I was wrong. One by one, cancer knocked on each of their doors too. Cancer didn't care if they allowed him in; he was coming in with or without a formal invite.

Lila looked at us and began weeping as her body crumbled. My sisters went to her, hugging her, trying to stop her fear and sadness. I couldn't go to her. I could not hold her. I couldn't be the support she needed. She allowed her sisters to be the strength she needed to help her accept the truth of her fate.

Tugging at my leg, young Adam looked up at me and said, "Don't worry Aunt Beth, I'm angry too. I was hoping for someone better and for someone my age," disappointedly slumping off to find something else to do. Adam couldn't have realized how truly disappointed I was. My sister, Lila, made a promise to me and clearly she didn't fulfill it. Broken promises were the equivalent to shattered hopes, both left an empty void of despair.

There

"Does anyone care what I think?" I screamed as I slammed my aunt's bedroom door. I couldn't figure out how people could even think about arguing over the clothes a person wore to be buried in. Who cared? The person was dead. DEAD. It wasn't like my Aunt Lila was going to wake up, look at her outfit and say, "Oh no, not this. This'll certainly not be appropriate for eternity under the soil, fraternizing with the worms, maggots, and potato bugs." It was absurd to even care, let alone fight over it.

My sister, Darby, was acting like Aunt Lila was going to her prom and must be the Belle of the Ball. I knew I sounded harsh and cold, but why do families always break out into a World War when making funeral arrangements? Why does death force families to battle one another when they should really be clinging to one another for love and support? Arguing about flowers, obituaries, clothing for the dead, and where the after-burial luncheon was going to be just baffled me.

Death should teach people that life is entirely too short to "sweat the small stuff," but death makes people "sweat it" even more. Arguing over the clothing of a corpse seemed awfully trite and meaningless if you asked me. However, nobody ever asked me. It didn't matter how old I was, how many college degrees I earned, or how much my yearly income grossed, I'd forever be the baby of the family and with that title, I relinquished all rights to decision-making and opinion-giving. The baby of the family always remained the "baby," and all other family members continually treated them as such. My mom was the "baby," the youngest out of six girls. My aunts were devastated when they realized that they couldn't protect her and save her from her terminal diagnosis. Her sisters sat with her and took care of her in her final months, proving that the bond, the love between sisters, was unbreakable and strong.

My mom was adamant about what she wanted to be buried in. She figured that since she was going to be asleep that she should be in a nice, frilly, pink nightgown. By God, she was too. I thought that Aunt Lila should also wear a nightgown. Hell, I hadn't seen her in anything other than a nightgown in over a year, so I was sure that's what she'd want to wear. (Nobody asked me though.) I couldn't believe that we didn't talk to her about this before; we obviously knew this day was looming.

My sister wanted to put my Aunt Lila in a pink business suit that she'd bought for her at a local department store. My aunt never wore a suit in her entire life, for all I knew. She'd been a waitress for most of her working life. A blush pink business suit with white piping just seemed freak-diculous to be buried in. The person was in the ground; why wear a suit for that?

My mother planned her entire funeral and all of the arrangements that went along with the Big Day. Actually, at times, you'd have thought that she was planning her wedding the way she talked about flowers, colors, and nightgowns. I still get a sick feeling in my stomach when I see or smell roses, yellow roses specifically. Aunt Lila, on the other hand, just kept telling us, and anyone else who'd listen, that she was going to be fine. She never accepted her cancer, swearing unconvincingly that her arthritis was just acting up, not that bone cancer was slowly deteriorating her entire body, like aggressive little termites eating away at the bone structure that made her who she was.

My mom, on the other hand, probably wanted to help us, her three kids, by making sure that her children did not have too much preparation for her funeral, considering that we'd have to figure out how to live the rest of our entire lives without parents.

Chapter 3
Here

Everyone began to settle in for what we normally referred to as the "horror-telling." Once our "newly arriveds" accepted that they were actually the newly departed, they began to tell the woes of their final days and the events that led up to their final gasp of earthly air. Lila needed a few minutes to just look at us, her five sisters. Lila hadn't see Patricia in seven years; she hadn't seen me in ten years. As a newly arrived, it was inexplicable as to how we all looked to them. Upon that final gasp of earthly air, our minds and souls were taken back to the time when we were the happiest, felt the most beautiful, and were the most optimistic and carefree. Then, we get to stay appearing that beautiful, that young, and that joyous for the rest of eternity. Many people are adorned in their wedding gowns. Others are in their hospital gowns from the day they gave birth to a child. The hospital gowns do not lack modesty and the wedding gowns are said to be unimaginably comfortable and cozy. Nobody here wants to fight with a girdle, garter belt, or airy backsides forever. Forever.

Oftentimes, the attire one appears in can start arguments among couples or families and friends. My oldest sister, Anna, appeared in the Coco Chanel dress that my brother-in-law proposed to her in. She couldn't understand why when Tom arrived, he was wearing a gray sweatshirt and sweat pants. For a long time, he wouldn't tell her why he was wearing such an outfit, considering it did nothing to compliment her yellow and white designer summer dress. Anna was the fashionista of all my sisters and loved to wear the latest styles. Since I was just a kid, being 15 years younger than she, she was my idol. I wanted to be just like her, and test the rules, just like her.

Much later, Anna realized that her husband, the man whom she'd been married to for over 30 years was the happiest, the most optimistic, and felt the youngest when Ohio State beat Michigan in overtime. Apparently, Anna'd been feeling ill that day, still recovering from a botched appendectomy. Tom was in the den watching the football game with his fifteen-year-old and ten-year-old sons. Once Ohio State clinched the win, he couldn't have felt more euphoria being there with his two boys and celebrating all together, as men. He admitted that he'd even allowed them to celebrate with a beer, a typical masculine male-bonding moment. We don't have many terrible arguments here since we've gone through the experience and ultimately have evolved, but Tom and Anna really fought that one out. I'm not saying that arguments don't happen, because they do. They're just rare.

Upon my arrival, seeing Carl, in his wedding day tuxedo brought back a flood of memories and love. He wasn't upset or angry about my attire, however, just confused. Looking at me, he immediately realized that there had to be a story behind my beyond-ordinary outfit. My casual black slacks and nondescript green blouse didn't reveal a setting or explanation for the moment of my greatest joy.

I still feel guilty wearing this particular outfit, because it reveals to everyone that my happiest day was a day years after my husband died. I feel like I should occasionally get to wear my wedding gown, the hospital gown that I gave birth in, or even the outfit that I was wearing when I discovered that my cancer was in remission, shortest "remission" on record. I don't want people to think that I don't love my husband and three children.

However, I'm eternally secured to black pants and a green shirt. Believe me, the day in question was the happiest day of my life, which is not to say that I didn't feel utter joy, contentment, and wonder on my wedding day or on the days that my three children were born. I did; I truly did. Those days were the greatest days of my life up until the most significant day in my life occurred. However, the day that I wore the black pants and green shirt, I knew that I'd succeeded. I wasn't a failure, which was something that I continually questioned at the time. I questioned if I'd taught my children the right lessons in life: how to love, how to forgive, and how to be strong in times of struggle and pain. To me, those were the lessons that all parents must teach their children, the only lessons really worth learning.

At first, I didn't even remember why I was wearing this particular outfit. I looked around and saw motley of clothing choices. Carl explained why people were wearing their particular outfits, explaining the bliss that coupled the outfit. It even took me a considerable amount of time to figure out where and when I had worn such a bland outfit, especially since it was supposed to be such a monumental occasion. Then all at once, the feelings and emotions flooded through me, and my thoughts were transported back to that stadium, to the place that taught me that I wasn't a failure. My happiness and pride overtook me, and I remembered every last detail of the day that I wore this particularly hideous outfit.

If I could go back to that glorious day, then I would absolutely change my choice of tired, old, boring clothing, but I wouldn't, absolutely would not, change one detail about that day. I would not change the torrential downpour. I wouldn't change the fact that there were four of us in our family, in a jam-packed audience with only one teeny, tiny umbrella. I wouldn't change the pride I felt in my heart as I watched my son receive his degree from The Ohio State University. I looked at him as my success. When a son grows up without a father, it's almost expected that the son will not amount to anything and that he will become unruly and wayward. I needed to negate the theories and defy the statistics. I wanted my son to be a success in all of his endeavors. I needed to know that I wasn't a failure as a mother, and as a father too. I had two roles to play, and I didn't take either one of them lightly.

When my husband saw my clothes, his quizzical expression was enough to make me immediately apologize for not being in a more stereotypical feminine choice, but once I revealed to him what my slacks and blouse represented, I think that Carl wanted to wear the outfit himself. He wanted to hear every detail of the day. He even laughed gutturally when he heard that Lila's infamous bouffant was pulverized by the downpour. I nearly relive those events with Carl daily, just so he can feel my pride and my joy, and know that the years he had with his son made an impact and did not leave him struggling with unanswered questions and guidance.

There

I have a place that I like to go to when I need to think or decompress, as I often put it. Growing up, I spent many days at the "mudhole" swimming with my friends and family. The "mudhole" was a man-made lake in my neighborhood. Each family was required to pay a seasonal membership of $50.00 to swim there. As a child, having a place to swim every day was like hitting the lottery. In retrospect, the "mudhole" was only one step up from being a giant mud puddle with a dock. However, my childhood was in that the lake, on that dock, on the swings and within the confines of that old barbed-wire fence. As is most things from my childhood, the neighborhood is now rundown and quite shabby. The "mudhole" is still in existence, but grass is beginning to grow up over where the water once was. The swings are missing their seats; the roof's nearly torn off of the old picnic pavilion. Even the giant hill that was a struggle to walk up and a joy to sled ride down now seems old, worn out, and not as ominous as it once was. Whenever I needed time to reflect, time to rest, time to think, or just time to be, I found myself shimmying under the still-broken fence off to the south corner of the park. This hole under the fence was the "in" for those neighbors who didn't pay their summer dues. Basically, the summer pass was based on a not-so-honorary honor system.

I found myself sitting on a decrepit picnic table, trying to find the perfect words, the words that would say it all. Typically, my brother, the family success and eloquence, was chosen to deliver the eulogies at my family members' funeral services. Lucky him. My brother did the eulogy for three of my aunts and was expected to do my Aunt Lila's as well. Vaughn, however, didn't do my Aunt Virginia's. Her granddaughter, Aisley, who was only 7-years-old at the time, spoke at her grandmother's funeral. Other than hers, Vaughn delivered all the other eulogies, with eloquence, emotion, and inspiration. My brother was quite the orator.

Since my Aunt Lila did not have children of her own or a husband, Vaughn wasn't asked to speak at her funeral; he just pretty much appointed himself as the eulogist. I found this rather insulting and perplexing. Why wouldn't he assume that I'd want to speak? I was a high school English teacher. I taught speech and debate and directed the drama production. A speaker I was. Surely, I could find the right words and the right delivery for a heartfelt and meaningful eulogy.

When my brother stated that he would deliver the eulogy, I explained that I wanted to speak on behalf of my aunt, honoring her life. My sister and brother both protested. Apparently, we all felt that our words, our feelings, and our thoughts should be heard. Now, despite what the priest may have said, we were all three going to eulogize our last aunt, which was what actually brought me to my childhood spot in the first place. I was looking for the words, the emotions, and the perfect delivery for the recitation of my heart. Unfortunately, the words that I was searching for, the feelings that I had hidden so deep within myself were not sequestered somewhere at the "mudhole."

"I knew you'd be here." The voice stopped all my thoughts, sending shivers up my spine.

Oh crap! I didn't want to see him. I did not want to have to deal with this, not now, not ever actually. I knew that he'd show up. Death brings people out of the woodwork. People used death as a free pass to go anywhere and do anything they wanted. I never understood that. When my mom died, people called me "to talk" and offer their sympathy, even if the previous conversation I'd had with them was volatile and horrendous. Somehow, death equaled a free pass back into people's lives.

"Hi Chance," I said, dropping my head and my eyes from his gaze. As he reached out to hug me, I shied away. I noticed the small grimace on his face and ignored the pangs in my heart. "How're ya doing? How's Mallory?" I asked, wondering about his daughter.

"I'm fine," he said, giving me my space. "She's fine. She misses you. How're you doing?" He asked, dropping his sympathetic eyes.

"I'm good. I'm just wrapping up here and heading back to my brother's house." I started walking toward the hill.

"Here, let me help," he proffered. As he took my laptop satchel from me, he pulled the handle, and I fell into him. He embraced me, and told me how sorry he was. Naturally, he told me that I if I needed anything that I knew where to find him. My heart wrenched. I wanted to wrap my arms around him and hold on to him forever, but I didn't, because I couldn't. It was always better to keep the past in the past.

"Chance, you didn't have to come here," I said, letting him off the hook. "You and I, we're okay. We don't have to follow all these etiquette protocols. I know you care." I didn't want or need Chance's pity. We had our chance a long time ago. (I loved using his name "punfully." The English teacher in me always got a good giggle out of it.) Chance and I, we didn't work out. He's a great guy—just not the guy for me. Our relationship was over; he needed to understand that and move on.

"I more than care, Shelby Lynn. Even though you and I aren't together--"

"And haven't been for nearly a year," I piped in too quickly and way too rudely. I always did that to him—had always done that to him. I'm an interrupter. It used to drive Chance bonkers that he was never able to finish his statements. I'd cut him off in midsentence repeatedly. Actually, I do it to everyone. It's a flaw. I bet that he's happy that all of this thoughts and words are finally meeting their endpoints.

"I know that, but that does not mean that I don't worry about you, care about you, but more importantly Shelby Lynn, I loved Aunt Lila."

"Oh Bullshit! She drove you crazy, and you know it," I said, smiling as I remembered how he used to love to get her riled up, boiling her old school Italian-tempered blood.

"Of course she did! That's what I loved about her," he said. I noticed a faraway look of pain on his face. "I loved to get her going, get her talking, and just sit back and relish in her humor and the stories she told." He stopped, stopping me at the same time. He turned to me, put a hand on my arm and said, "It's nuts, every time I think of the parties we had or the holidays we shared, I always think about how no matter what, she was always there."

That was it. I'd sat at the mudhole for almost two hours and couldn't get it right. I could not find the right words. Chance was with me for less than five minutes and already found the words, the two perfect words: Always There.

Chapter 4

Here

I heard Lila telling everyone about her final days, describing the fear and loneliness she felt going through those horrifying nights without someone to comfort her, someone to hold her, and someone to distract her from the agony. I remembered those nights, and I was glad to conquer them alone. I never wanted my kids to see the torture their mother endured each and every night. Darby would get glimpses of my agony, but I masked it as much as possible. Parents never want their children to see them in pain, but more importantly, it's hard as a mother to accept that you're the reason for their agony. We spend our lives trying to protect them from being hurt, but in the end, I was the reason that my children we so full of hurt.

Lila just babbled on and on about how she was there for us and nobody was there for her. Did she really believe that we owed her anything? She was the one who got to experience life and happiness with all of our children—our children! How could she even believe that she was entitled to any form of complaint or our sympathy? She had what we all wanted. She was the lucky one. Lila had time, time that was stolen from each of us.

"...and then Vaughn, oh boy, he handled everything for me--"

That was it. I'd heard way more than I'd already wanted to hear. Now, she was specifically bringing up my children, my son. No way. "How dare you?" I screamed, shutting her up, charging toward her.

"Beth, Oh Betheny!" Lila rose from her chair. I froze. I did not want her talking to me, coming near me, or even looking at me. "Oh Bethie Boo, I have so much to tell--."

"No! You have nothing to say to me; I don't want to hear it... No!" I was beginning to tremble, feeling emotions that I didn't know were possible here." Carl looped his arm through the crook of my arm and eased me away from her. He could always extinguish a situation and calm anyone down. He was a pacifist and so tranquil—even at the most chaotic times.

As we walked away, Carl cleared his throat and stumbled with the words, "Uh...honey, I love you and support you, but I really want to know--"

"No Carl! I cannot bear to hear it. I wanted her with them. They've nobody now," I cried, trembling with fear. "They're still not old enough to be all alone without someone to guide them." I pleaded with him, lamenting at our loss and the abandonment that they must feel.

"I know that you still see them as your babies, but you've gotta realize that it's been 10 years since you've seen them. They've grown; they've changed," he said, holding me, stroking my hair. "They're not your little babies anymore. Betheny, they were adults when you left them."

What? Was he kidding right now? I pushed myself back from him, glaring at his face. "What did you just say to me?" I bellowed. Closing in on him, as I pointed back at myself for emphasis, I said,

"Me? Me? I left them? I'm sorry, but where are you right now?" I raged.

Stuttering and realizing he'd chosen the wrong words, he backpedaled and said, "No Beth, I didn't mean--"

"No! How dare you!" I exclaimed. Carl reached for me, trying to pull me back to him, to comfort my rage. I pushed him off of me, screaming, "You left...you left first. You left when they were just kids." I was done. I couldn't listen to another bit of this. Not from Lila. Not from Carl. Not from anyone.

There

When my brother finished speaking, there wasn't a dry eye in the church. My sister attempted her eulogy, and she didn't get farther than, "I cannot believe--" before she broke down and her friend had to nearly carry her back to her seat. My sister's a crier and a hugger. I've always thought that she should be a professional funeral goer. She'd fit right in with all that wailing, sobbing, and hugging. At the very least, she should own her own funeral home. With the amount of tears she'd shed in the last few days, I was shocked that she could even make it to the podium without keeling over from dehydration. Darby's an emotional person. She has more feelings and emotion in her little pinky than a room full of new mothers suffering from post-partum. My sister feels. Me? Not so much. And what I did feel, I locked it up, not sharing any of it with another living soul. It was better that way.

When Darby was in high school, she was voted "Most Caring," which my mom deemed "Nosiest." I understand that there is a fine line between caring and being nosy, but I don't think curiosity is what motivates my sister. Sure, if someone's diary were laying about, my sister would find a way to break the lock, read the words, and repair the lock all in time for the owner to return from the refrigerator with a glass of water. But, it's more than that with her. My sister cares. She loves. She feels. Her emotions are fragile and raw and oftentimes explosive, which was why I was so shocked that she was even able to begin a eulogy for someone she was closer to than any of us were.

I realized then that the church was silent. I was still thinking about my brother's eloquent words and my sister's raw pain. I hadn't even noticed how the silence was being muffled by the quiet sobs and sniffles of those around me. My brother put his hand on my shoulder and said, "It's Go Time." He was so bizarre. I chuckled, because it reminded me of my Aunt Virginia's funeral. Man, we've been to a lot of funerals together.

My brother and I were sitting next to my Aunt Lila at a different aunt's funeral. My little cousin had just given a beautiful eulogy (the only one that Vaughn didn't do). The eulogy was extraordinarily special, because my cousin, Aisley was only 7-years-old at the time that she spoke of her memories and her love for her "Nonnie." Aisley'd always been a special little girl, especially since she'd endured the death of her older brother at such a young age. Aisley was only four when her older brother died. Adam was eight at the time. Adam had a rare heart defect; he wasn't expected to live as long has he had. His life was tragic, spending more time in the hospital than out. Adam had 12 heart surgeries in his short eight years of life. He died one sunny afternoon playing "Kick the Can," a game they probably shouldn't have been playing in the backyard with his sister and dad. Aisley watched, screaming for her brother as her father tried to revive him. There was no revival; Adam's life was over. Children should never have to die—ever. A part of Aisley died that day as she watched the paramedics wheel her brother's lifeless body from the very spot he moments before had kicked an old, rusty can.

Aisley's words tore everyone up; the sounds of hearts breaking filled the church. Crying, my brother needed a tissue; Aunt Lila gave him one. After blowing his nose, my brother tried to hand me his soaked, disgusting, used tissue, which I quickly and successfully refused. Needing somewhere to place his used Kleenex, because Vaughn wouldn't be one to pocket his own tissue, my brother placed it in my Aunt Lila's coat pocket without making her aware. We found this funny, yet inappropriate too. Vaughn was satisfied and pleased with himself for being able to dispose of the used tissue discreetly.

But shortly after his deceptive move, the priest spoke, invoking more tears from his listeners, at which time, my aunt took the same used tissue from her pocket, opened it completely, and wiped her eyes and nose. My brother and I witnessed the entire event in sheer shock, repulsion, and hilarity. All we could do was put our heads on the pew in front of us, and laugh until tears soaked our eyes and cheeks. To others, the tear-stained faces and trembling shoulders revealed our agony and sadness for the loss of our aunt and luckily, not for the hysterical and repulsive event my brother caused that we both witnessed. My brother has a tendency to take the saddest of times and turn them into a wonderful dinner party-worthy story.

"Go Shelby Lynn," my sister urged.

I walked up to the podium, the same podium my mother's best friend spoke from when my mom died ten years earlier. I was shocked by how calm and peaceful I felt as I looked at my family and at the closed, flower-laden casket. I wanted to say the words that would truly reveal how special Aunt Lila was to everyone. I lowered the microphone, just a tad from where my brother needed it, smiled my nervous-I-am-about-to-speak-publicly smile, and took a deep breath.

"My brother, sister, and I argued over who was going to talk here today," I said, my voice cracking and betraying me. Clearing my throat for a moment, I continued, "As you all know, my brother has always been our designated speaker, the chosen eulogist, and my sister was extremely close to her godmother, my Aunt Lila." I stopped, looked at them for support. Darby was crying; Vaughn nodded his encouragement. "What some of you may not know is that I have the utmost respect and admiration for my Aunt Lila, and there was a major aspect of her that I aspire to, which is why I really wanted to speak on her behalf today."

I nodded, taking a deep breath, "I know that whether or not you want to admit it, but before Aunt Lila got sick and definitely before she died, when you first thought of Lila DiBellini, many of you would roll your eyes and grumble about some argument you may have had with her recently or even remember a fight in the faraway past." I paused as people nodded their assent and chuckled at their own memories of Aunt Lila. Aunt Lila was a feisty, argumentative one.

"And that is probably true. She was a very strong-willed, opinionated woman, who did not let her voice and feelings go unheard. She was a fighter with every ounce of her being—even right down to her final minutes. But beyond those arguments, those opinions, and those words, Aunt Lila was so much more." My voice cracked; I could barely get out the "so much more." I couldn't stop though; it was important for me to be able to tell these people, our family and friends, how much my aunt meant to me.

"First of all, nobody called her "Lila," not her co-workers, not her friends, no one. She was "Aunt Lila" to so many; she welcomed so many people into her life and considered everyone, even acquaintances as family members to her, which is why everyone called her 'Aunt Lila.' But, she was so much more to my brother, to my sister, and to me." Crying, I wiped my eyes, and tried to compose myself for the next part of the eulogy.

"I'm not sure how many of you remember, but I was still in college at Ohio State when my mother died. She died at the end of April, and Darby, Vaughn and Aunt Lila came to Columbus to see me that very first weekend in May, because they didn't want me to spend Mother's Day alone...probably they didn't want spend it alone either." I looked at Darby and Vaughn, and saw Vaughn grab Darby's hand. I wanted to be with them, feel their strength. Being up at the podium talking about my aunt made me feel more alone than I'd ever felt before.

"That Mother's Day, we went to Damon's and they were passing out flowers to 'all the mothers' in the restaurant. The maître d' gave Aunt Lila a flower and said, 'these are for all the mothers.' Aunt Lila began to cry and said, 'I'm not their mother.' Vaughn immediately gave the flower to Aunt Lila and said, 'Take it, Aunt Lila, you deserve it.' Aunt Lila did deserve that flower; she was there for us, when nobody else was. So naturally, she took the flower and cried."

I knew that day that my aunt was suffering from losing her sister; I hated that she had to be reminded that she never had children too. Her baby sister had died; she wasn't married. And now, some stranger was reminding her that she wasn't a mother. She was already a childless mother. But now, after her baby sister's death, she lost another title. She was no longer someone's "big sister." Losing a title is a painful loss in itself. One day you're a big sister, and the next day, you're not.

Continuing on, I said, "As I look around and see all the people who called her 'aunt,' I realize that Vaughn was right. She deserved that flower. She filled in for us. She was our mother, our parent, and our guardian when there was nobody else to fill the role. When there was no longer a mom, she took the position willingly and proudly. She loved us unconditionally and we loved her the same."

Aunt Lila may not have realized it, but she quickly became a much-needed mother-figure in my life, something I never told her. I hate that we never remember or realize how many kind words, loving words, go unsaid, unuttered. Why don't we shout our feelings from the rooftops, so we don't live with guilt and "what ifs" for the rest of our lives?

Looking at the packed churched and making eye contact with many teary eyes, I said, "I want to ask all of you something right now, because most of us now are saying goodbye to our last aunt, the last of the DiBellinis. I want you to remember your happiest moments. Think about your wedding day. Think about the times when you graduated, gave birth, did something fantastic. Now, I want you to think about those hard times, the times when money was tight, when work was hard, when your marriage ended or when you had to say goodbye to a parent, to a spouse, or even to a child. Most of you, the majority of you, are just like us, just like me, when you think of those highs and you think of those lows, there is probably one common factor in all of the events, those moments were not faced without Aunt Lila. So, the one thing that I can try to emulate and aspire to is that Aunt Lila was always there. Always there."

Always there. Saying the final two words of the eulogy, I was too choked up to get them out a second time. While I tried to un-garble the words, I looked up and around at the people whose emotions I was stirring. I looked away, at the back of the church, and finally said "Always there" to the man who was standing in the back, next to the Holy water, swaying from side to side in his normal, nervous, fidgety fashion. To Chance. Always there.

Chapter 5

Here

"It's not fair. She got to be there. She was always there. Carl, how can you not feel envious?" My husband was making me angry. I didn't want to sit and listen to Lila talk to everyone about how she was the one who got be a part of our children's lives. She didn't even have kids. She wasn't a mother; why did she get to play mother for all of us? We wanted to be the mother for our children—not forfeit the role to her.

"Beth, I love you more than words can explain, but I don't understand this anger and animosity coming from you. Out of all of your sisters, you loved Lila the most," he said, trying to calm me down. "You relied on her the most and were closer to her than anyone. How could you ignore the fact that your closest sister, whom you haven't seen in 10 years is standing right here for you to talk to, to love, and to embrace?"

"I'm not gonna talk to you about this; you obviously don't get it," I said, turning my back on him, again.

"I just said that I don't get--" I stormed away before my husband could say anything more. Lila's arrival was certainly doing a number on my marriage. Hell, I'd said until death do us part; I guess that technically he wasn't even my husband any longer. Right now, that thought just made me feel a lot better, although I knew it shouldn't. I'm just so frustrated and full of anger. I was experiencing feelings that we didn't normally feel here; they almost made me feel more alive.

Honestly, I'm jealous of my sister. I cannot believe that Carl wants me to sit back and listen to her talk about my children, my kids, my nieces, my nephews and even listen to her complain about having to leave them. She doesn't know the half of it. She doesn't know what it was like lying in bed night after night, wondering if I would even wake up the next day, wondering what would happen to my kids. I would lie in the dark, wide-awake, praying that they would survive another death of a parent. I'd pray that they would still be together and rely on one another for strength and support. I worried that my death would tear them apart and destroy the relationships that I worked so hard to foster and create. I was terrified that I hadn't prepared them enough, emotionally and financially for my pending death. I would toss and turn, wondering if I raised them well enough to carry on and grow and mature into strong adults, loving spouses, and caring parents. I struggled and agonized over the thought that all the death and suffering that they had seen would create cold, unloving, and unfeeling people. I would finally fall into a fitful sleep, wondering if it was my fault. . . if I could have done anything to prevent the inevitable. Wondering. . . praying ...hoping...fearing...crying.

There

"I swear to God if one more person hugs me and tells me that they're sorry, I'm gonna lose my freaking mind. I just want people to stop touching me." I grumbled to my brother before I walked out of the luncheon

"Classy, nice Shelb!" Vaughn called after me. Vaughn always knew how to make me feel better. Do funerals bring out the jerk in everyone?

In his defense, I'd been ranting for the past half an hour. I didn't care who heard me either. For Christ's sake, if I wanted to scream, yell, and rage, then damn it, I was going to. At this point, who was going to stop me? It wasn't like I had parents to argue with or someone to tell me what to do anymore. Now that Aunt Lila was dead, there wasn't anyone that I ever had to listen to again. Darby and Vaughn had their own families, who cared what I did or said? I actually remembered being this incorrigible at my mom's funeral too. Maybe funerals didn't bring out the jerk in everyone else, but just brought out the bitch in me. That was probably more likely.

We had calling hours for my mom from like 3:00 to 9:00 p.m., which was entirely too long for any one person to spend at a funeral home. Plus they'd "graciously" let us come at 2:00 p.m., so we could get used to the dead body mom-look-alike before the "guests" arrived to view my mom's lifeless corpse. Good times. (Funerals and all the hoopla that go with them are so morbid.)

Around 6:30 p.m. or so, I was just done, completely fried and numb. To the dismay of my brother and sister, I decided that I was hungry and went across the street to get a value meal from McDonald's. To this day, I find it pretty funny when I think about it. People came up the front steps of the funeral home, preparing themselves to see the grieving orphaned children of the woman who passed away, but what did they find instead? The youngest child snacking on a Quarter Pounder with cheese and drinking a medium Diet Coke to greet them as they entered the condolences line. Their faces were priceless and so relieved that they were not called upon to help lessen my mourning and pain. I didn't need people hugging me and telling me that it was going to be okay. I needed the jackass cashier at McDonald's to listen to me when I said, "No pickles or onions."

I didn't need the sympathy of people I'd never really spoken to or had any idea who they were at my mom's calling hours and funeral, and I certainly didn't need it now at my aunt's. I surely did not need to hear the "Aunt Lila is finally with her sisters now" comments. People lose their senses at funerals and make the dumbest comments.

I could sincerely write a book about how to act at funerals, because it really is quite easy. It's a simple rule: Do whatever the living loved ones are doing. If they are crying and suffering, then cry and suffer with them. If they are trying to be strong, upbeat, and light-hearted, then be strong, upbeat, and light-hearted with them. Consider the grieving loved ones as the cruise directors of the SS Death and follow their lead. Whatever you do, do not try to make them sad if they are happy and happy if they are sad. Just do what they do. Seriously, how hard is that?

People feel so compelled to say and do something. The only thing, and I mean the only thing, appropriate to say is, "I'm so sorry." Since I am an old hat at this, I often throw in a "This just sucks, sucks so bad, I'm so sorry." If I'm really close to the grieving person, then I just lay it all on the line with "Man, this fucking blows." And believe me, death does fucking blow.

At my mom's funeral, I felt like the priest didn't think Vaughn, Darby, and I were sad enough. When he spoke, he evidently wanted us to cry harder, more agonizingly. He actually said, "Look at these three kids, now alone, without any parents. How're they going to feel next week on Mother's Day, or at Thanksgiving and Christmas without their parents? What about their wedding days, who's going to walk them down the aisle, pick out gowns with them...?" And on and on.... Like we weren't already thinking those horrific thoughts, he took it upon his "religious" self to remind us what was looming. Yep, death fucking blows.

People try to be therapists, Buddhists, priests or something helpful, when they really should just leave all of those trite comments like, "She's in a better place" or "She's with the Lord now" in the car before they even think about entering the funeral home. Those asinine comments just make people angry and do nothing to ease the pain. My least favorite has always been, "At least the suffering is over." I always want to respond to people who say that with, "Really? Because my suffering isn't, you fuckhole, so thanks a lot." Also, people should be very careful of, "I know how you feel." People have no idea how others feel, how others grieve, or how they suffer. It's just absurd to think otherwise.

My friend, Violet, her baby was eight days old and that beautiful baby girl died in her arms. Sure, Violet knew that her baby was suffering and that she was probably going to die. She tried to prepare herself, but how does anyone really prepare for a death of a loved one, especially the death of a brand new baby, a baby that she waited nine months for? Mothers should never have to say, "goodbye" to their children. It's almost impossible to fathom the pain that comes with losing a baby, a pain that I'm sure never really lessens.

I think that people always know that someday their parents are going to die. It's almost expected at some point. People keep the thought in the back of their minds that their siblings or spouses may die before them as well. But children, parents can't fathom that pain, that tragedy; it would be the epitome of Hell. Children are people's lifelines. When parents lose a child, that lifeline gets cut off, making it hard for mothers and fathers to continue living, living in a way they once knew. All life, all happiness that they once knew and embraced, ceases to exist. Those parents, the childless parents, have to learn how to live without their lifelines, and we all know it's impossible to live without a lifeline.

Anyway, at Violet's daughter's funeral, someone actually said to her, "at least you're young; you can have more children." What the mother fuck are people thinking? Do they suddenly undergo some emergency lobotomy, making them lose all common sense? Anyone with half a brain should realize that another baby would never take the place of a baby who died. I'm not even a mother, and I get that. If I were Violet, I would have kicked that old bitch right in the crotch and said something crude like, "At least you haven't been using it lately anyway."

I know what people are thinking about me. I have angst, anger, and most definitely could use a world of therapy. Yeah, I was wrong before. Death doesn't bring out the worst in everyone else; it brings out the swearing, whining, angry witch in me. People probably think that I am some cold, unfeeling woman, because I don't want to be touched, cry on their shoulders, and cling to strangers for strength. My sister, she does. She's emotional. She's touchy-feely. She wants to hug, to cry, to tell stories, and cry all over again. They can go hang all over her and keep their pity paws off of me. My brother likes being the strength behind the weak. They're a perfect pair. I've never really known where I fit in. They're the perfect equation. I'm not even a variable in their equation.

"I knew I'd find you here." As I heard his voice, I stiffened and shot back a quick quip.

"That is all you say any more," I sniped at him. "Where else would I be, Captain Obvious? Was I not going to attend the luncheon after my aunt's funeral?" Seriously, I had to get a grip. Chance wasn't a punching bag, and he certainly wasn't my punching bag, any longer.

"Of course, you would. I just meant that I knew I'd find you outside, away from everyone." Chance was trying. I should give him some credit for that. Everyone who knows me knows it's best to just steer clear of me at times like this. I get too angry, too argumentative. He used to know me better than anyone. He should know to stay away from me right now.

"Oh right, because I hate people, I'm just gonna hide away from everyone, is that what you're saying?" Even when I knew I was out of line, I couldn't stop myself, and couldn't reel myself back in.

"Shelby, I just came out here to be with you, to be there for you," he said, closing the space between us. "Come on, come here." As Chance reached for my hand and tried to pull me close to him, I slinked back quickly and abruptly. His faced looked like I'd slapped him, pain surfaced in his eyes. It may have actually hurt less if I had struck him.

"What part of this do you not get? We're not together. We are not going to be together. Just because my aunt died does not mean that you get a free pass back into my life," I screamed. "Chance, we're over and have been for quite some time." If I thought I had hurt him when I pulled away from his embrace, then I just now destroyed him. Seconds before he dropped his head, I watched as his eyes filled with tears. He turned from me and said, "I hear you, but I just don't understand you." As he walked away, I wondered how one person could be so cold and another could be so warm.

Chapter 6
Here

"Betheny, we need to talk." My sister, Patricia, approached me with a concerned look in her eyes. My sister, Rosemary, was also with her. Ro and Patti are my caring, loving sisters, who would do anything and everything for anyone. We all have our titles and our strengths, along with our weaknesses. Anna, our oldest sister, is not the typical eldest daughter of six girls. She does not possess all of those stereotypical birth order traits. She is a strong-willed fighter. She breaks the rules and has more fire in her than the other five of us put together. She is beautiful and feisty, a fashion-wonder, even though we never really had any money. She worked hard, married a hard-worker and saw to it that she and her children were hugely provided for and nurtured. She was a strong disciplinarian and our role model. We always looked to her for advice, companionship, and humor, still do, even here.

Virginia is the introvert of the family. She married young and had a loving, caring family. Once she got married, her sisters were still her family, but they were no longer her top priority. She focused on her own children and her husband. She always loved and needed her sisters, but her priorities changed. Virgie married very young, but loved him with all of her being. Ray was taken from her early after a quick and fatal car accident. She never loved another, never even bothered to look at another, because Raymond was her world, her love, her life.

My sister, Rosemary, found her love, her life, early, but she was forbidden to be with him. It was strange, because she was the obedient, "good" one of the family, but then she just up and left the house to be with him for a while. It turned out; she met up with him when he was on leave from the military, married him, spent the night with him, and then returned home without our parents ever knowing. Months later, he was released from the military (his service had ended), and they had to reveal to everyone that they were already married. It was catastrophic. My mother, a full-blooded, non-English-speaking Italian woman, went ballistic on everyone and everything. It was not a loving or pretty sight at all. She threw objects; she screamed. She yelled; she formulated English profanity that we didn't even know she knew or understood. After time, Rosemary was welcomed back into our home and her new husband, John-Mitchell, was finally welcomed as well. However, out of all of my brothers-in-law, it seemed like my mother never really trusted John-Mitchell. I loved him like my own brother and enjoyed his Southern drawl and hospitality, but my mother couldn't get past her loss of a wedding.

It was Rosemary who sat by my side night after night when I was in agony and didn't want my children to see me suffering. She and Darby were my at-home nurses and caregivers. Being the youngest, my sisters had the hardest time watching me suffer. I was their baby sister, and they always promised to protect me and take care of me. It was hard on them when that promise couldn't be kept.

It always seemed so strange to me. I was the youngest, but the one who always experienced all of the hardships first. My husband died first; my death sentence came first. How can the youngest be put through all of the agony first? It's a question that I still cannot answer, even here. Maybe, it's one that my baby, my daughter, Shelby can answer. We were taken from her entirely too soon as well. Our lives are eerily parallel.

Moving on, my sister Patricia is the lovable one of all of my sisters. Everyone always considered her the "airhead" of the family, but she had everyone fooled. She wanted to be regarded as such, because she didn't want to get embroiled in all of the family hoopla. She chose to just look the other way and not listen to the messes that our family created and enjoyed. When she was getting older, it was obvious that she really did need a hearing aid. However, family brawls would surface, and Patricia would sit there with this goofy, clueless look on her face. To a bystander, it would appear that she was too ignorant to figure out what was being said or going on. To us though, we knew that as soon as an airy word was stated and another retorted, Patricia would simply reach up, turn down her hearing aid, and sit in silent bliss while verbal attacks and battles would go on right near her.

Patricia is a woman filled with love. She married Frank, who adored her and believed the world revolved around her. He was at her beck and call and did everything that she asked—even when she asked him to do handyman jobs for all of her sisters at their homes. He was a silent, grunting man, who fulfilled her every wish, despite the grunts and groans. They were a funny and crowd-pleasing couple. People were reminded what true love is when in their presence. Much of their adoration for each other was contagious and rubbed off on others.

Now Lila, she's the crazy one. She outlived us all, because she's just too stubborn to do otherwise. Lila's story is one of true epic complications and wonderment. I always believed that Lila had a love of soap operas, because they were the only stories or programs that came remotely close to her everyday happenings. Her life was a soap opera, filled with drama, betrayal, seduction, and disappointment. To tell her story, I'd have to like her right now, but I don't. Therefore, I can't tell it, because it would soften me, reliving her life and feeling her pain. People adored Lila. I adored Lila. People flocked to Lila; I flocked to Lila. Children worshipped Lila; my children worshipped Lila.

I looked at Rosemary and Patricia, and gave them my canned response: "I don't wanna talk about it."

Patricia looked me in the eye and tried to be stern, (anger does not work for her), "You may not want to talk, but we do. So, you listen," she said, pointing at me.

Rosemary chimed in with, "Do you realize how long it's been since you've seen your children, spoken to your sister?" When I didn't respond, she continued. "You're being childish. You may be the smartest one of us, but you're acting stupid. Lila couldn't help her death any more than you could." Rosemary knew my innermost fears; I told her everything in those long, dark agonizing nights. My worries had quickly become hers as she promised me nightly that she'd be there for my kids. I knew that her promises were meant to ease my worry and fear. But, I also knew that she couldn't keep those promises; Ro had a husband and children of her own to tend to, as did the rest of my sisters, except for Lila. Lila had us. Lila was supposed to be the one who took care of my kids for me, watched after them and protected them in those times of devastation and uncertainty.

"Beth, you remember first being here, alone, scared, and clinging to Carl. All you wanted were answers, reassurance, and love. How can you not give that to Lila right now?" Patti added. Patti always wanted to smooth things over for people, and we usually allowed her to do so. But not this time.

"I just can't. I feel like...I mean...I can't." I didn't know how to explain this to them, to Carl, or even to myself. How could I tell the people whom I loved the most and needed the most right now that I was terrified of the truth?

There

I met Chance almost four years ago. Even I can admit that it was a "fairy tale" meeting. It was May, and my sister had just bought her first computer. It was back in the time when online chat rooms had just gotten popular, and people were trying their luck at technological dating or mating, whatever you wanted to call it. My sister and I were no exception. One night, I was online chatting with the most magnificent and charming man of all time. Technologically, I was already smitten. He was sensitive, romantic, clever, and said all of the right things. For instance, one night while he was at home in Pennsylvania, and I was at my house in Ohio, he told me to go outside and look at the moon. I did. When I came in, he said that he could see the same moon and that we were not as far away as I thought. He told me to imagine him every time I looked at that moon and when I did his arms would be around me. He was wonderfully romantic. And I was falling fast.

During this magical conversation, I received an instant message. I was also dabbling in some chat rooms, one called Chance Encounters at the time. I was still new to the online chat room world, so it was pretty fun and exciting to me.

Anyway, this Instant Message popped up and said, "How can it be a chance encounter if you deliberately went to the chat room?"

Despite the fact that I found this question clever and relevant, I was completely annoyed at this random person, who interrupted my romantic moon conversation, which I later began to call my "moon swoon", so I just responded with a "shut up." The stranger, a male, based on his screen name and profile link, countered by expressing that he expected a better response from an Ohio State graduate. (Apparently, he'd read my online profile as well.) I retorted with some profane vulgarity, figuring that I would certainly silence him.

He said (typed), "With an English degree from Ohio State, your vocabulary could use some help."

Now, I'd always prided myself on my diction, extensive vocabulary, and my effective communication skills, so this goaded me right into a full out battle. I was forced to excuse myself from my online "sweet nothings" in order to wage a verbal assault on this romance saboteur.

This guy and I were different in every way. After perusing my online profile, he commented on my choice of foreign cars, because he would only "Buy American." At the time, I had a sporty 2-door, shiny silver Honda Civic. Of course, he owned a giant Ford pickup truck.

Additionally, as I sang my praises for Toad the Wet Sprocket, Hootie and the Blowfish, and Pearl Jam, he couldn't fathom that anyone in this day and age would not love country music, specifically Garth Brooks and George Strait. I hated that he drove a giant pickup truck, listened to country music, wore cowboy boots and a cowboy hat, and to add to the horror, he even had a daughter.

The having a daughter business gave me an ample amount of ammunition to shoot at him. I explained that safe sex was not a new invention and that he should try it out. That comment did not go over too well, igniting anger and hurt in him immediately. I did wager an online apologetic retraction after he blasted me with his rant about not having any regrets and loving his daughter and his time with her unconditionally. That was the first glimpse I received of the real man behind the keyboard; his loyalty shone through his type strokes.

The real battle began when he discovered that I was desperately in love with former president, Bill Clinton. He went on a tirade (typed) about the glory days of Reagan, a president that I was sure he didn't really remember, based on his age. After long over an hour of belittling ping-pong, my online enemy, and I were finished. However, every time I signed online thereafter, he and I would spend a few minutes or so, in angry combat.

Meanwhile, I was falling head over heels in like with Rob, my online "moon swoon" suitor. Since I'd just graduated from Ohio State and was an unemployed teacher, looking for work, and he was on leave from the Navy, we had plenty of time to swoon and flirt over the computer. Rob and I spent the majority of the summer falling in likable lust over the Internet. I do believe that true love can be found hundreds of miles away online. It can happen for anyone that way.

After nearly three and a half months of chatting and getting to know one another, it was time for Rob to go back to the Navy base; he'd reenlisted. He needed to travel to Chicago to get his orders and find out where he was going and when he was shipping out. Since I was in Ohio, and he was leaving Pennsylvania, our face-to-face meeting was inevitable. I agreed to meet him at a shopping mall that was 25 minutes from my house. By this point, I thoroughly trusted him, but I'm not an idiot. I know that there are crazies in this world. (I talked to a different one almost daily online). I gave my brother and my sister all the background information on Rob. I had pictures of him, and he even willingly gave me his address, social security number, and birth date. I knew that my brother and sister would know what to do if I mysteriously went missing. However, I wasn't afraid, because I had all the faith in the world in Rob.

We met at the Starbucks at the mall (I hate coffee). I was sitting there waiting for him, and he walked right up and enveloped me in his arms. It was instant. I adored him. It did not seem like we had met seconds ago; it seemed as if we had known each other for our entire lives. He knew truths about me that I'd be too frightened to tell someone face-to-face. He knew my fears, my hopes, my funny stories, and my sexy desires. We had the most wonderful afternoon, evening, and night. It was the date that neither of us wanted to end. When he went back to his hotel, our first kiss (in the parking lot) was perfect, and long awaited. No, I didn't go into his hotel room, but his kisses melted my insides and made my heart skip pitter-pattering beats. I stepped back, looked at him, and knew that I had met Mr. Right....Now.

The next morning, he showed up at my house (I'd willingly given him directions) with roses and a stuffed animal. He said that I brought out the romantic and the kid in him, so roses and toys were appropriate. He was perfect. Our day was perfect. We spent the entire afternoon at a nearby amusement park. We had a wonderful time. Then, in the evening, we had a romantic dinner at a lakeside restaurant watching the boats dock and set sail again.

On his third day, we spent the day with my brother and sister. They loved him and thought that they had certainly met their soon-to-be brother-in-law. They were so thrilled that I had found someone who made me so happy and who was so supremely smitten with me. I was blissful and giddy, something they had not seen in years. On his last morning, before leaving for Chicago, he gave me three airline tickets to visit him in three weeks. One ticket was for me, and the other two were for my sister and my friend. He wanted to be certain that I would not back out of the visit by ensuring that I had traveling companions. He even booked us in a pretty nice hotel in the heart of Chicago.

The three weeks I had to wait until my visit were torture. I was miserable not being with him. I longed for him, his smile, his scent, and his embrace. Online chatting was not cutting it any longer. He had so much going on in Chicago, even our phone calls were strained and rushed. I hated every second of it. However, once we were reunited, we were back to the happy, loving, falling couple. We had a whirlwind romance in Chicago. He took me to all the fabulous places that I had seen in movies. We walked everywhere hand-in-hand, arm-in-arm, and heart-in-heart. My sister and friend couldn't believe how perfect two people were for one another.

Then on our final day, saying goodbye, standing curbside, waiting for the taxi to take us to the airport to leave Chicago, my conversation with Rob went like this:

(A wonderfully hot and passionate kiss ended.)

Rob: When can I see you again?

Shelby Lynn: I don't think that we should see each other anymore.

I was shocked that those words just came out of my mouth, as was my sister and my friend.

Rob: What're you talking about?

Rob was visibly shocked and hurt.

Shelby: I don't wanna do this with you. I don't wanna be a military wife. I don't want to say "goodbye" to you to all the time. Goodbyes hurt. I don't wanna hurt anymore. I'm not a military woman. I want a man who works 9:00 a.m.—5:00 p.m. and comes home every night to me. I've experienced too much loss. With you, with the military, with all the goodbyes, the chances of you being another loss is way too great. And....and...you don't even use the right "your" in emails.

Rob stood there astonished, nodding, knowing the past pain I'd endured, realizing that he didn't

want to add to it. My sister and my friend looked on in disbelief; I got in the cab and was ready to leave Rob, my online "moon swoon" for good.

To this day, I have no idea where those words came from. As I stood there on the curb, saying goodbye to him again, I knew that I couldn't live a life of him shipping out and leaving me alone all the time. I spent enough of my life being alone, and being left by people I loved. I was not about to do it on a regular basis, but I had not thought all of this through. I had no idea that I was going to say those words. They were as much a surprise to me as they were to everyone who heard them.

In the cab, my sister started in on me. She told me that if I continued to push everyone away that I would spend my life alone. She even went as far to say that he was the one for me. I could not stand her babbling any longer, so I asked the cab driver to please turn up the radio. The song, "I Can Love You Like That," by All-4-One was on the radio, and it was at the part that goes:

"They read you Cinderella

You hoped it would come true

That one day your Prince Charming

Would come rescue you..."

My sister piped in with "See Shelb, he's your Prince Charming. He's here to rescue you. You just blew it." It was hard to say goodbye to Rob, but in my heart of hearts, I knew I'd made the right decision, even though that decision crumbled my already broken heart.

I glared at her and asked the cab driver to turn off the radio as I looked out the window and sulked. I was definitely hurting, even though I knew it was the only decision and the right thing to do.

For the next month, I ended up homebound and couldn't find the pep in my step again. I found myself back online spending my nights (and even some days) arguing and debating with my online archenemy. I actually came to start relying on him to be there to fight with. He was helping me get through a rough spot with my unfortunate and surprising breakup with Rob. However, this online fighter didn't know that though, because we never had a real or meaningful conversation. All he and I ever did online was argue and bicker and debate over whatever topic came up. I knew nothing of importance about him, or he about me. He was safe, safe to fight with and release my pent up anger with.

Imagine my surprise one day in late September when he asked if he could take me out. I was shocked and rather disgusted. This was a guy that I really couldn't stand, let alone like and want to spend time with. He had to be kidding me.

I typed, "Yeah right. You and I go out together, that'll happen."

I must've shocked him with my response, because it took a while for his typed response to appear on screen. Then I saw:

"Shelby, I'm serious. Let me take you to a movie tonight. We both live in Akron; we're bound to meet sooner or later." Wow. He correctly used a semicolon; that was impressive.

Still shocked, I typed, "I don't even know your last name. You could be the next Jeffrey Dahmer." Jeffrey Dahmer was a serial killer from our state who killed people, and then ate their remains. I wasn't about to date a Jeffrey Dahmer. Surely, I wasn't that desperate and lonely. Was I?

Being the crude jerk that he was, he responded with, "First of all, if I ate you, then you wouldn't be complaining. . ."

Although, I do love a good pun, I found his vulgarity disgusting, out of place, and completely inappropriate at this time. I was about to tell him so, when he typed, "Michaels."

Chance Michaels. Michaels. Michaels. I recognized the name. Holy Mary Mother of God! Then, with shaky fingers and total disbelief, I typed, "Do you know Steve Kline and Debbie Maine?" and waited for his response.

Then I saw the words that I couldn't believe, "Yes, I'm in their wedding in November."

Crap!

Crap!

Crap!

Slowly and carefully, I typed, "You're my partner," and I immediately signed off the computer. I'd been helping my friend, Debbie, plan her wedding for months now. She told me a long time ago that Chance Michaels would be my partner. Naturally, I didn't think anything of it. I just knew the name of the male who would be escorting me down the aisle and dancing with me during the bridal party introductions. I hadn't thought too much about it. I was already stressing over Debbie's wedding, because of Nate. Oh Christ, Nate.

Nate. Now, I can honestly say that at that point in my life, I'd only been in love with one person ever. My first boyfriend, my first love, my first. . . well everything...was with Nate. I fell hard and completely in love with him. Actually, I loved Nate all through high school and a few years into college. There hadn't been anyone I was even remotely interested in since Nate. After four years of being alone and dealing with my Nate-shattered heart, I met Rob, my moon-swoon.

With Nate, it was the typical first love feelings. I wanted to eat, sleep, breathe Nate at all times. When he wasn't around, the world felt too big, and I never felt that I could breathe fully. He was my air. Ahhh first love. I believe that he felt the same way. However, we were young, and we eventually realized that our futures were not going in the same direction. We were not on the same types of paths. (He discovered it long before I did though.)

My first love was also my first heartbreak. Wow, does that first one hurt like Hell, too. Nate now came back into the picture, because he's Debbie's cousin. I was already worried about her wedding, because Nate would be at her wedding with his hot, young, new fiancé. Fiancé. He had a fiancé, and I had a guy in Chicago who used the wrong "your" and an online nemesis. One of us had fared much better after our break up four years ago. Four years! What was I doing with my life?

Christ! Now, I had to worry about meeting Mr. Cowboy Republican Daddy Man in the midst of all of this. What were the chances? Chance! Fan-freaking-tastic. Then wouldn't you know it, right in the middle of my mid-afternoon freak-out, my phone rang.

"Hello?"

"Shelby Lynn?" Although I'd never heard his voice, I didn't have to ask; I immediately knew who it was.

"Oh my God, how'd you get my phone number?" I asked panic-stricken.

"You know, sometimes, you're not very bright for a college graduate," I could hear the humor in his voice. It was gentle and fun. He added, "I called Debbie, and she gave me your number. She told me to go easy on you."

Debbie. Crap. I'd kill her. "So what's up?" I'm dumb. I do say dumb things. I didn't know what it was about this guy that made me so dumb and garble-mouthed.

"I wanna take you to a movie tonight. Let's go to dinner and movie," he said, so casually.

"Yeah, I'm sorry, but that's not gonna happen." I countered. Holy moly, this was all too much for me. "I'm not looking to date." Who says that? All girls in their mid-twenties are looking to date. I couldn't handle this. How did my online fighter get to be the guy on the phone asking me out? Who also just so happened to be the guy that was going to be my partner in an upcoming, dreaded wedding? The gods were playing me with me. I was sure of it now, and I was certainly losing.

"Easy killer, I'm not looking to go steady or anything; I just wanna take you to a movie," he mocked. "Ya figure, we're gonna meet in two months anyway." He was very articulate and quite persuasive, but he had a way of making me feel like an idiot. Maybe because I am an idiot.

"So, we'll meet then, in November. I gotta go." I hung up the phone immediately.

I spent the rest of the afternoon and early evening in a state of worry and panic. I could not calm down. Rob was somewhere in Chicago, long gone. I hadn't heard from him once since I'd gotten in that cab. I guess my sister, Darby, was wrong. He was not my "Prince Charming" after all. Everyone knows that Prince Charming always comes back.

Nate, my first love, was about to marry a girl who looked like "Robin from General Hospital," according to Debbie. Really? Deb couldn't sugar-coat it for me and change it to Lila Quartermaine? Christ! Now, I had to worry that Chance Michaels, AKA the Rhinestone Cowboy, was going to embarrass the crap out of me at Debbie's wedding in front of Nate, the only person I'd ever really loved.

I couldn't take the tension, frustration, and worry. I ended up going for a run. (I'm really and truly not a runner either.) I just needed to do something to calm my nerves and clear my head. Seeing me run is not a pretty sight. I sweat more than an overweight teenage boy in gym class. I'm ridiculous. However, when I got home, I was more relaxed and had a better sense of clarity. I did not like-like (as my students would say) this guy, but he would be a fun partner at the wedding. He'd be a distraction from Nate and his Robin Scorpio look-alike fiancé. Granted, this Chance guy and I would fight the entire day, but he would keep me on my toes and away from being a huddled, sobbing, loser-mess on the floor after seeing who I thought was the "one who got away."

I had to pull myself together. Initially, I was mourning the loss of Navy Rob, but now I was re-mourning the loss of my first love, as well as fretting the meeting of my online political debater. For someone who was normally, dateless and clueless, I sure had my hands full with non-love-affair affairs. As my worries were finally subsiding and my rationality finally setting in, the phone rang.

"Okay, so I wanna go to dinner and see Juno." Chance said, with an air of confidence in his voice. Geez, this guy was persistent; I needed to be firm in my stance. He was even a little creepy, in the Oh-my-God-you're-as-charming-as-Hell, kind of way. But I still wasn't budging.

"Wow, you don't get it; I'm not gonna out with you," I said in an exasperated tone. "You're like a stalker."

"A stalker? That's funny you should say that," he laughed. At that moment, my doorbell rang.

"Hold on a second," I said, opening my door. I couldn't believe it. A stranger was on my front porch holding a cell phone. Chance. I was going to kill Debbie.

He looked me up and down (I'd just returned from running), wrinkled his nose, and said, "Ewww, I'll give you an hour to get ready." Ewww??? Really!

Insulted, I said, "You aren't that ugly." I was oddly surprised that he was attractive. He was just under six feet, I estimated. I wasn't that great at judging height. Everyone was taller than me, since I stood at a whopping five foot nothing. Looking at him, I knew that I didn't have to ask; he'd played football and/or baseball in high school. He just had "that athletic" look about him, complete with the broad shoulders, strong back, and small waist. Catcher. I bet he was a catcher.

Chance had dark, thick hair, and very, almost-black, eyes. What I found the most attractive about his eyes were his eyebrows. They were beautifully arched and expressive, but untouched; these brows weren't manicured, but were perfectly naturally sculpted.

They said so much, but what I heard was "Protect your heart honey; it's gonna get broken."

When he looked at me, his eyes pierced through me, sending chills up my back. He was good-looking, better looking than Rob by far. More manly and mature than Nate, definitely more educated than both Rob and Nate put together. Hmmmm...I was intrigued. Why hadn't Debbie fixed me up with this guy before? Maybe by pairing us up at the wedding, she was in a sense trying to fix us up. Or she knew my Liberal views were way too Left for his Right-Winged crap. Strangely though, my stomach began to flutter. Surprising myself yet again, I said, "I'll see you in 60." I closed the door and got into the shower.

Oddly enough, I was pretty excited and acting awfully girlie about my impromptu date with this online creeper. He intrigued me to say the least. He was witty, sarcastic, intelligent, and he used the right "your." I found myself trying to choose the perfect outfit and hoping for a good hair day. I was remorseful that I didn't have time for a manicure and pedicure. I was such a girl at times, fickle to the core. I went from hating this guy, to avoiding this guy, to worrying about my cuticles for this guy. Being a girl was so tiring.

Over an hour later, as we were getting into his Ford pickup truck (I hate trucks), he told me that we had 55 minutes until the movie started. Chance suggested that we eat after the movie. He asked me what I wanted to do to kill time, and I told him that I didn't care. I left it open and told him that we could do whatever he wanted for the next 55 minutes.

He said, "We could have sex," with a devilish, sexy grin.

Finally understanding my role in this verbal game of cat and mouse, I said, "What would we do for the other 50 minutes?" Nice, take that. An attack on a man's performance always hits hard. Pun intended.

Laughing loudly, he looked at me, clearly impressed. Chance nodded appreciatively, smiled genuinely, turned on the radio, and said, "We're gonna get married, aren't we?"

At that moment, the song, that same song, "I Can Love You Like That," came on the radio; alternatively this was the remake by John Michael Montgomery (Remember, Chance's a country fan).

"They read you Cinderella

You hoped it would come true

That one day your Prince Charming

Would come rescue you..."

Not believing the lyrics that were blaring (unnecessarily) out of the speakers, I said, "Yeah, it looks that way." And that was the beginning of the story of Chance and me. Now, it's four years later. We are unmarried, and I am back to avoiding that same guy in his newer, fancier pickup truck after an already very bumpy ride.

Chapter 7

Here

My husband died after we'd been married almost 20 years. His death destroyed me. I overheard my sisters and my friends talking once about whether or not I was going to pull through his death. I couldn't eat, drink, sleep, talk, or even parent my own children. My kids spent the months after Carl's death being raised by my sisters and friends. My youngest, who was only ten-years-old at the time, even asked me why so many people bought her birthday presents when they had never bought her presents before. I guess that people didn't typically turn their backs on a little girl and her 11th birthday, especially when it fell a month after her daddy's death.

Carl died a month before Shelby's birthday, and everyone was still in our house by the time her birthday came around. My house was filled with people for months, helping me cope and keeping a watch on me. All I did was sit on the corner of the couch, cry, and rub the armrest. I couldn't stop rubbing the armrest; it gave me comfort to keep my hands moving. The couch's armrest was another fatality in my husband's death. Within two months, there was a large, gaping hole in the couch from all of the friction from my incessant rubbing. The hole in the couch began to represent the void I felt in my heart, the more I rubbed the couch, the more comfort I felt, making me feel somewhat closer to my husband. Made no sense then; makes no sense now. But it did help. Believe me, I needed all the help I could get.

We didn't have a storybook start to our love affair. It was rather the opposite. At first sight, I despised him and wanted nothing to do with him. I was in my mid-twenties, working as a cocktail waitress in a local dive bar/restaurant. (Don't ever tell my children, we told them that we met at church.) I liked to flaunt my assets to increase my nightly take home gratuity. Alright, I wore low-cut shirts to get better tips. It doesn't sound nearly as trashy saying it the other way.

A creepy regular at the bar enjoyed gawking at my flaunted material; he often boasted that he was a "boob man." My friends and I at the bar often mocked him privately, saying that he was definitely a "boob" of a man.

One of his first visits to the bar was the first night that I realized just how disgusting this man was. On a bet with his work buddies and apparently over-the-top intoxicated, when I came over to see if anyone needed any "top offs," he begged to see my "top off." Scoffing, I began to turn away and leave, when he grabbed my waist, turned me around and shoved his face/head into my décolletage. Instantly, I was repulsed and furious. From that moment on, I refused to ever wait on him and his obnoxious buddies again. To make matters worse, his name was "Carl;" I hated the name Carl. It reminded me of a name that you would give to a duck or a platypus. I don't know why someone would name a platypus, but if someone were looking to name a platypus, then Carl would be a good name for it.

Still, he was in the bar nightly, gawking, leaving next to nothing as tips, and annoying me and the rest of the workers. He was relentless about asking me to join him. Obviously, he couldn't understand that I was working and that he was more of a nuisance than a possible beau for me. After a year of his gaping, annoying and oftentimes repulsive behavior, he gave me an offer I couldn't resist. Carl said that if I would agree to go on one date with him, then he would not only stop asking me out and stop gawking at me, but he would also never step foot in the whole establishment again. My co-workers said that after a year with this man bothering everyone that I owed it to them and to the other patrons to go out with him and deter his future misbehavior and conduct. Reluctantly, I agreed to a single two-hour date with him, in daylight hours only.

On the afternoon of our date, I wasn't too eager to impress Carl. I wore clothing that wouldn't impress a vagabond on the street, let alone a gentleman caller. I did not wash or set my hair; makeup was minimal. As a rule, I never left the house without lipstick, but today, I didn't want to draw attention to my lips or any other assets that might invite his grotesque salivating attention. Therefore, my shirt was a crew neck, covering all but my collarbone, and my lips went un-glossed for the afternoon.

When I heard the overzealous and raucous knocking at the door, my heart sank, and I knew that this would be a date unlike any other. Imagine my surprise, when Carl seemed more underdressed and unkempt than I. This man was unbelievable. To think that he didn't even try to shine when all he'd done for the last year was beg for an outing with me. Men!

Then I nearly ended the date when the first words out of his mouth were, "I see you're hiding my favorites," as he stared only at my chest. I was speechless and did not have a clever comeback. The man was appalling, but I promised everyone at the bar that I would fulfill my civic duty and ensure that he never stepped foot into our establishment again.

As we stepped out onto my front porch, I noticed that there wasn't a car parked in my driveway or along the road. I asked him where his car was and almost fell over when he said, "My buddy, Butch, dropped me off." I looked at him in disbelief, and he said, "I don't have a car, but don't worry, I don't expect ya to drive," he said walking toward the sidewalk. "We're only goin' a few blocks away, down to the sandlot. It wouldn't kill ya to walk a few blocks."

"Sandlot? Excuse me? You expect me to play baseball in this?" I couldn't believe what he was saying and that I was actually hearing these words. How'd I get myself into these situations?

Chuckling, "Well, no, we're not playing baseball. We're gonna watch a game. Anyway, that getup would be fine for a game of stickball in the street," he said, stopping, and looking me up and down. "You're not winning any beauty pageants in that, honey." When he smiled, I knew that he was kidding, but then he added, "Darling, I'm just fooling with ya. I knew that you weren't gonna take me or this date seriously. You look wonderful in anything ya wear," he said, staring at me as he placed a lose strand of hair behind my ear. Oddly enough, I felt a chill when his hand brushed the back of my ear, which I quickly dismissed and accepted as a tremble of repulsion.

Carl was strange. When he wasn't around his friends, he seemed a little intimidated, a little shy, and pretty witty in a goofy way. However, the clock was set, and I only had about 110 more minutes with this guy, thankfully.

"So, we're gonna watch baseball? Who's playing?" I guessed that I could handle two hours in this gorgeous sunlight, watching a baseball game. Seemed public and harmless enough.

"Johnny. He's my next-door-neighbor. He's eleven and loves playing ball," Carl's face lit up as he talked about his neighbor. "I like throwing the ball around with him. His daddy died in service...he really is a nice kid," Carl said, shaking his head, as if to remove the memory from his mind. "I figured since he was playing just a few blocks away from you that I'd kill two birds with one stone."

"That's terrible about his father. How's the rest of his family?" I always hated stories about children losing their parents, especially little boys who had to grow up without their fathers to guide them and teach them. I instinctively assumed that a mother just couldn't fill in that sort of role. Little did I know, right?

"His mom pretty much gave up on his daddy long before he died. When he shipped out the first time, she started finding comfort in anyone who'd offer it up," Carl explained. "She took no time in finding another man...other men...you name it. She disgusts me; that's why I try to spend time with Johnny." Carl kicked a rock and watched it hit the metal part of the sewer grate. "A kid needs someone he can count on." Carl just shook his head and kicked another small stone on the sidewalk. The rock went out onto the brick road. Carl seemed less sure of himself now, awkward and shy, maybe. We were closing in on Firestone Park, and I found myself strangely enough wishing that we had a little longer to walk and talk.

Normally, I'm a really good judge of people and their characters, so I was having trouble getting my head on straight. From the moment that Carl starting speaking today, it seemed as if a whole new person was talking to me. This wasn't the wimpy, slurring, obnoxious, "boob" of a man who frequented the bar. He was charming, sensitive, and more down to earth than many of the men I'd met in a long time.

As far as Carl's appearance, I could never be attracted to someone like him. His beer belly hung way out over his pants. He had hair coming out of his ears and his nose. Gray was not his predominant hair color, but it was apparent that gray would overtake the dark brown. Glancing at him, there wasn't a feature that anyone would be ga-ga over, but his eyes were the kindest and softest eyes that had ever looked at me. And as hypocritical as this was, I would never date a smoker. I say hypocritical, because I'm a smoker, but I'm so turned off by male smokers. I think women who smoke are classy, sophisticated and exude maturity and mystery. Men who smoke are repulsive, smell, and lack class and sophistication. Carl didn't have a whole lot going for him, but adding smoker to the resume certainly did not get him the job, if you catch my drift. And who could get past the name, Carl? Terrible name. As these thoughts were running through my head, I felt shocked that I found myself so compelled to repeatedly list his downfalls and character flaws. It was almost as if I were trying to remind myself of how truly undatable he was.

"Hey Johnny!" Carl's face lit up and just beamed with pride as the most hideous-looking boy came running up to him and punched him square in the gut. Carl laughed, doubled over, and "pretended" that it hurt. I believe that it really did hurt him. He was pretending to pretend. Carl was not a stud, let's be honest. There was a lot of gut there.

When Carl spoke of Johnny, I pictured a saddened, angelic little boy that anyone would love to take home. The little boy before me needed hosed down, some soap, toothpaste, a brush, and a couple plates of manicotti to start with. His uniform was far dirtier than any of the other players' uniforms, especially since the game had not yet even begun. It was evident that this little boy did not bathe regularly, eat often, have any form of oral hygiene or wash his clothing. Johnny was a disgusting little waif.

I prayed that he didn't reach out to shake my hand during our introductions, as I finished my prayer, he said, "Hi Miss Betheny, Mr. Carl told me everything about you." Before I could respond, he was wrapped around my waist, smiling a very blackened and foul-smelling grin. "Thanks for coming to m'game...yeah...uh... thanks for finally saying you'd go out with him too. Talks about ya all the time. Almost as much as he talks about sports." Carl reached over, pried him from my skirt, covered his mouth, took off his ball cap and mussed his hair. Johnny smiled and squealed for the duration. I would've assumed that an eleven-year-old would be embarrassed by this display of childish fun, but he was relishing every moment of it.

"Alright champ-a-rific, go play some ball and remember, get your mitt in the dirt for those grounders. Don't let any balls by you today. For every error you get today is another day that you have to weed our flower beds," Carl joked easily with him.

"Yes Sir! No errors!" Johnny said, saluting us. Johnny ran back to his team to finish warming up with his friends. Despite his waiflike appearance, his team seemed to really welcome him and respect him. As it turned out, Johnny was one of the best players on the team. He only had one error from what I saw, but it seemed rather intentional. Johnny was the first baseman and the pitcher threw the ball straight to him. He caught the ball dead on, but then dropped it at the last second. Johnny looked straight at Carl, grinned and shrugged his shoulders. Then as if lightning struck him, he picked up the ball and drilled it to the second baseman, getting the boy out on a slide. He made the out, but Carl still claimed it was an error. I couldn't believe that the runner even attempted to get to second when the ball was just at the foot of the first baseman, but what do I know about baseball? It was obvious that he wanted to have errors to just spend more time with Carl. Their friendship was sweet; they needed each other.

As far as my date with Carl was going, I really did not feel like we were on a first date or any date at all for that matter. He watched the game. I watched the game. We cheered for the Green Crush and clapped and hooted when Johnny got a triple. Our only conversation during the game was about a certain play or about Johnny and his love of baseball. It was pretty fun and enjoyable— laid back and relaxing. All that fun changed in the bottom of the fifth inning when a skinnier, more attractive, classier man, but still resembling Carl came running into the park in a frantic frenzy. He stood at the third baseline and yelled for Carl to come quick. Carl's face immediately displayed fear and panic. He bolted right off the back of the bleachers and ran around to the back of the park. I hesitated, not knowing what to do, until he called, "Betheny, come on!"

I ran down the bleachers and joined the men, upon coming up on the two of them I heard, "heart attack." Confused, I looked into the similar faces of the men. Brothers. Carl looked at me and said, "Betheny, my mom just had a heart attack; they're taking her to City Hospital. I've gotta go." Tears were filling his eyes, and his hands were trembling.

I grabbed both of his hands in mine, nodded, told him to call me, and kissed his knuckles." He and his brother ran to the parking lot and jumped into his brother's car and drove off. I stood there, not quite knowing what to do next. Out of respect for everyone involved, I went back to my spot on the bleachers and decided to cheer for Johnny until the game ended. I assumed it was the least I could do. Carl's mother needed him. Johnny needed him. I could fill in for now.

Once the game ended, Johnny walked up the bleachers and asked me where Carl and Mr. David had gone. (Dave must be Carl's younger brother.) I explained to him that their mother was in the hospital.

"Did Mrs. LeeMaster have another heart attack?" I hadn't realized that she had suffered a heart attack before. Johnny and Carl must be closer than I'd actually understood. He sure knew a great deal about Carl and Carl's life. I found it strange that Carl felt comfortable talking to a small boy about his family, about his life, and even about me. How could an adult ever have a friendship with a child that wasn't his? They were really friends, the real definition of friendship.

"Yes honey, she did." I truly did not know what to say to this little boy. He seemed so sad. As I contemplated what I should do next, he hugged me again and said, "We'd better go to the hospital and check on Mrs. LeeMaster. Carl'd want us to be with him."

I was certain that wouldn't be a good idea. "Johnny, I think that Carl needs to be with his family right now. We need to give them space." I didn't even know Carl, let alone his family. The last place that I needed to be was with strangers while they endured the horrors of their mother's second heart attack.

"Miss Betheny, I am his family. Sometimes, friends feel more like family than real family ever feels like family." Although the way he said it was confusing and slightly incoherent, I knew exactly what he meant. I knew that Johnny was going to the hospital to check on his friend with or without me. I also knew that I wasn't letting a little boy walk across town at dusk by himself; it was at least 18 city blocks to the hospital. The sun was beginning to set; we weren't in the best part of town. As much as I wanted to deny it, I was going to finish my date with Carl at the hospital while his mother suffered the aftermath of a heart attack.

As Johnny and I entered the ER, Carl, David, a woman, who appeared to be a little older than Carl, and an older man were walking out of one of the makeshift curtained-off rooms. The woman was sobbing, Carl and David were on either side of her, supporting her as she walked. The older man had his hands in his pockets; his face was stoic and drawn. Carl was crying and Dave was shaking his head and clicking his tongue. Instantly and certainly, I knew that their mother hadn't survived this heart attack.

I wanted to protect Johnny from the truth and the horrors of being around death, but he was too wise and fast for me. He let go of my hand and ran straight toward the woman, saying, "Mrs. Lora, I'm so sorry." Glancing at the older man, he added, "Mr. LeeMaster, I'm so sorry." The woman, Lora, held him and cried openly into the top of his matted, messy hair. Carl rubbed his back. David and the older man just stood, observing the scene in front of them. Evidently, Dave and the older man were not as close to young Johnny as Lora and Carl were. David noticed me standing back, he took a step toward Carl, hit his shoulder and pointed to me.

Carl looked me in the eyes, and nodded, mouthing a sincere, "Thank you."

I walked over to the family, and said, "I'm sorry to intrude; I didn't want Johnny to walk over here alone." Carl immediately hugged me and cried into my shoulder. His embrace was strong, but revealed a weakness in him. This suffering and raw pain was new to him, to his family. He was uncertain and was holding on, fearful to let go. I let him hold me. From that day on, I never made him let go.

There

I hadn't told anyone about my aunt's last words to me, which was surprising, because I do have a tendency to talk about everything with anyone and everyone. I try not to have any secrets; I'm an open book....usually. Lately, I had in fact been keeping a few secrets, which was very unlike me.

I just didn't want people hanging and fawning all over me. It's strange though; I'll tell anyone about myself. Additionally, I will listen, hear the problems of just about anybody, and offer advice, guidance, and even a bit of wisdom to ponder, some of which has profundity and insight. However, what I try not to do is rely too much on others for their advice or their profound thoughts and infinite wisdom. I like solving my own problems and not enlist the help of others. I like to believe that I'm a forager of sorts and that I can sift through and clear away all of the weeds to get the heart of any problem or quandary I'm facing. Oftentimes, I'm wrong and end up getting more lost in my jungle of a life than necessary.

This particular issue had me stumped. I thought that my aunt was telling me that she loved me and those would be her final words to me. However, I was wrong, dead wrong; I had no way of ever really knowing what she wanted to say to me or what she meant by "I forgive you." I'd never done anything too terribly wrong to her. Like anyone in today's society, I probably could have been nicer to her before it was too late. I could've spent more time with her, appreciated her more, been more available emotionally and physically to her. But to have actually needed to be forgiven for something, I didn't understand what that could mean.

I couldn't comprehend what she could've meant or intended by that. I always had an above average relationship with my aunt. Although, she was much closer to Darby and Vaughn than she ever was to me. Before I was born, my Aunt Lila actually lived with my family. She never lived with us once I was born; maybe she forgave me for taking her spot in the family.

I doubted that was the big secret though. Once my parents realized that they were pregnant again (with me) and having a child in their 30s, they decided that they wanted to move the family out of Firestone Park and make sure that their children had a safer and more academically sound environment in which to grow up. That was what my mom told people anyway. To my very liberal father's dismay, my mom wanted to move out of Firestone Park, because she and her sisters believed that the neighborhood was going to Hell with all the minorities moving in.

As a teacher, racism confused me. It's so blatantly absurd to dislike people based on their appearance or even their beliefs and cultural upbringing. Truthfully, my racism unit is the hardest to teach. I struggle with the fact that I have to tell my students that racism is wrong. Oh, it's wrong. Believe me, I know it's wrong. See, I teach To Kill a Mockingbird, which portrays the horrors of racism. If my student already believes in the horrors and ridiculousness of racism, then it connects us on a deeper, more intellectual level. Many students are enthralled with the novel and learn a little more about tolerance and acceptance, but others are so resistant. Their parents are obviously teaching them that conformity and intolerance is acceptable. Therefore, when students are bigoted and prejudice, my lessons of the absurdity of racist acts and behaviors puts a wedge between us, severing whatever bond I'd attempted to create.

How do I, as their English teacher, explain to them that the very parents they idolize and often try to emulate are wrong? It's a catch-22 and extremely difficult to handle in the classroom. For me, I was lucky that I was not so ignorantly misinformed. My father got to my mother before she got to us. What I mean is that my mom was raised by some very intolerant, old-school Italian parents; therefore she was pretty ignorant and quite the product of her environment. My father agreed to move us out of Firestone Park, not because of the minorities, but because the school district we relocated to was known for its arts, academics, and athletics. Even though my father was not a well-educated man, or even a moderately educated man, he valued all three of the As. He knew that more opportunities would arise for his children in a prominent suburban school district. However, he kept after my mom to open her mind and her heart to all types of people.

Little by little, he broke down her initial bigotry, and she began to become more educated and more accepting of others. She had to; my father had two best friends when I was young. One was a younger African-American man; the other was a homosexual man from Scotland. My father cherished his friendships with both of them. They worked together, laughed together, and often drank together. After my father forced these men on my mother and required that she nurture lasting friendships with them, her racist and homophobic viewpoints dwindled considerably....entirely. Can I fault my mother for being so closed-minded when that is what she was taught? My mom was ignorant and closed-minded to what she didn't know, but then learned the errors of her ways. My mother ended up being the most open-minded out of all of her sisters.

My aunts used to call African-Americans, "colored" people. They never understood or caught on when I looked at them square in the eye and asked, "What 'color' were they? Purple?" My aunts had no idea that I was mocking them and challenging their old, ignorant, racist mindsets. Therefore, shouldn't I be proud of my mom for evolving and not embarrassed by how and what she was before? I'd never been sure of what to think. I do know that I had never in my life heard her say an ill word about anyone, especially against a minority. My father spurned her acceptance of people, helping her to evolve.

I was glad that my dad got to her. I was glad that by the time I was growing up, that both of my parents were evolved enough to teach me that a life without differences and diversity would not only lack color, but would lack a certain verve that makes living worthwhile. I felt lucky that I could thank my father for my open-mindedness and for my bleeding heart.

I don't think that I could be an effective teacher without those qualities, which is why I struggle so much with my viewpoints about my students. I want to hate my racist, bigoted students, but wouldn't that make me no better than they are? I can't hate them or judge them for how they think; I can just hate what they think.

Anyway, right before I was born, my family moved away from all of their aunts, uncles, sisters and cousins in the city and moved to an all-white suburb. My father was like a fish out of water. He hated being away from the city; he valued diversity, culture, and city living. My mom, she was in her element. My mother loved being the suburban mom and reveled in the catty chatty mothers and the neighborhood gatherings. Maybe my aunt resented me for coming along and moving the family away.

I had to figure out what my aunt meant, but I didn't know how. My brother would think I was silly for even fretting about it. Vaughn would most likely say something like, "she was dying; she probably didn't even know what she was saying." My sister would go completely berserk and become all-encompassed with finding out the truth behind her dying words. So for the third time in my life, I was keeping a secret, while still wanting the truth.

"Miss LeeMaster do you have a sec?" I'd been staring at the same essay for over 15 minutes without getting beyond the thesis-less introductory paragraph. Of course, I had a second; I certainly could be using my planning period for better use than daydreaming.

"Sure Janessa, whaddya need?" I'd known Janessa for almost five full years now. When I started teaching, she was in my little seventh grade honors English class. She was so quiet and mousy, barely noticeable. She earned high grades, showed signs of creativity, and exuded a scholarly mentality. Janessa hid behind her thick glasses, reading and absorbing everything she read.

After teaching seventh grade for one year, I moved up to ninth grade at the high school. When I ran a cheerleading clinic for tryouts, I hadn't seen Janessa in a year. It was in the spring of her eighth grade year, and she was going to see if she had what it took to be a high school cheerleader. Apparently, the new "Nessa" learned a lot more than the eighth grade curricula in the past year. Her body developed. She traded in her glasses for contacts, and boys replaced those books she cared so much about. Being a new teacher, I didn't realize that one 365-day period could be so crucial to a girl of 13. (Additionally, age-wise, Janessa was a year behind all of the other students in her grade.) Her maturation was surprisingly astonishing.

Janessa ended up being an incredible cheerleader and gymnast. She'd made the squad with scores higher than most of the seniors at the time. As her cheerleading coach and ninth grade English teacher, I spent many evenings trying to counter the peer pressure that Janessa was facing. I repeatedly lost my battles. It is devastating to watch students make poor choices and have to live with the consequences. Often, I just want to make all of their decisions for them, because it is just so hard for them to make smart decisions on their own. For some reason, it's harder for them to do the right thing, because they'd rather be doing the "cool" thing.

"I have a problem. . ." It was strange to see her so uncomfortable talking to me. Here it was, the end of her junior year, and she and I had encountered and surmounted many obstacles together. Janessa's father died when she was in ninth grade, which rocked her world, forcing her to make a long slew of poor decisions. She had a pregnancy scare shortly thereafter, and attempted to end her own life in the middle of tenth grade. Her junior year had gone shockingly well after those two years of turmoil and distress. And now, at nearly the half-way point of her senior year, she was doing remarkably well and waiting to hear back from a few Ivy League schools. Despite all that she had endured, she was still very well-liked, very intelligent (academically), and very involved in the school. She was the truth behind what the high school sweetheart often was, gorgeous and perfect on the outside, hurt, damaged, and full of angst on the inside.

"Miss LeeMaster, I don't know how to say this." She was truly agonizing over something, but what? I had no idea.

"What Janessa? What're ya trying to tell me?" I'd never had to pry anything out of her since I met her. She'd always been so verbose and loose with her tongue. This had to be big, and I was curious and nervous at the same time.

"Okay...ummm...well...you know how Shane and I had sex right?" I nodded, remembering the pregnancy scare and how upset she was and how equally terrified he was. I also knew that the two of them broke up a few months ago and both of them had been quite "free" in the past months. Teenagers were thrill-seekers and truth deniers. Shane was a good guy for the most part though, despite a few flawed decisions here and there.

"Well, one time...ummm...we...uhhh...made a tape..." Wow! My mind hadn't gone there. I was convinced that she found out he cheated on her or gave her some STD. I even thought that this could have been another pregnancy scare. Porn? No, my mind hadn't gone to child pornography. Oh my God! I should've chosen another profession.

"Okay, so you made a tape and...?" I had to keep my composure, otherwise, I'd scare her away, and she'd have nobody to confide in.

"Well, Shane thought it would be funny since me and him broke up that he would like show everyone at Ken's party. Miss LeeMaster, they've been making fun of me and saying shit, I mean, crap to me all day. What am I gonna to do?" She whined, throwing herself on the table top of the desk.

I wanted to tell her to start using her brain and stop getting herself into these messes, but it wasn't the time for an adult lecture. This was clearly a time for an adolescence and coping with high school and gossip lecture.

"Whew...okay," this was a tough one for me. When I was in high school, I was so far from making tapes. Heck, I barely made out with boys. I didn't have much personal experience or knowledge to go on here. "Well, at cheerleading camp in the dorms, I can barely get you dressed." Janessa was very proud of her body and flaunted it at every opportunity she could—even in a room full of girls.

Continuing, since I had her attention, I said, "You always walk up and down the halls in your thong underwear and bras. You always tell me that you love your body. When the kids say things, and they will, make no mistake about that, just say to them, 'it was dumb to make that video, but wow don't I look good?"

I found that if kids don't think that you're phased by what people are saying to you, then they give up on the berating comments much quicker than if you cry, yell, and carry on. "High school ridicule and degradation can only continue if you allow the belittling fools to get the best of you," I explained. "You have to act like it doesn't phase you at all."

"I can't! That's the problem! I don't look good," she pouted childishly. "We made the tape in eighth grade. I don't have any boobs or hips or anything!" Christ, she wasn't upset, because people saw the video. She was upset, because her body was underdeveloped at the time of the taping of the video. What was I doing? I had students in middle school video-taping themselves screwing, trying to kill themselves, getting pregnant, and experimenting with drugs and alcohol and my main concern at work was supposed to be whether or not they pass the damn Ohio Graduation Test. Plus, on top of all of that, I had to figure out what "I forgive you" meant. I was just too tired and getting too old for all this.

"Okay, first of all, stop being this person. Stop getting yourself into these kinds of messes," I lectured, knowing that I shouldn't be admonishing her, but not being able to help myself. "You've got to start using your head. You're eight months away from going to college. With your grades, you're probably going to get into any one of those colleges and get a free ride." Sometimes, I cannot even talk myself out of the parental, adult-like lectures. She just nodded and agreed with me. I always wondered if when I started talking if that was the time they opened up the air passage that traveled between their ears, so the words went right in and floated right back out. I think my words are the magic key to opening that mythical portal.

"Secondly, I'll talk to Shane. He's essentially a pretty good guy. He's eighteen right?" She nodded again, with that adolescent glazed-over look that teenagers often got when adults were speaking to them.

Now, I was certain that she truly wasn't listening to me. I'd scare the crap out of him. Janessa was only seventeen; I'd tell him that if her parents found out that he was distributing or publicly viewing that tape, he could be brought up on child pornography charges, since she was seventeen and he was eighteen. I had no idea if I was right or not, but it would scare him enough to destroy the tapes.

"And Janessa..." she looked at me, remorsefully. "You know I'm gonna have to call your mom and his parents about this." She grumbled and begged, but in the end, I told her that her sex life wasn't important enough to me to jeopardize my job by keeping a secret as destructive as this one. Reluctantly, she laughed, nodded, and ending up apologizing to me. I knew she hated letting me down; I'd become pretty important to her in the last four years. What I never told her was that she'd become pretty important to me too. Not having a husband, a boyfriend, or kids of my own, my students were my family. I cared about them. Oftentimes, I even cared for them when nobody else would.

When she started walking away, I stopped her. "Janessa, someday, you're gonna meet Mr. Wonderful. He's gonna sweep you off your feet and teach you what forever means." She walked back to me, holding on to my every word. Girls loved hearing stories about true love, dreaming about Prince Charming. "One night, that wonderful man is going to look into your beautiful eyes and ask you how many men you've been with." She dropped her head in humiliation.

She started to speak, but I cut her off. "You're gonna have to be honest, so make sure you realize that number, whatever it may be, can make Mr. Wonderful not want you, not want to be with you like you want him to." I said, forcing her to look me in the eyes. "So make sure that number isn't something that embarrasses or mortifies you. Hopefully, you'll start learning from these mistakes and stop giving yourself so freely to these guys. You're only seventeen." Nodding, she cried openly and hugged me.

"I'm so dumb," she cried into my shoulder.

"Actually Janessa, you're really smart; you just make dumb decisions," I said letting her go. I walked across my classroom to get her a tissue. "Here's the thing, I know a lot of girls who tell me that they wish they wouldn't have slept with so many guys in high school and in college," I said handing her a few Kleenex. I waited while she wiped her eyes, blew her nose, and was listening to me again. I wanted her undivided attention; I wanted this wisdom to sink in, all the way in.

"But I don't know any girls who ever say, 'Man, I wish I would've slept with more.' You just need to start thinking things through before you act on them. Slow down; you have the rest of your life to be a 'grown up' and do adult things, Janessa." I brushed the hair out of her eyes, looking at her and still seeing that insecure seventh grade girl. "Hold on to your childhood, honey. It's the one thing that you'll never get back."

"I'm sorry, Miss LeeMaster. I'm so sorry." She cried, wiping her tears.

"Honey, you don't have to apologize to me. I'm always here for you, and I'll always forgive you." Again, those words. I forgive you. I needed the truth behind those words.

Chapter 8

Here

I needed to talk to someone. I couldn't handle being around Carl, my sisters, or my other family members and friends. Each of them agreed that I should welcome Lila and let her tell me all about my kids and their lives. I remember how ignorant I used to be when I was still there. I used to believe that my parents were watching over me, protecting me, like guardian angels. Little did I know that they were sitting here hoping that they'd made all the right decisions to ensure our happy and healthy futures. Like me, they were nervously awaiting new arrivals to fill in the gaps of what had occurred after their departures. Whoever came up with the notion that we became guardian angels? It was a comforting notion, but a fairy tale nonetheless. It was only something to ease the fear and uncertainty of the unknown. Trust me, I'd love to watch over my children; I'd kill to see them again...

Julian. I needed to talk to Julian. He'd advise me, guide me. Rumor had it that he'd ignored the firm recommendation that we never try to reconnect, because the pain was too unbearable. He'd needed to finish something, something so pressing, so monumental that he was granted permission to return for a moment. People claimed that he went back and did what he was supposed to do, but the pain that coupled it was interminable. Whenever I saw him, his eyes didn't posses the joy and life we all had here. Sadness and loneliness were still feelings that we endured, but they never possessed us or overwhelmed us. Our souls didn't allow such negative feelings to linger; negativity evaporated quickly here. I was actually surprised by how long my anger for Lila's arrival actually remained. Soon, it would be gone, but for now, I was reveling in the fury I felt toward her and toward the rest of my family.

"I thought you'd come see me," Julian said to me without looking up from the painting he was working on. Julian really was a mystery to everyone here. We all knew he'd gone back and come back more broken when he returned. All that was special or unique about him was that he was the only one we'd ever heard of that had gone back.

"Really?" This was surprising to me. "Do you even know me?" I questioned, skeptically.

"Betheny DiBellini-LeeMaster. Married to Carl LeeMaster. Died early, leaving behind three kids, all over the age of 18. Horrible colon cancer did ya in, but lucked out, because ya didn't have to watch all yer sisters die in the exact same, abhorrent way," he blurted out without ever making eye contact with me. I wondered what his clothes and look represented, what it all meant to him. His torn jeans and stained shirt was odd here, as was his long, blond scraggly hair. His eyes were the softest, clearest blue, but seemed so tortured and pained, even here.

Stunned, I shook my head, trying to formulate my thoughts. "I....uh...was..."

"You were wondering what it was like to go back," he said, mixing colors into the most vibrant shade of purple I'd ever seen. "It's miraculously and magically horrifying, and I wouldn't recommend it to my worst enemy." He finally stopped, put down the paintbrush and looked straight into my eyes. "But if you're here, your mind is made up, you wanna go back, your 'unfinished business' is more important than everyone else's."

I didn't really want to go back; I didn't. But I needed some answers. I needed to know if my children were okay, going to be okay, were on the road to okay... I just hated this.

"If you're so worried, so curious, then just ask your sister; she just saw them." Whoa. We don't have special powers here; how could he have known what I was thinking, what was on my mind?

"How'd you..."

"Your husband, Carl, talked me a little while ago." He said as he started painting again; I couldn't tell what he was painting, but I could tell how serene it made him, serenity I hadn't experienced lately, but missed terribly. "With all the drama going on in your family, I'd think I was back there and not here." He smirked as he continued a series of methodic strokes, highlighting and emphasizing the lines of the painting.

"Julian, what's the punishment, or the forfeit....for...ummm... going back?" I asked, knowing he wouldn't tell me the truth. He never told anyone.

He put his brush down, wiped off his hands, took both of my hands tightly in his and said, "Hell."

There

Ever since our school went to block scheduling, lunch had become the most wonderful aspect of the teaching day. Teachers now had 90-minute lunch breaks. By freeing up that time, we actually felt like real human beings with professional jobs. It was remarkable how a little free time within the workday made life more tolerable and enjoyable.

My two teacher friends, Nina and Amy, and I met each day at the track, walked two miles, and then spent the rest of the lunch break eating lunch at a picnic table away from the always-listening ears of the students and other nosy teachers. Nina and I'd been friends since our first day of new teacher training. At the new teacher orientation, we immediately clicked, because both of us visibly despised the antics of the "meet & greet ice breaker activities." With a commonality like that, nothing could come between us. A few years ago, Nina hosted a student teacher that quickly became our sidekick. Nina was the most valued and respected teacher in the building, so with Nina's recommendation, her student teacher, Amy, was hired and therefore, never left our lunchtime shadow. I'd come to value Amy's friendship and camaraderie; Nina still had trouble viewing her as our friend, and not as a student.

After I told the two of them about Janessa's latest "sexual escapade," leaving out her name, Amy went on a rant about how promiscuous teenagers were. Nearing 30, I felt much older and wiser than my students. But Amy was pushing 25-years-old, she couldn't possibly view them as children yet, like I did.

Cutting off Amy's tirade, Nina asked, "Shelb, have you cleaned out your aunt's condo yet?" She'd known that I'd been forcing my brother and sister to stall on the inevitable. First of all, my aunt was a low-grade hoarder, which made the job that much more disgustingly repulsive. But secondly, cleaning the condo meant officially closing the chapter of that part of our lives, something I wasn't ready to face.

"Nah, we're meeting this Sunday for lunch and then going to the condo," I explained. "I wish we'd just all chip in and pay someone to go in and clean the whole thing out for us. Hell, I bet I could pay a few students and they'd loot the whole place," I joked, knowing that was a real possibility though. It would be so much easier if we didn't have to do all the work and face the memories simultaneously. Cleaning out an entire condo was going to be tiring, hard labor, but adding in the memories and the mementos we'd have to sift through just made the whole ordeal grueling and draining. "Then to add to our day of morbid fun, we're going over to Darby's in the evening to write the thank you cards and shit," I whined with clear agitation in my voice.

"Christ, why do ya have to do it all this weekend?" Nina groaned. "Haven't ya dealt with enough lately?"

"Darby and Vaughn want to get all this over with. I get it; they've been away from their families for so long, caring for Aunt Lila. They just wanna get it done." I just hated the fact that as soon as we closed this chapter of our lives, that this particular book would never be opened again. The DiBellinis were gone, and I had to accept that.

"Do ya want Ame and I to come help write thank yous?" Nina offered; Amy nodded. "We will ya know?" Nina was a good friend, always said and did the right things. She had friendship in the bag. I had friends in my present life that could learn quite a bit from her.

I knew they'd help too, but this was something that Vaughn, Darby, and I needed to face alone. "Nah, we're good, but thanks." I didn't know why in the world we had to write thank yous for flowers or food we didn't necessarily want in the first place. I could totally grasp a thank you card for a Christmas gift or a birthday gift, but for flowers at a funeral? I didn't ask for them, expect them, or even want them for that matter. Why would I have to thank someone for them? And for the 12 lasagnas in the freezer? What were we going to do with all that pasta? Other than having to start the South Beach Diet after devouring it all...

Talking about cleaning out her house seemed like the perfect transition into my aunt's last words to me. I told them both the story, hoping for some sort of insight from them. Amy was terrified; she seemed to think that it had ominous undertones. Whatever the Hell that meant. Maybe Nina was right, maybe Amy was too young for our friendship.

Nina wasn't as concerned. She was like Vaughn in that manner. She believed that the pain meds were doing the talking, not necessarily my Aunt Lila. Nina then gave me a sense of some optimism. "Hey maybe when you clean out her house, you can find something there to let you know what she meant...if...she did mean anything by it."

I hadn't thought about that. "Ooooh, you might have something there," I said. I hadn't considered that at all. Cleaning out the condo would give me every opportunity to go through all of my aunt's belongings. "There's a chance the answer's there." Damn it...I knew better than to use that word in front of Nina.

"Speaking of 'Chance,' have you heard from him?" Nina never missed a beat when it came to Chance. I was usually on "Chance alert" and tried to avoid any and all conversations pertaining to him or even using the term, "chance."

"Not since the luncheon," I answered. I was going to have this conversation devoid of all emotion.

"That's too bad," she said. "You should've seen Mallory at her dance recital; she was the most beautiful girl there."

"What? What're you talking about?" Damn it, she got me again. Her lips smirked triumphantly. My shoulders sagged, accepting defeat. "When did you see her?" I muffled.

"Well Chance called me the other day, because he didn't wanna bother you," she explained. "Mallory was upset, because he'd forgotten to make her a hair appointment for the recital."

"Did you do Mallory's hair?" I asked reluctantly. I could feel my heart fall, feeling betrayed.

"No, I knew you'd freak if I did, so I got her an appointment with my stylist." Nina reassured me.

"I wouldn't--"

"Uh...yeah...ya would," she said. "I'm well aware that those two are off limits to anyone in a 60 mile radius of you." That wasn't technically true, but if Chance started spending time with Nina, then that would be a little too close for my comfort. "Once I got her in with Jorge, I asked Chance where and when the recital was," she explained.

Nina had shown up at the recital before Mallory went on and snuck back to the 7-year-old "dancing darlings" holding room. She said that Mallory was ecstatic to see her, hoping that I was with her. My heartstrings felt taut, nearing their breaking point. "She was sad that you couldn't be there, but was happy that you sent her flowers and lip gloss."

"What?" I was going to kill her. "You gave her flowers and said they were from me?" I was livid. It wasn't right to play with a little girl's heart like that.

"Don't be pissed. We both know that you would've done her hair, done her makeup, bought her flowers and sat in the front row if Chance would've told you about it." She countered. "Just because you're not with Chance doesn't change how you feel about that little girl."

"Nina, you have no right to play with her heart and give her hope like that." I felt terribly.

"And neither do you. You know her dead-beat douchebag mom wasn't going to show up and save the day. You would've been there if you hadn't been dealing with all this shit," she said, making sense, but pissing me off equally. "I was just filling in." She smiled, knowing that she had easily won this particular battle.

"But what if Chance--"

"Chance was well aware of my plans and intentions. He knows that you don't want anything to do with him. We talked about that on the phone too...several times." She explained.

"Several times? What's that mean?" I asked too quickly but, terrified of the answer. What was going on? Were Nina and Chance developing some sort of friendship, or worse, a relationship?

"He calls me a lot, Shelb. He checks on you all the time. That's one man you're not getting rid of all that easily." Nina said.

"We've been broken up for over a year; he needs to move on--"

"Believe me, the only moving on he's ever gonna do is gonna be right beside you. He's not going anywhere." She put her arm around me, pulled me to her and whispered in my ear, "Just give him another chance."

Chance? No way. Now how. No chance.

Chapter 9

Here

Remember, when you almost died during your C-section with Darby?" Carl asked, coming up behind me, massaging my shoulders.

"Not really, seeing as how I was knocked out," I quipped snidely at him, shrugging his hands off my shoulders.

"Well, I do, and it was at that moment that I realized that I'd never stop worrying about you or our children," he said. He walked around to face me, sitting on the ground. "The whole time you were pregnant, I guess I never realized that I should worry about it. Everyone gets pregnant and has kids, no big deal." I knew what he meant. Once you realize what could truly go wrong in a pregnancy is when you realize the true meaning behind "ignorance is bliss." Then, you start to realize how precious life is, how precious those children really are, so fragile and so perfect, growing so innocently inside you.

I nodded, remembering why I loved him so much, "Carl, after all of these years, you never told me how scared you were." This confession of his worry was new to me, yet so important too. When Darby was born, men stayed in the waiting room, pacing the corridors, waiting to be told if they had a daughter or a son. Based on what I knew about the birthing process and even the C-sections now, the fathers were right there in the heart of it all. If everything went well, their hearts filled and bloomed right along with the mothers. If problems occurred, then the fathers' hearts broke too. Carl had never before mentioned anything about that time he spent alone worrying in the waiting room.

Carl grabbed my hands and pulled me to him. "I've been afraid of losing you, of not being able to protect you or to take care of you, since the day you held me and supported me when my mom died." He kissed me lightly and tenderly. "Betheny, I don't want to hurt you or to upset you. Ever. But, I miss our kids; I miss knowing about their lives. They've stayed stagnant for seven years now. I need answers, honey." He was being so tender, so open and honest. No wonder I fell in love with him, graying hair, sloppy clothes and protruding gut and all. You can't always choose who you fall in love with. Sometimes love just chooses you.

I knew I wasn't being fair to him. My guilt shouldn't stop him from getting to know which direction our kids' lives went. He left them so long ago; he didn't know them like I did. Carl didn't really know their flaws or the wrong paths they were capable of taking. I did, and it scared me to know the truth.

"Do you know why I fell in love with you?" he asked me. It was so odd that all of this would come up after all of these years. I'd thought we exhausted all of these confessions and revelations years ago, lifetimes ago.

"Yeah, because my boobs were the biggest you'd ever seen," I rolled my eyes and shook my head at him.

"Well that," he said, nodding and chuckling. "And...because you're the most open-minded and stubborn woman I've ever met.

It never made sense, and still doesn't," he was looking at me awestruck, just like he used to when we were falling in love. "You're so stubborn in your wants and beliefs, but yet you listen to people and really hear them, oftentimes opening your mind to ideas and situations that you'd never thought of before." Carl never ceased to amaze me. He wasn't an educated man, but he was so smart, so insightful. I still loved him with every fiber of my being. Or soul. He'd taught me so much in our years together. He'd broken down so many preconceived notions I'd had about people. Carl taught me acceptance, opening my mind to so many things and so many people.

"But you don't understand," I took a deep breath, trying to find the right words. "I made so many mistakes with them, mistakes that could've ruined them, ruined their lives."

Carl embraced me, stroking my hair, "Shh honey, don't you think that every mother has regrets, worries that they didn't do everything they were supposed to?" He asked me, calmly and rationally. He was always so rational and calm, especially when I was flying off the handle. We really were a perfect match; he was the ying to my yang. What I lacked, he had, and what he lacked, I had. But right now, I just couldn't handle his lecture on rationality.

My husband didn't understand. He loved me so much and believed in me so much that he couldn't believe that I could've made mistakes, devastating mistakes that could've damaged our children for the rest of their lives. He didn't know it, but I did.

There

Driving to my aunt's house, I was worried that I wouldn't discover what she'd meant by "I forgive you." But, I also felt terrified to know what she did mean by "I forgive you." I hated having conflicting emotions. I hated that I couldn't just sit down and talk to her about what was behind those cryptic words. I'd watched so many people die, and yet I still had so many words left unsaid, things left undone. It amazed me that I still hadn't learned from all of my previous mistakes.

When I was 10-years-old, my father died. He worked nights, therefore, I rarely saw him. Sadly, I don't have many memories of spending time with him. I do vividly remember the last thing I ever said to him on that final morning I spent with him.

My mother was off on Thursdays, so she often slept late those days, forcing my dad to get up with me on Thursday mornings. I'd heard through the 5th grade elementary grapevine that Tim Novack was going to ask me to "go with him" that day during recess. I wanted to look extra good in my Cavaricci pants with my big, permed hair. However, I was having a fifth grade catastrophic hair day, and I couldn't find my pants anywhere. I kept trying to wake up my mom, so she could help with my hair. My dad wouldn't let me wake her, hushing me all morning long. Being a prepubescent brat, I got louder and louder in hopes of stirring her from their bedroom. She didn't wake up and help me with my hair, so I had to settle for my neighbor's hand-me-down Levi's and a slicked back pony tail with an old, non-matching scrunchie.

Grumbling, I left the house in hatred and anger with horrible hair and hideous jeans. My dad stood on the front porch waving to me as the bus approached our house, telling me that he loved me. I turned around, half-way across the front yard and said, "I hate you; I hope you never get up with me again." The words were caustic and biting, and I loved spitting them at my father, feeling cool and mature, showing my independence. He just continued to smile and wave, not caring that I wished him away. I didn't have a heads up penny or a four-leaf clover. I never saw a bottle with a genie. But none of that mattered. I got my wish. I got that horrendous and unforgiveable wish.

That night, my father came home at midnight from his second shift job, got his glass of Coke and settled in the basement recliner to watch television to unwind after a long day of work. My mom was asleep upstairs in their bed. At some point, between 1:00 a.m. and 2:00 a.m., my dad, the man who I hoped would never get up with me again, suffered a fatal heart attack, dying instantly in his chair, while watching television and drinking his Coca~Cola.

My older sister, Darby, was seventeen, a senior in high school when she walked down the stairs the next morning to get her clothes out of the dryer. She never got those clothes. Instead, she found my dad's body, cold, hard, and lifeless in the recliner in our basement, wrecking our lives for the first time. I woke to blood-curdling screams of "Mom, Dad's dead!" over and over. Actually, I awoke to those words for many years after, but my sister wasn't screaming them anymore; they were in my head, in my nightmares, and in my regrets.

I should've learned then that life changes and can destroy you in an instant. I should've learned then that the people you love the most in life aren't always going to be there to do your hair, make you breakfast, or hug you goodbye. But when those people are there, you need to cherish those moments. I should've learned it then, but I didn't. Even if I did learn it, I soon forgot again. We always seem to forget, even when it's the most important lesson we ever learn.

Pulling into my aunt's driveway, I noticed that Darby and Vaughn's cars weren't there yet. Darby had the keys, so I walked around back to the patio and sat on the swing, wishing my aunt was with me, sipping iced tea as we talked about what books we'd read recently. Darby hated reading. My mom loved to read. My friend, Nina was the only English teacher in the building who hated reading for fun. I didn't have anyone to talk to about reading and what books to read next. I made a mental note to start or join a book club; I cringed at the thought of not having someone to talk to about my passion. Reading was my escape, even if my escape meant that I'd have to face reality soon enough once the book ended.

Sometimes, I wished I could make a real escape and not face reality ever again. I could skip town, move to Jamaica, and braid hair on the beach for tourists who want to look like islanders. I'd spend my days carefree, without a worry in the world. I'd bask in the sunshine, reading and relaxing, forgetting the pains I'd endured throughout my life. Often, I'd have these whims, but then reality would set back in, reminding me that there were so many flaws in that plan. I hated sand. I hated touching people's hair. I really couldn't braid that well, and I wasn't a big fan of the heat. I'd die in the tropics. I'm pretty fond of 72 degrees and sunny or just cranked up air conditioning. Jamaica was out; reality was in.

"Are you ready?" Vaughn's voice startled me, shooting me up off the swing. My scream scared him so badly that he fell backward into the bushes, tearing his shorts on the branches. "Holy shit Shelby, calm down," he yelled, trying to get up from the bush.

My fear turned to unadulterated laughter and uncontrollable giggles, causing my brother to scowl and glare at me. I walked over and offered him my hand, but he knocked it away, grumbling an "I got it." He hated to look like a fool, but sometimes he needed to be knocked down a few pegs.

Vaughn had it all. He was extremely good-looking. Honestly, I'd even call him "hot," if he weren't my brother. Vaughn had all of my mom's Italian features: dark eyes, dark, thick hair, and dark olive skin. He accepted nothing but perfection in his life; therefore, he exercised like a fiend and dressed only in the latest professional styles, complete with monogrammed dress shirts, engraved cufflinks, and silk ties. What he lacked in height; he made up for in presence and prestige. Vaughn was the CEO of an international real estate company. Ultimately, he was raking in the big bucks, while looking like a million bucks.

Vaughn's wife, Rachel, was pretty much the most gorgeous and even nicest woman on the planet. It sucked that I couldn't hate her. The first time I saw her, I hated her with a passion. Rachel was almost too pretty to look at; I wanted to kick her. But then, when I talked to her, I was even more pissed off. Rachel's smart, articulate, caring, and as sweet as can be. For the first year, I kept trying to find her flaws, but when searching for her flaws, I ended up finding more and more of my own. So, I quit looking, because my self-esteem was taking a serious beating. She's the real deal. His kids are adorable, well-behaved, and freakishly intelligent. Vaughn has the perfect life, in a pretty package, all wrapped up with a big, shiny bow.

Once Vaughn finally got out of the bushes, we walked together to the front of the condo. Darby was already unloading plastic totes, trash bags, brooms, and cleaning supplies out of her small SUV. Leave it to Darby to bring even more items to a "cleaning out" pity party. She was always prepared, always thinking. Darby had been a "mom" long before she ever had Becca. Darby prided herself on taking care of everyone, whoever needed it. Darby even looked the part; she had that "mom look" for years, even when it wasn't yet acceptable to have it.

Darby kept her overly highlighted dark hair styled and cut in layers, framing her round face, but emphasizing her dark eyes. Oddly, she was the tallest of the three of us, at just over 5'5". Her divorce and our parents' death had aged her, but hadn't hardened her look. Her face was still soft, vibrant, and expressive like it always was. Since she'd begun running, she'd thinned out and toned up. Her body was extraordinarily fit and tight, especially if you considered how soft and chubby she was in high school.

Darby looked amazing, I was thoroughly awed and proud of her, and even a little envious. I loved my brother and sister so much, needed them much more than they ever realized. I looked at Vaughn and Darby, trying hard to hold back my tears. They were all I had. Darby and Vaughn. My big sister and my big brother.

I couldn't believe that I'd come from such a large, crazy, boisterous family, and I was standing in the driveway with the two remaining members of my family. Of course, I had cousins, but once our aunts started dying, one by one, we all started to drift apart, leaving only Vaughn and Darby as my family. It was hard to accept, hard to digest. But what was harder to take was that I wasn't all they had. Vaughn had his wife and his two sons.

Darby's husband left her years ago, but she and Becca had built a wonderful family life together, being active members of their community. Once he left, Becca never saw him again, but Darby was the type of mother who could fill in for a man easily. Becca never mentioned him or acted as if she was missing out on anyone or anything. I'd hoped that Darby would meet someone and would fall in love again, but for now, she was just fine on her own, raising her daughter better than any mother I'd ever known.

Vaughn and Rachel had been married for over seven years now and had a cushy, happy life. Their sons were hysterical, but a handful as well. I adored my niece and nephews, but I'd never felt as connected to them as I had to my aunts growing up. I was certainly not their "Aunt Lila." I wasn't filling in that role for anyone. Truthfully, the boys didn't really know me. Once Vaughn married Rachel, he'd defected to her side of the family. We didn't see him on the holidays or anything like that. He'd gotten married and left us. Darby'd been okay with it; she had Becca. I missed Vaughn though. He'd always been my father-figure, the man in my life. It was hard to see him with someone else's family, being the man in their lives. I missed him, but was beyond proud of him and who he was.

Darby immersed herself in Becca's life. She was very active in Becca's preschool and extra curricular activities. I just didn't know where I fit in. I was the drifter, drifting aimlessly. I had no idea what the rest of my life had in store for me. I had four titles: aunt, friend, sister, and teacher. I'd come to accept that I'd never have any other titles. I'd never be a daughter or a niece again. When I first realized that I was no longer someone's daughter, it hit hard. I cried for days, sobbing in fetal position in my bed. People take their titles so lightly, but when they're ripped from you abruptly and permanently, it's devastating and debilitating. It's a difficult vicissitude to accept. I doubted I'd ever add wife or mother to my resume either. Yeah, those were definitely titles I'd never have. Four titles were enough, right?

"Hello, Earth to Shelby," my sister snapped her fingers in front of my face. "Are you here to help or stare off into some strange space all day?" Luckily, they didn't question me about my thoughts, leaving me alone to my reverie. I was known for daydreaming and not paying attention to my surroundings; I just needed brought back every now and again.

We spent the afternoon cleaning. We found many items that we laughed and cried over. The whole process left us feeling closer to Aunt Lila, even though it felt like we were purging her from our lives. Since we'd done this before, two times before, we didn't fight or bicker about who was getting what. None of us seemed to want anything. We loved having Aunt Lila, but she didn't own things that we'd actually want. We just wanted her. There were a few items that we divvied up out of convenience. I needed a foyer table; Aunt Lila had one. Vaughn needed a box spring for his spare bedroom bed; he took Aunt Lila's. Darby wanted the sentimental things: her photo albums, old letters, and cards; things she could sift through and cry all night over.

The process didn't take as long as I'd originally predicted. We were done within five hours and eating pizza back at Darby's shortly thereafter. Vaughn had picked up Rachel and the boys. The boys were playing some virtual sports video game with Becca in the great room. Rachel was addressing envelopes while Vaughn, Darby, and I wrote heartfelt and meaningful thank you cards in honor of Aunt Lila. Aunt Lila hated "canned" responses and cards. She wanted her cards to always have meaning and be personal, which thoroughly lengthened the process, but we'd do anything for her.

Once we'd finally finished, we weren't in any hurry to go home to our houses. We were still in the mourning stages, saddened from the day's events, so we hung around the kitchen table, telling Rachel stories of our aunts and their epic weekend-long card games. Darby was perusing boxes of cards and mementos.

"Hey Shelby," she said handing me an envelope. "This is yours."

My heart fell. Darby gave me the envelope, looking at me quizzically. "Thanks." I didn't want to look too excited or scared; I didn't want to draw attention to my eagerness or apprehension. The envelope looked old, very old. "It's probably just a card or letter that she meant to send me at Ohio State." Aunt Lila was the best at postal correspondence. I received a letter, a package, or money from her every Wednesday when I lived in the dorms. Not having kids of her own, she often spoiled us as such.

In college, I'd gotten a package from her every Wednesday, usually filled with one-dollar bills. Being a waitress, Aunt Lila always had a lot of cash on her. She would wad up a roll of ones, stuff them in an old sock or a purple velvet Crown Royal sack and mail it all to me in a large yellow envelope. For the longest time, I had my roommates convinced that my older aunt was a stripper in an eccentric strip club for older gentlemen only.

"Open it," Darby said excitedly.

"Darby, leave her alone; she probably wants to open it in private," Vaughn jumped in to my rescue. There was no way Darby was going to accept that. I'd known her my entire life. I was surprised that the suspense hadn't already killed her; it was killing me.

"Nah, I'll open it," I said, hearing Darby sigh with relief. I slid my finger under the flap, tearing the paper from the adhesive. I unfolded the paper and saw the date. The date. "Actually, I'm just gonna read it at home." I folded the paper back up with shaky hands, trying unsuccessfully to put it back in the envelope. Finally, I just shoved the letter and envelope into my purse.

Vaughn, Darby, and even Rachel were eyeing me suspiciously now. I wasn't reading this with them around, especially after I saw the date. I'd wait until I was at home, on the couch, in my pajamas, drinking a glass of Merlot. The date scared me, making my heart beat loudly and ominously. My aunt had kept a letter that she'd written to me ten years ago on the very day that my mom died. What could my aunt have wanted to say to me the day mom died that she hadn't found the time (or courage) to say to me in the last ten years?

Chapter 10

Here

"She went to Homecoming?' Virginia questioned excitedly. "You saw her?"

"Oh Virgie, she was beautiful in such a classy and tasteful emerald green gown; all of her friends looked like hussies. But oh no, not her, she was exquisite," Lila said, telling my sister, Virginia about Aisley, her granddaughter's, first homecoming dance.

"And she wore emerald green." Virgie stated, glancing at her husband Raymond; both were beaming with pride. Emerald green was Virginia's favorite color.

"I told her that her Nonnie loved emerald green and that she'd be so proud of the young woman she was turning into," I heard Virginia sniffle. "You would too Virgie; she's at the top of her class and so sassy. She doesn't take anything from anyone—not even her mother."

Virginia laughed, snorting through her nose. "Serves her right; she was my toughest child, always testing my limits. Remember that time she ran away with that deadbeat to Florida....on a fucking pile of tin motorcycle?" She looked around, waiting for our memories to kick in.

All my sisters laughed remembering when our niece told Virginia to "stuff it" and rode off with some hoodlum to Florida to "see the Pacific ocean." Despite lingering discreetly in the back, not wanting to really be part of this "reunion," I could hear their words and chuckled with them, remembering how mad Virgie was at her daughter for taking off with that scumbag and for being so ignorant in geography. Even upon her arrival home, she still hadn't realized that she'd seen the Gulf of Mexico and not the Pacific Ocean.

Virgie grounded her "for life" and forced her to study geography every night for two hours. My niece knew every state, every capital, and every country in North America. Virgie even made her learn the countries and capitals in South America, as well as the oceans and rivers too. She could accurately label them on a map, spelling them all correctly. Once my niece realized it, she was devastated that she still hadn't seen the Pacific Ocean. I wondered if she'd ever gotten there since the last time I saw her. I hoped she had.

Patricia got excited, "Do me! Do me next." Lila's face fell, making Patricia anxious and troubled. "What Lila? Tell me." Worry suddenly clouded Patricia's face, making Frank tuck his arm tightly and quickly around her waist for support and stability.

Lila hated telling Patricia that her son had lost his job and had been unemployed for a few years, mooching off of his ex in-laws and not really looking for work. Patricia cried at the news, but was delighted that he was still the coach of his son's baseball team. She'd wanted to make sure she raised a good father, because her husband, Frank, had been such a great role model all around. Again sadness shadowed Lila's face as she explained that his wife had given up on him and found solace in the arms of another man.

It was apparent that the news was hard for Patricia to hear; she'd had such high hopes for her son. Being here, we want the news, but sometimes the news is very difficult and hard to hear. Oftentimes, the truth weighs more heavily on you than the curiosity of not knowing anything at all.

"I never liked her anyway; why'd he marry a Protestant in the first place? I told him to marry a good Catholic girl, an Italian who could cook," she complained. "No wonder he lost his job, he probably hated his wife and her subpar cooking." We all laughed. Even here, our children could do no wrong in our eyes (or minds).

Patricia was pleased to hear that her daughter's marriage was still going strong and that she had three healthy granddaughters; she'd only met two of those granddaughters. Patricia's daughter had gone back to college and finished her degree in nursing, something she'd always wanted to do.

"I always told her that she'd make a wonderful nurse," Patricia cried. "She was so good with me when I was sick; she ain't afraid of no needles, blood, or even shit and piss." We all laughed feeling happy that our niece had done so well for herself and feeling even happier that Patricia could feel pride for her daughter even when her son was still struggling.

Life was a series of gives and takes, pulls and pushes. Patricia had one child faring well and another still flailing around in adulthood. As parents, we cannot expect perfection, and yet we can't shelter our children from pain and setbacks. It's the pain and setbacks that make a person strong and resilient. In that case, I guessed my children must be the ultimate successes. Powerhouses of strength and tenacity.

My children were the youngest out of all the cousins, since there was a 15-year age gap between my oldest sister, Anna, and me. I felt badly thinking that only my children were the ones suffering, when I knew that each of my sisters and their husbands left their children. But Carl and I were the first to leave, and we did have the youngest children. By the time my sisters and brothers-in-law arrived, all of their children were married and most of them had children of their own. My kids, Darby, Vaughn, and Shelby Lynn, hadn't fallen in love, didn't have children, and were still struggling with being "orphaned" in their twenties. My last update was that Darby and Vaughn had recently found stable careers and were beginning to date new people. Shelby Lynn was still hoping to be a teacher and figure out what she wanted to do with her life. I wanted to know my children found happiness, success, and most importantly true love, someone to share their lives with, create memories with. That was seven years ago. Seven long, lonely years. I realize that seven years can feel like a lifetime and many milestones could be met in such an amount of time. I just worried that my children were stuck in a stagnant seven-year rut.

I finally excused myself from the group. I loved hearing about the lives of my nieces and nephews, but the longer that I sat listening, the more I doubted whether or not I had prepared my children for adulthood. I knew Carl was dying (odd phrase here) to know the paths our children had taken too, but I wasn't ready, wondered really if I'd ever be ready.

"Betheny?" Patricia followed me away from the group. "I was just thinking about something--" she said, looking away nervously, afraid to make eye contact.

"Don't try to talk me into staying over there---" I cut her off.

She shook her head, cutting me right back off. She looked me directly in the eyes. "Believe me, I've met you. You can't make an ass do anything it doesn't wanna do." She said curtly.

"Did you just call me an ass?" I was shocked. Patricia was my non-confrontational sister.

"If the butt fits..." She said, grinning victoriously.

Patricia obviously hadn't stopped me to come argue with me; she was being playful. I didn't know why I was so abrupt and short with her. She was the sister that I was least likely to fight with, all of us were; she was our Switzerland.

Alright Patti," I succumbed. "Let's talk."

"Has anyone ever told you, really sat you down and told you about the day that we all found out you had cancer?" She asked me, staring at me intently, searching my face for the truth before the words were revealed.

"What's to tell? Cancer. Dead. Not much more to the story," I said, trying to rid my voice and face of all emotion, hoping Patti wouldn't see right through it.

Actually the answer was, "No." I'd never heard the story. All I was ever told were the medical findings of that day:

Colon Cancer.

Over ¾ of my body riddled with cancer.

Stage 4.

Three months to live.

I remembered two things about that day. I was angry that they'd told Shelby Lynn that I had cancer. She was just a junior in high school, seventeen years old; she was too young to hear that news. They should've let me decide if and when I wanted to tell my children about this terminal diagnosis.

Additionally and inexplicably, I was devastated that they took out my belly button. My belly button! Not only was I being taken from my children in three months, but those doctors took away my body part that gave them life and nutrients for the nine months that they lived inside of me. It also connected me to my mother. It was our lifeline to generations of family bonding and connection. Was there anything I was going to be allowed to save and cherish between my children and me? It was a crushing blow. My belly button. I cried about it and lamented for days.

Finally, a doctor, a nice female doctor, who I soon became quite close to, listened to me and told me that many parents nowadays opted to laser off umbilical cords, so their children didn't have unsightly belly buttons. Apparently, belly buttons were going to be a thing of the past. (I wondered if that ever did happen. Seemed strange that a body part might become extinct.)

Then the doctor even revealed that at no point was my belly button connected to my children, but that it was in fact connected to my mother. I thought my belly button fed my children. I was horribly anatomically mistaken. Therefore, I couldn't and shouldn't think of it as a connection to my mother, my grandmother, and my own children, because that just wasn't the case. Instead of learning about my cancer and my upcoming treatments, I was getting lessons in navel history. I'd been more upset about my belly button than I was about the cancer, the colostomy bag, and my life expectancy.

The cancer news just angered me and sparked a fire in me. Those doctors could kiss my 3-months-to-live ass. I was not about to die in three months. That was just utter bullshit. Anyone who knew me, knew that I wasn't going to stand, sit, or lie down for that bullshit news. I lived three more years, two of them in "remission." Bastards were certainly not going to tell me that I couldn't watch my daughter, my baby, go to her senior prom, walk across the stage on her graduation day, or move in to dormitory on her first day of college. I had plans and by no means was colon cancer going to make me change my plans.

Eventually, that colon cancer won, but not before I fulfilled those particular dreams. I'd set milestone goals that I'd wanted to see; I only saw about ¼ of them. But what I saw, what I got to witness and feel, still floods me with love and pride each and every day of my....eternal existence.

"Beth, I want to tell you about that day---" Patti said, bringing me back to the conversation.

"Why now?" I asked. "Isn't it a little late, a little irrelevant?" I didn't know where she was going with this.

"Just sit down and let me tell you, and you can decide if it's important." She sat down next to me and told me the story of my diagnosis day, my dying diagnosis day.

It was May, a gorgeous spring day. I was scheduled for an "exploratory surgery" to possibly scrape the polyps from my colon at 6:00 a.m. I'd been in and out of the hospital for nearly six weeks with stomach pains and severe vomiting and diarrhea. I'd had horrible flu-like symptoms that the doctors were convinced were caused by polyps on my colon. Having poor health insurance with my job, the doctors were reluctant to do superfluous tests or procedures to determine the cause of my symptoms. Finally, after much pressure from Vaughn, Darby, and my five angry older Italian sisters, an exploratory surgery was reluctantly scheduled.

I was thrilled to be having the surgery, because the pain and suffering from the vomiting and diarrhea exceeded what I could endure much longer. The surgery was expected to last one to two hours at most, counting the recovery room time, depending how well I came out of the anesthesia. My sisters and children were there with hugs, kisses, and "I love yous," as they rolled me off to the operating room. Rolling away, looking at their worried faces, I prayed that I'd never see such worry on their faces again, and that I'd never be the source of their anguish again. A lot of good those prayers did me. That was the last thing of the morning that I could recall—until I was given my diagnosis and the news of my belly button.

Patricia filled me in on the story, a pretty significant story that nobody ever bothered to tell me. It was heart-wrenching to hear, but crucial to my mental well-being and current state of mind. Apparently, by 6:00 p.m., 12 hours later, the entire family, nieces, nephews, cousins, and brothers-in-law, were assembled in the waiting room, frantically pacing back and forth since no doctors or nurses had ever reported back with news or updates on my surgery. The family just sat in fear, together, but alone in their thoughts and worry. My heart broke for them, hearing this now. How could those medical professionals do that to my loved ones, not update them on the progress of my surgery? All they knew or were told was that the surgery was still going on. Patricia said that they were terrified that a 1-2 hour exploratory surgery could turn into a 12-hour surgery. Everyone thought the worst; nobody talked. Everyone feared.

Finally, a doctor that Patricia described as looking like Ichabod Crane with evil-beady eyes, required that they all file into an all-glass walled conference room for privacy, but the room was transparent, so everyone walking by could witness what was occurring within this dreaded "see-all" conference room. Once the family was all gathered together, shoulder-to-shoulder in the tiny glass room, the doctor broke the news, fast, cold, and carelessly, looking only at my children.

"Your mother has cancer over ¾ of her body," he said without feeling and matter-of-factly, destroying all hearts and hopes within earshot.

My son, Vaughn, began asking medical questions, while Darby cried loudly and uncontrollably into her hands. Then, without warning and completely out of her happy, humorous, obnoxious character, my Shelby Lynn, my seventeen-year-old daughter, screamed, "NOOO!" shocking the entire room into silence and awe. Being towards the back of the room, she stood, while still screaming "No," over and over again. Shelby pushed and shoved her way out of the glass room of doom and ran as fast as she could down the hospital corridor, not knowing where she was going.

Darby and Vaughn ran after her, while my sisters, nieces, nephews, and brothers-in-law sat sadly and painfully in silence and despair. Darby, still crying and losing momentum, slowed down while Patricia and Lila finally caught up to her, holding Darby as she cried. All three of them watched as Vaughn tackled Shelby Lynn to the ground.

"Please don't go, we need you, I need you," he cried into her arms. "Don't go, Shelby." He said those words over and over as Patricia, Lila, and Darby approached them in the hallway. Darby sat down on the floor, and they all three hugged in a heap, holding on to each other for dear life, never wanting to let the others go.

They held on, they held on to each other, because there was nobody else to hold.

My heart lurched; my stomach twisted. I'd never felt these feelings here. I didn't know how to handle them, how to deal with them. Why had nobody ever told me this story? Why was it ten, no thirteen years later, and I was just hearing it? And why was I hearing it now? Why did Patricia want to hurt me like this? I looked at her in agony, questioning her motive, falling to the ground in waves of sobbing emotion.

"Don't you get it Betheny?" She said, sitting down, holding me in her arms. "They're us. You raised them to cling to each other—just as we've always done. Their bond is unbreakable." She stroked my hair and kissed the top of my head. Sisters and brothers are the truest, purest forms of love, family, and friendship, knowing when to hold you and when to challenge you, but always being a part of you. How could I have questioned any of them, especially Lila?

"Talk to Lila, you've got nothing to be afraid of, not the past, and definitely not the truth." She said, wiping away my tears. "And if by chance there is, then you know we're gonna face it right there with you."

There

I'd just finished my second glass of Merlot, silently staring at the envelope sitting on the coffee table in front of me, the same coffee table that my mom and I'd purchased my junior year in high school, five months before her terminal diagnosis. I looked around the house, crestfallen. I hadn't changed a thing, not one aspect of my parents' house since the day my mom died. Vaughn and Darby'd moved out, bought houses, gotten married, and had children of their own. If someone, a friend from my high school days, walked into my house now, they'd think they entered a time warp.

Vaughn and Darby relentlessly tried to get me to change the house, rearrange the house, or just do something to it. I couldn't; I wouldn't. Vaughn had even offered to buy me all new furniture, get the house painted, and hire a decorator for me. I just didn't want to change it. I did however mount a flat screen HD television to my bedroom (my parents' old room) wall. They'd never had a TV in their room, said they didn't need it, would snicker and grin while saying so. As a child, a ten-year-old, I never understood what they meant or why they didn't have one in their room. All of my friends' parents had a television in their room. Once I hit adulthood and understood what the snickering and knowing glances meant, I vowed to never have a television in my room as well, especially if it meant that I could be as happy as my parents were together. However, one day, I came home from work and Chance had bought one and mounted it for me; he was so excited and proud of himself. I just couldn't break the news to him that I didn't want it or need it. Anyway, all I did in my room was sleep in there anyway. I guess at the time, I was doing Chance in there too. But now, I was back to only sleeping in my room.

I couldn't bear the thought of ever not living here. I loved living where where each room was flooded with memories and stories told of people of the past. I glanced down the hallway to the closet, the closet that Vaughn, Darby, and I hid from my mom in. The same closet that the three of us were in when Vaughn closed the door, not knowing that my finger was stuck in the door's hinges, cutting off my pinkie finger when I was two years old. A closet could have memories, loads of them, keeping those memories safe and guarded.

All parts of this house were filled with memories, overflowing with special moments in my life that I held dear to my heart. I chuckled looking at the remote control, remembering when I came home one night after a date with my high school boyfriend, Nate, to a very frustrated mother. She couldn't change the channel and was frantically losing her patience. Hysterically, Nate and I explained to her that she was using the cordless phone and not the remote control. She was livid and threw the remote and cordless phone at Nate. Luckily, he was quick enough to dodge the items. He'd been around her long enough to never underestimate her Italian temper.

Man, she was such a riot, and the most wonderful woman I'd ever known. This was my parents' home and now it was my house. I didn't have to let it go; I'd created my own memories here too. I glanced at the front door, remembering when Chance stood on that front porch looking through the screen door on his cell phone. I'd closed that door a long time ago too, but held that memory close to my heart.

Maybe everyone was right; maybe since it was my house, I should make it look like my house, not like my parents' house, not like the house I'd grown up in, not like the house both of my parents died in, but my house with my own style and décor, with a touch of vitality and more color. The wallpaper in the kitchen was hideous, orange and yellow, straight from the Seventies. I got up and walked into the kitchen and pulled a small piece of the paper from the wall. It hit me hard, changing this house, stripping this wallpaper, packing up Aunt Lila's mementos of a lifetime was the ultimate farewell. Ripping that paper off the wall, crumpling it into a haphazard ball was too horrifying; it was letting go, saying goodbye, moving on, alone, without the people I loved most in life. How could anyone ever be expected to do such a thing? It wasn't like I'd ever be able to smooth the paper back out and put it right back where it belonged, on my wall, surrounding me, keeping me safe within my home, with my memories and family. But honestly, it wasn't like I could smooth out my past either and surround myself with those I loved ever again either. My security, my "wallpaper," had been stripped and thrown out a long time ago.

Shaking myself free of those thoughts, I walked straight back into the living room and grabbed the letter off of the coffee table, glanced at the date at the top, and immediately began reading:

Dear Shelby Lynn,

I'm no writer but I've got things to say to you. Your mom would be so angry with me if I said any of them, but right now my mind is in jumbles. She made me promise never to tell you what I thought, but what good is that promise now? I just watched as Hospice took my baby sister's body away. My baby sister is dead. She's dead. How could you Shelby? You could've saved her and you didn't. Why didn't you save her? She was sick for so long, but you didn't tell us. We could've convinced her to go to the hospital. Forced her to go. Why didn't you tell us? You were living alone with her; you saw how sick she was, vomiting and diarrhea. Why did you wait two months to tell Vaughn and Darby? Those two months could've saved her life. Were you so preoccupied with your own life, your cheerleading and friends, to even care about your own mother? She would've done anything for you and you did nothing for her. I would have my baby sister right here, right now with me, instead of in a funeral home waiting to be six feet under. Shelby, I will never forgive you.

Lila

I couldn't breathe; I read the letter over and over. My eyes blurred; I could no longer see her words as the tears clouded my eyes, as they soaked the paper. Every worry, every fear was just confirmed in this letter. It was my fault. My mom was dead, because I was too selfish, too focused on everything, but her, to pay attention to her suffering. I'd spent the last ten years wondering if I could've done anything to help her, prevent the tragic end, and my aunt just made my worst fears a reality. My mom was dead because of me. Reading the letter the final time, I saw that she didn't even sign it "Aunt Lila." My aunt blamed me for my mother's death and our relationship was a fatality of that truth. My aunt didn't want to claim me as family any longer, because I'd taken her most important family member from her.

Chapter 11

Here

Patricia and I walked back to our sisters and the rest of our family, arm-in-arm. They really were my strength. Carl met us and grabbed my other arm, as each member of our family watched as he led me over to Lila, my Lila, my closest sister. She looked at me with such love, devotion, and loss; I didn't think anything could stop me at that point from going to her. I let go of Patricia and Carl, enveloping Lila into my arms, holding her as if it were the last time I'd ever get to embrace my beautiful sister.

For the first time, I noticed her clothes. I was horrified by her attire. Now Anna was indisputably our best-dressed sister, but Lila loved clothes and fashion as much as anyone, more so than I. Her outfit was more nondescript and ordinary than my own putrid green shirt and old black slacks. Lila had on awful brown-colored pants with a mustard yellow shirt with a brown collar. It was hideous. She watched my line of vision and looked down at herself, laughing, understanding my confusion and astonishment. I recognized that I'd seen her in it before, but I couldn't recall where or when. I just remembered that I'd told her that she resembled a rotten banana, one that nobody would ever be interested in eating.

Lila smiled at me, nodded, and said, "The doctor's office, the day we found out your cancer was in remission." That was my Lila. Her happiest day didn't have anything to do with her, but had everything to do with me. She was my older sister, closest to me in age and in heart.

"Oh Lila," I hugged her again. "Tell me, tell me everything, don't leave anything out." I could feel her arms around me and feel Carl's hand on my lower back. He sighed an audible breath of relief; the suspense had been too much for him as well.

The rest of our sisters left us alone, knowing that this solitude was integral to our relationship, a relationship that for the first time in our lives, and beyond our lives, needed mending. Carl stayed with us, but at an arm-length's distance; he didn't want to crowd our repair, but needed to be a part of the knowledge that Lila was soon going to impart upon us.

"Betheny, they're wonderful. Every day they amaze me more and more." Her face fell, realizing her words. "Or they did...Oh God...thank you for letting me in their lives for as long as I could." She hugged me again; both of us holding and supporting the other. I saw how agonizing this was for her as well. She'd lived in the same house as Darby and Vaughn until we'd moved to the suburbs. She'd been with them, as their only "parent" for the past ten years; she was separating now from her children too. This, I finally understood. We'd shared everything growing up, and to my amazement, I realized now that we shared my children too. She loved them as I did.

"Start with Darby. I wanna know it all," I said, motioning Carl up to us; he needed to be right beside us, as the three of us talked about my children, Carl's children, and even Lila's children. Our children.

"Darby and Becca are perfect, you'd be so proud--" she started.

"Becca? Who's Becca?" In my early, naïve years, my mind had been so closed and cut off from accepting people. I was judgmental and opinionated, but Carl opened my mind to everyone. Carl was the soft-hearted liberal one, who had a heart of gold. He taught me about accepting people for who they were, not for how they looked or chose to live their lives. Admittedly, I was shocked to hear that Darby was with a woman; she'd never exhibited such signs before. Okay, that was fine; I could accept anything and anyone that made my daughter happy and filled her with love. Right? Of course, I could.

Darby was so full of love and if this Becca loved her as she deserved to be loved, then who could fault them for that love? I wouldn't. I'd grown. I learned the importance of finding and holding on to love, because you just never know who you're going to fall in love with or how long you're going to be blessed with that love. Love just happens. I looked at Carl, remembering that initial repulsion I'd had for him so many years ago. Yes, it's true; love just happens. There really is no rhyme or reason. It just happens.

"Becca, her daughter, her beautiful daughter. You don't know about Becca?" She looked at me puzzled, searching my face for answers that weren't there. "Oh...that's right...you wouldn't, she's only six years old. Patricia died seven years ago." Lila was calculating the numbers, determining how it could be that I didn't know who Becca was.

Daughter? She said daughter. My granddaughter. I had a granddaughter. A grandbaby. I was a "Nana." Tears flooded my eyes. Oh why couldn't I hold her, spoil her, bake cookies with her, have her spend the night with me, and relish in every moment of being a Nana? I felt Carl's hand lovingly stroke my back. I knew his emotions were doing a number on him too. How could they not at this point? We were grandparents without grandchildren to hold and love. It seemed so cruel and unfair. A title without the reward.

Carl and I listened as we heard all about Darby's quick love affair with her husband, who'd left her and Becca when Becca was only two-years-old, and he never looked back. I hated him whoever he was, and knew he didn't deserve my perfect granddaughter and my Darby. My eyes pooled with tears as I heard that Darby'd worn my wedding gown and tiara; she'd always loved looking at my wedding pictures, planning her own wedding. It melted my heart to know that she still found a way to keep me with her, even on her wedding day. That was my Darby; she'd pull sentiment into anything, hold on to love with all of her might. She was the most selfless and giving child I'd ever encountered. While she was growing up, I'd never seen a child so sensitive and selfless; she'd always amazed me. I was thrilled to know that nothing had changed and that she centered all of that love and generosity to her own daughter. Maybe there were some things that I did do right.

I was surprised that she was in the business world, working in human resources. I'd always thought she'd find her way into a profession that worked directly with aiding and helping people. Hiring people and making their dreams come true seemed perfect, but if she had to terminate their employment, then I knew that she'd never be able to face those people without a heavy heart. Darby wore her heart on her sleeve. I was sure it was a struggle each time she had to face a person and destroy their hopes and dreams; that was not my Darby. I hoped audibly that her past, what she'd endured throughout her life, hadn't hardened her.

"Oh Beth, no!" Lila exclaimed. "Darby was with me, giving all of herself to me, until the very end. She couldn't go 48-hours without checking on me." My worry subsided as Lila explained the truth to me. "Actually, she's grown more giving and selfless since she became a mother. She's even working on taking classes to become a foster parent." Lila grasped my hands, looking directly into my eyes, showing me how truthful she was being. "There are some extra hoops she has to go through since she's a single mother, but nothing is going to stop her from helping a child in need." Lila affirmed, assuaging my fears. Carl hugged me to him; I knew he was dying to know about Vaughn, his only son.

"Wow, a foster mother, she really is who I thought she'd be, selfless in every way." I said, looking between Carl and Lila, feeling pride well inside my heart.

"Oh and Betheny, if you saw her, you'd never believe your eyes," Lila said. "She's a tiny, little, workout fanatic." Lila was right; that was hard to believe. Darby'd struggled with her weight her entire life (from what I knew). Apparently after that deadbeat, scum-of-the-earth husband left her, she was devastated. Darby, my lie-on-the-couch and eat pizza daughter, started running and watching every morsel of food that entered her mouth, realizing that she needed to get it together, because she was the lone provider, caregiver, and role model for my granddaughter, Becca. My granddaughter.

Darby realized how beneficial the calorie counting and exercise was for her health as well as for her mental well-being. After a few years of being healthy and fit, she decided to expand her plans. Always looking to help others, she started a local running club, called Running From Problems.

Lila said, "The club meets twice a week; Darby often hosts at her house. They start the meetings with a typical 'Hello my name is_____ and I'm running from:_____ (my recent divorce, my husband's affair, the loss of my mother, or my daughter's drug addiction).' They go around the room, expressing their pains. Then, they run in pack for three to five miles, depending upon the day. Finally they end the club meetings with a pot-of-luck healthy food for the future dinner." It really was a brilliant and inspiring concept, and my Darby had come up with it. Darby. My oldest daughter was truly amazing.

Listening to Lila explain it all, I could just hear Darby's wheels spinning as she got excited about the club and how it would all pan out. Darby loved planning events, ensuring the pleasure and fun in people's lives. Although I was floored, no, downright dumbfounded, that Darby had become a runner, I wasn't surprised that she'd initiated something to help herself, but in turn ended up helping her entire community too. "She was even honored by the mayor," Lila said, smiling with pride, at her goddaughter's success.

"Lila," Carl said, "How's Vaughn?" He looked nervous. Carl hated leaving Vaughn when he was only 16-years-old. Vaughn was a small child, a "late bloomer." Carl'd spent many days and nights here, lamenting that he'd never even taught Vaughn how to shave. I'd tried to ease his worry, explain to him that I'd covered it. I'd been shaving my legs for years; it wasn't too extremely tough to teach a young man how to shave. The difficulty only came when his teenage boy angst and his resistance to my lessons transpired.

"Vaughn? Christ...oops, can I say that here?" Lila looked like she'd committed the highest-level crime in the world. Carl and I laughed, remembering how difficult it was acclimating to this place, a place of acceptance and tolerance, one devoid of ridicule and judgment.

"Lila relax," I said. "You're in the heart of unconditional love and absolution. Your words are just that, words. They reflect fleeting moments of thought, nothing more, nothing less." She looked as if she was more confused than ever before.

"Once you go through the experience in a few days, you'll understand more clearly." Carl added in hopes of refocusing her back to Vaughn.

"Experience? What's--"

"Nothing we could ever do justice in explaining," Carl said, knowing that neither of us would be able to find the words that would give her a clear vision of the experience.

"You'll see; you'll understand everything soon enough." I said, rubbing her back and calming her down. "The experience is just that, an experience, different and monumental for everyone.

"Betheny, can I ask you something before I go on about Vaughn?" she asked, seeming nervous and uncertain.

"Of course." I reassured her; she looked worried.

"Why haven't I seen...." She struggled with the words, not being able to finish her sentence.

Knowing where she was going with her question, I helped her out, not forcing her to finish her thought. "You'll see him after the experience; we all thought it'd be better for everyone involved that way." Even though she didn't know what the experience was, Lila trusted all of us and knew that whatever it may be was probably the wisest choice when it came to him.

Everyone's experience here is different, but oddly enough, the same. Confusing, I know. The experience is instantaneous, but lasts throughout an eternity. It is best if our first few days here allow us to remain with our "earthly" thoughts and feelings. Through the experience, we lose many feelings that are obsolete and unnecessary here. However, when a new person arrives, someone from our past, we are able to gain those "earthly" feelings yet again to fully empathize and accept the arrival of our loved ones, acclimating them to their new status.

For instance, the jealousy I am feeling for Lila, the anger, and nervousness will be gone once she goes through the experience, which is why I enjoy these feelings and holding on to them. I haven't experienced them in seven years. We need to be able to relate to our arrivals, otherwise, they'd just think that we're crazies with lobotomies, going around smiling, like children with a secret that they cannot wait to tell. Once Lila goes through the experience, then we'll all gradually return to our serenity and euphoria once again, looking goofy, yet blissfully happy. Sure, I'm enjoying my anger, frustration, and worry, but don't get me wrong, I much prefer the evolved feelings of here.

Julian made it seem like I wanted to return. He was right in assuming that I grappled with those thoughts, especially once I gained my "earthly" and obsolete feelings again. If I did want to return, then I'd have to decide to go back before Lila's experience, because within time, I'd be back to evolved feelings, feelings and knowledge of the big picture and all that the experience revealed.

The experience grants us a glimpse of a lifetime, a "what's it all mean?" Think of George Bailey in It's A Wonderful Life, he got to see how his life mattered to his friends and family and what the true picture really was. I suppose that is the best way to describe the experience, but on a much grander scheme. Imagine being George. Imagine being able to see how your life mattered to the entire world and what your life meant, not just to your family and friends, but also to everyone and everything. We tend to view our lives as the smallest, most infinitesimal aspects of the universe, seeing ourselves as tiny blurbs on a map, but the experience allows us to understand that we're really more comparable to small gears on a machine that make the entire world work smoothly and swiftly. It truly is amazing and breathtakingly beautiful. It's an experience.

Once, I stopped to pick up a penny in the grocery store parking lot with Shelby as a toddler, we bent over and took a moment to get it, momentarily delaying a young woman from getting into her car. Within my experience, I saw that in that split second that I'd paused to get the penny, it prevented that young woman from having to swerve to hit a deer on the highway moments later, crossing the median, killing a family of four. That "good luck" penny, which I'd prayed would bring us luck and put Carl back on dayshifts at work, actually brought luck to the woman behind me and a beautiful family of four traveling out of town for a wedding.

In another snippet, I allowed a young man to go ahead of me at the bank in the teller's line; he seemed anxious to get somewhere. Upon leaving the bank in a hurry, he ran into a young woman, literally running into her, knocking paperwork out of her arms. As they both bent down to pick up the scattered papers, their eyes met, immediately falling in love. Their second child, a young boy, grew up to be one of the best pediatric heart surgeons in America, saving the lives of many young children.

One of Carl's snippets was closer to home. One night, when he was in his early twenties, he came home from his job as a cashier at a convenience store. He'd gotten sent home for work early, because he'd been coughing and hacking all night, due to a bronchial infection. Customers started to complain. He walked in and his younger brother, Dave, who was fourteen at the time, was looking for medicine to add to his bourbon and scotch concoction, hoping to down enough pills to end his life. When Carl came in, he didn't notice his brother's mixed drink, but did offer to watch television and play a little cards with him. Dave immediately accepted, quickly postponing and eventually forgetting his suicidal thoughts. All Dave ever wanted was his big brother's attention; Carl gave it to him, without knowing how truly important it was at that moment.

The next day, the teenage girl who'd broken young David's heart wanted him back. He married her eight years later. The experience allows us to see just how truly precious our lives are, all life is. Our lives are precious to us, to our family, and even to the rest of the world. It really is magical; that one moment of true clarity erases all negativity, regret, and resentment, leaving nothing but gracious peace.

Carl's voice brought me back to my sister and my husband, "So Lila, can you tell us something, anything about Vaughn?" His eagerness was evident; when emotions allowed, Carl was in a constant state of worry, wondering about his son. Being a nightshift, working father and dying early, Carl often feared that

Vaughn's knowledge of manhood would end up skewed in some way.

"Perfection."

Carl and I waited, staring expectantly at Lila. Carl waved his hands at her, in a "go on" gesture. She just shook her head.

"Carl, there's nothing else to say. Truly." Lila added. She looked from Carl to me and then back to Carl again. Finally, she said, "He's everything you ever hoped for and more."

"Lila, please spoon-feed Carl, tell him any and everything that he'd ever want to know." I rubbed Carl's back, reassuring him that it was going to be okay.

Carl sobbed throughout Lila's recapitulation of Vaughn's life, focusing primarily on his successes. Actually, Lila repeatedly reconfirmed that there were no stories of setback or failure. Basically, since Vaughn suffered through the death of his father and the prolonged agonizing death of his mother, Vaughn had been smooth sailing, enjoying a life blessed by fortune and prestige, paid for by hard work and intelligence.

"He has millions? Like of dollars?" Carl couldn't believe it. "Are you kidding me?" he questioned again for the tenth time.

"Millions upon millions," Lila confirmed again. "He's so generous with it; you would both be so proud." Lila started listing all of the generous acts Vaughn paid for with his earnings. He'd bought a practice football field at Ohio State and named it after us. Carl beamed with pride, knowing his son would pay for such a thing and that he still loved sports as much as when he was a child, something Carl had instilled in him. I sobbed when I heard that he'd covered the cost of Shelby's education and Darby's first wedding to that less than worthy wuss.

"His wife is gorgeous; his boys are hysterical. Oh Carl, you'd love how athletic they already are." Boys? We had grandsons too. Carl's emotions couldn't take much more. He'd missed out on so much of our kids' lives, working nights and dying early. The knowledge that he was missing out on his grandsons' lives too was a bit much for him. Carl needed a break.

"But Carl, what about Shelby?" I asked, pleading with him to stay.

"Beth, I understood when you needed time before confronting Lila, grant me that please." Lines of pain shadowed the corners of his eyes. How could I push him? He was always so gentle and understanding with me. How could I not afford him the same?

Understanding, and actually listening, I said, "Of course, honey, we're talking about Shelby Lynne; she's always been our strongest, most independent fighter. If the other two fared beyond our wildest dreams, then there wasn't anything really to worry about now." I looked at Lila for confirmation, "Right?"

"Uhhh..."

There

In the midst of my full out, ugly crying, the kind of crying nobody other than your Siamese twin should ever witness, my doorbell rang. I decided to put the pillow over my head and finish my crying into the security of the already snot-ridden couch pillow. The doorbell rang again at the same time my cell phone alerted me to a text message. I moved the pillow and glanced at my phone:

Thought I'd stop by. Know you're in there. Heard you crying. Open up, Shelby.

Son of a... Why did Chance always seem to show up and be there at the most inopportune times? I knew he'd never leave if he'd heard me crying; he'd insist on making sure I was okay first. I got up, wiped my nose, and well, basically, my entire face on the pillow, and opened the door.

"Hey Chance, what's up?" I asked as casually as I could, trying to seem completely and totally "fine."

"Don't 'Hey Chance' me. What's going on? Why're you crying?" he asked, not wasting any time with frivolous niceties. He walked past me and surveyed the place, looking around for the source of my grief.

"Oh that, you know me, just watching She's Having a Baby." He knew firsthand how that particular movie reduced me to a pile of sobbing goo. He looked at the black television, picked up the remote, turned on the TV, and saw that reruns of Friends were on

Nick at Nite. Still giving me the benefit of the doubt, he hit the guide button, and searched for She's Having a Baby.

Seriously! Nothing. Really? It couldn't be on ONE channel this entire month? That's just great. Thanks cable company. I was changing providers first thing in the morning.

"What the Hell, Chance?" I grabbed the remote from him, turning Friends off. "Don't worry about it; I'm fine." I plopped down on the chair, the farthest chair away from him.

"I'm gonna worry about it. When the woman that I..." he stopped himself, rephrasing his statement. "When I can hear you crying from the front porch with the door closed, then there's something to worry about." He looked around, saw the letter on the coffee table, and immediately picked it up. I bolted up, trying to sprint across the living room at break-neck speed. It was already in his possession. He unfolded the letter and began reading, turning his back to me.

I knew I'd lost. I knew defeat. I sat back down and put my head in my hands, trying to hold back the tears that had already started pouring back down my face. When I looked up, he was staring at me; I saw the tears in his eyes and the slight quiver of his lip. He made no attempt to hide his pain and pity for me.

"Shelb..."

I raised my hand, cutting him off. "Don't...Chance...just don't."

He got up and walked over to me, kneeling down in front of me. He lifted my chin, urging me to look at him. "Pie...I mean..." he shook his head, knowing that he shouldn't use his old nickname for me. "Shelby, this letter was written ten years ago.... on the day your mom died." I tried to drop my head and break eye contact with him. He held my head, not letting me look away. "Aunt Lila, your

Aunt Lila, did not feel this way about you. She wrote this when she was grief-stricken. Her sister'd just died. She was just looking for an outlet."

"Stop...Chance... I can't." I said, pushing him away as I got up and went to the refrigerator, getting out the wine bottle. Chilled wine, even if it wasn't supposed to be refrigerated, always made me feel better. I poured myself another glass of Merlot.

"Listen to me. Your aunt loved you, like her own daughter. You know that." He came up behind me, turned me around, so I'd face him. "Shelby, what would you tell one of your students if this happened to her?" He asked. I stared at him blankly, not responding. "Tell me, what would you say to her?"

Chance always did this to me. He always said that I gave my students or my friends the best advice, heartfelt, wise, and insightful advice, but never took it myself, always ignoring my little rational voice inside. He was right. I do tend to think that I'm not worthy of my best advice. Advice is a strange thing. People are always looking for advice, someone's opinion, on what they should or shouldn't do. But ultimately, in the end, they do or believe what they'd wanted to all along. I have so many students come to me about their boyfriends or girlfriends or even their best friends. They ask for advice. I give it to them, usually my best, well-thought out, and devised words of wisdom, and they end up doing what they want anyway, disregarding all of my warnings or recommendations.

My friend, Nina, from work; she's the worst culprit. We talk our mouths off over what should or shouldn't happen about something, anything, and she always ends up doing something entirely different and completely new from whatever we'd discussed in the first place. People don't really want advice; they just want to talk and be heard. However, my student, Janessa, she always does what I advise. I think that's why I like her so much. I just wish she'd stop every now and then, and think about what I might say before she made any poor decisions on her own.

"I'd tell them... I'd say..." I didn't know. I knew that if Janessa found some letter like this, I'd make her stop and think about it. I would tell her basically the same things that Chance was saying to me. "But... you don't get it..."

"What don't I get? That you've been beating yourself up about the same thing for the last decade?" He said, silencing me. "Oh I get it Shelby. I've gotten it for a long time," he said, pulling me into his arms. I was so beaten, so tired; I let him hold me. His arms felt comforting, safe. I buried my face into the warmth and security of his chest.

He continued, as he stroked my hair and spoke into the top of my head, "Oh Honey, don't you realize, I'm a casualty in your ten-year, senseless guilt, so I get it. You're no more to blame for your mom's death as you are for Aunt Lila's death." He pulled me back, staring into my eyes, bending over to look directly into mine. He wiped my tears and said, "You're not the villain here. There's no villain, Shelby. Cancer's the villain." Cancer is always the villain.

Staring at him, feeling his strength, and the effects of the three glasses of wine, I couldn't resist the feelings he stirred in me. I put my arms up around his neck and pulled him slightly forward. He leaned down closer to me; I could feel the electricity between us, his warm breath on my cheek. I ran the tip of my tongue along my top lip, whetting it. I stood on my toes, closing in on his lips.

Momentarily our lips met and nothing else mattered. It was just Chance and me, me and Chance.

Chance pulled away angrily and remorsefully, shaking his head. "No...damn it... I can't do this..." He let go and distanced himself across the kitchen from me, sitting down in the chair. Shame and humiliation washed over me.

After what seemed like an interminable about of time, he finally said, "Shelby, I meant it.... I'm not gonna keep doing this." He spoke directly into his arms, face smashed down in the crook of his arm. Then he looked up and stared right at me. "Can you say it? Are you ready? Can you say it now?" He questioned, hope written all over his face.

I lowered my head. "No." it was barely audible, but I was certain that he could hear me as if I were screaming it with a megaphone from the rooftops.

"Damn it...Shelby...why?" he asked, lowering his head into his hands, supporting the weight of his head as the word filled his mind once again. The word was heavy and burdensome and would forever remain etched into his mind. "Answer that, just answer why?" He pleaded.

"Because I can't." I said.

I'd hurt him....again. He'd heard that line too many times. Abruptly, he got up from the table, pushed in the chair, and grabbed a glass out of the cupboard. He put ice in the glass, filling it with water from the faucet. I watched him as he walked back to bathroom; I could hear him rifling through the medicine cabinet. He came back with two aspirin and handed me the glass of water and three pills. "Take these; you're gonna wake up with a horrid headache from all that wine and crying. Make sure you drink at least two glasses of water before you go to bed." He stopped talking and gazed at me; his expression softened. His shoulders fell, admitting defeat. Quickly, he kissed the top of my head and then walked to the door. "Shelby, you're not at fault. At all. Don't forget that."

"Chance, wait!" I said, grabbing his hand, turning him around. "You know I love you, right?" I questioned.

"Yes, Shelby, I do," he said, looking at me sadly. "But it's still the same, I'm not budging on this again. Until you can tell me it's forever, then there's no point." He embraced me again and whispered in my ear. "I want always. With you. It's one word Shelb. It's so easy. Always."

Letting me go, he didn't look back and walked dejectedly to his car without saying anything more. Always? That was all he wanted, but I couldn't give it to him. Not now. Not ever. With Chance Michaels there was no always...just what used to be.

He was just about to get into his car, when I yelled "Chance!"

He turned around, looking at me expectantly, again with hope in his eyes. "I... I....why'd you stop by anyway?" I asked.

"Oh yeah," he said, chuckling. "I bought you a security system. It'll be installed Wednesday morning." He walked back up the sidewalk, stopping at the bottom of the porch, keeping a considerable amount of distance from me. "You know I hate you living here alone. I got a deal; I know a guy. They'll be here on Wednesday." He smiled smugly, knowing that I couldn't stop him. When Chance got something in his mind, there was no stopping him. It was one of his most charming and endearing qualities. It was also his most annoying quality. A security system? Only

Chance. Nothing says, "I love you," like a loud, beeping, alerting-the-world security system. He was crazy and incorrigible.

It was crazy to me that he'd bought a security system for me. I hadn't felt secure or safe for a long, long time. I wasn't afraid of what was "out there" lurking to get me. I was afraid of what was inside, in me, trying to hurt me. All the money and technology in the world couldn't protect me from that fear. The only time that I'd felt even remotely secure since my mom died was when I was with Chance. But then, my safety was threatened again—a fear unlike any I'd ever experienced before—which is when I knew our relationship was over.

I didn't know what to say. He really was a wonderful man. A perfect man. A perfect father. "Thanks Chance. Tell Mallory that I miss her." I said. His face grimaced in pain when I mentioned his daughter's name. It made my heart ache. For him. For her. For us.

"Yeah sure," he said. "I'll see ya around." I watched him walk away slowly, get into his car, and drive off. I loved him. I loved him more than I ever loved someone before in my entire life. I hated hurting him. But this was how it had to be. I just knew he was going to be a wonderful husband someday; I just hoped whoever he married realized just how lucky she truly was.

Chapter 12

Here

"Are you sure you're ready for more?" I asked Carl. I'd never seen him so downtrodden. He was my upbeat and positive support; nothing ever got him down.

"Yeah babe, I'm okay; it's just a lot." He was right. This was a lot to handle and hear. We'd missed the most integral parts of our children's lives, the monumental milestones. It was hard and agonizing to hear about those crucial moments when we didn't get to experience any of them with our kids. This was taking quite the toll on Carl; he'd missed so much.

Two months after he died, when Darby was only seventeen years old, she had to undergo surgery, a pretty invasive surgery. They'd admitted her to the hospital for nearly a week to remove one of her ovaries; an entire ovary was riddled with cysts. Thinking about it now, it could have been so much worse with our family history. My poor Darby could've been riddled with ovarian tumors, not just tiny, aggravating cysts. We didn't know then that we should be thanking our lucky stars and not thinking "why us again?"

Darby was terribly down after the surgery, knowing that she'd just reduced her chances of having children by 50 percent. Darby'd always dreamed of having a big family, being a stay-at-home-mother, cooking, baking, and just doting on her children. Oh, I'm so thankful she has Becca now. Oh Becca. If only...

Darby's spirits lifted when her boyfriend called the hospital room to check on her. Darby loved harder and stronger than anyone I'd ever known. When she fell for this boy, she fell hard. As far as first boyfriends go, he was fine, a little strange and quirky, but acceptable nonetheless. Harmless really.

The phone call didn't last long. He checked on her, told her that he hoped she felt better soon, and then broke up with her. Oh yes, he dumped her three hours after a major surgery. They'd spent nine months together, were planning on attending her senior prom together, and he broke up with her over the phone while she was still coming out of an anesthesia haze from surgery. That quirky and strange boy quickly became the biggest jackass I'd ever met. And boy was he able to harm my Darby, my sweet, caring, and trusting Darby. And I'd called him "harmless."

I didn't know which was harder, trying to help Darby heal from her surgery or trying to help heal her heart. The first heartbreak should never come simultaneously with a major surgery. Darby's recovery took longer than expected. She never did go back to school her senior year or go to her senior prom. Within four months' time, my Darby, my oldest daughter, lost her father, got her heart broken, had major surgery, missed her senior prom, and missed her final days of high school. It was defeating for her and for me. I hated witnessing such pain and numbing setbacks for her. All the while, I couldn't help but be angry with Carl for leaving me so soon, forcing me to handle all of our oldest child's physical and emotional pain alone.

About six months before Carl died, he failed a work physical. His cholesterol and blood pressure were morbidly high, causing the doctor a great deal of worry. Carl swore he'd cut back on his cigarette smoking and shed a few pounds. He'd even promised to get a little more active and get more frequent blood pressure checkups. Since he worked nights, I only witnessed his weekend behaviors. From what I saw, he was eating healthier and becoming more active. I was proud of the great strides he'd made towards prolonging his life for me and for the kids. Hearing what the doctor said terrified me. I trusted him to take care of himself, so he could in turn take care of the kids and me.

Years after I arrived here, Carl admitted the truth. It was shortly after Rosemary's arrival; so we still had "borrowed earthly emotions" to relate to Rosemary and empathize with her. Carl's grief multiplied, worse than I'd ever known. Rosemary had just revealed to us that Vaughn had bought his first house and paid cash, and Carl crumbled. I'd never witnessed emotional weakness here like that before. None of us had. He took me aside and confessed to me that he'd been lying to me all these years. He spent his nights at work smoking like a chimney, eating junk food, and sitting around whenever time allowed. He hadn't exercised or changed any of his habits at all. He was also pretty sure that the stress of his health forced him to drink more alcohol and smoke more cigarettes.

Over and over again, he kept saying "I could've been there. I could've been there." Yes, he was right; he could've been. But the fact remained; he wasn't. Sometimes even though the truth hurts, forces us to shatter, it unfortunately still remains the truth. Regrets and "what ifs" are parts of life: sad, debilitating parts of life.

Thankfully, the experience lets us discover comfort in that what we view as our regrets are just necessary moments of life.

Carl wasn't saying anything that we all hadn't thought a million times since we got here. We all grapple with the thought that there could've been something that we could've done to prolong our time with our loved ones there. I knew that if I would've acted like a "grown up" and gone to the doctor when I couldn't control my vomiting and diarrhea that there was a strong possibility that I could've stayed longer and enjoyed many more milestones and memories with my children. We all think that, but dwelling on "what ifs" doesn't help anyone or anything. The earthly emotions are tough to handle, but once the serenity of here returns, it's extremely easy to let the feelings and peace of the experience fully consume you and take you back to a clearer understanding of the importance of your life.

"Are you two sure you're ready for more?" Lila asked.

"Oh, we're sure," Carl confirmed, holding me close to him. "Tell us the worst, don't hold anything back or sugarcoat a thing."

"Well, I thought about that after you walked away," Lila explained. "Vaughn and Darby don't really have any bad things in their lives. Sure, Darby married a schmuck, but she came out on top." I felt Carl give my hip a little squeeze; I recognized it as an "I told you so" squeeze of victory. We'd done it.

Lila continued, "Darby still wears her heart on her sleeve, which causes her to get hurt a little more than most people. But she's good. She's strong, and a fighter."

Darby did wear her heart on her sleeve. She took on the weight of the world's problems and setbacks as her own. When I was sick, she was suffering too, but not from her own pending loss. But suffering with me, she couldn't bear to see me in agony. It pained her; I could see it in her eyes and face. She never voiced her pain and fear though; she was my "nurse," taking care of me, handling all of my medications and overall well-being.

"But there isn't anyone in her life right now? Someone to share it with?" I asked, worrying about her.

"Not right now," Lila admitted. "But after her divorce, she decided to focus on Becca for a while. She's not ready for that yet. I agree too. When Darby falls, she falls hard. She needs to wait a bit and not rush into anything." I understood where Lila was coming from, but I was afraid that she'd end up all alone. "She has causal dates with this man she works with, but they just see movies and have dinner. They're more like friends."

Carl chuckled. Lila and I looked at him with questioning eyes. He laughed again and said, "It's just so weird. When she was born, I swore I'd never let any boy near her. It's bizarre to be sitting here hoping that she finds someone." He was such a dad, worrying about boys getting near his little girl. I knew what he meant though. We made jokes that we'd never let someone break our kids' hearts, but what we really want is for them to fully experience true love, and all that goes with it, including the heart shattering feelings of total heartbreak. That kind of loss only makes people stronger. Heartbreak was a necessary and essential part of life.

"Oh don't worry Carl; she will. I'm not worried at all, and you know how much I worry about Darby." Lila said, smiling. But then her smile faded, and she added, "I mean, I know you guys worry; she's your daughter....you have every right--"

I cut her off, "Lila stop. I love that you love my children; I'm grateful that you loved them so much. I'm so sorry....for everything." Lila and I hugged again; being with her wasn't the torture I'd predicted. I hadn't realized how much of me she still had with her. She was my older sister, my best friend. Nothing could ever come between us.

Clearing his throat, Carl said, "What about Vaughn? What're his dark secrets?"

"I told you...nothing!" Lila said. "I mean, he's a bit uptight, wants everything his way, which he thinks is just perfect," Lila chuckled. "But nothing really. He's absolutely wonderful, wonderful with his kids, wonderful to his wife, and runs his company wonderfully. Carl, your son, your boy, is wonderful."

Lila went over to Carl, hugged her brother-in-law, and said, "Shelby calls him 'Vaughn-derful,' which usually pisses him off." We all laughed. Only Shelby would come up with such a perfect and appropriate name for her older brother.

Carl shook his head, almost in disbelief, having a hard time accepting that he'd pulled off raising a "Vaughn-derful" man when he'd only been blessed with "being a father" for only seventeen wonderful years.

"Alright Lila, tell us all the great and hysterical things you can about Shelby Lynn." I said, eager to hear about my youngest daughter's life. She was such a spitfire; this was going to be good.

"Oh Shelby, she's....she's... Shelby's all right." Lila was shaking her head, like a mother who just saw her toddler pee on the front bushes in the yard.

"I'm gonna need a little more than that." I joked, wanting details, stories that would crack me up and warm my heart.

"Well, she's a high school teacher...English...a great teacher really. Those kids go to her for everything....I mean everything."

Lila smiled. I wasn't surprised; Shelby had always regarded her teachers so highly, especially after I'd gotten sick. I'd always assumed that she'd find her way to education, helping young adolescents through their teenage angst and woes. She'd loved her teachers, and I knew that they were role models for her too. There was one teacher in particular that she adored and valued.

Darby and Vaughn always raved about their Advanced English teacher, Mr. Hannity. They'd both had him when they were in school. On the first day of her junior year when Shelby discovered that she had him for Advanced English, she was elated. She'd been waiting so many years to get him as a teacher, like her older brother and sister had. Darby and Vaughn made him out to be a God of English.

He really was an extraordinary man. His mother was rich, beyond wealthy. When she died, she'd left him millions of dollars. The money and new economic status didn't stop him from going to work every day in his BMW, donning an Armani suit, and teaching ungrateful teenagers all the facts behind American literature. Mr. Hannity treated those kids like adults; he respected and revered them unlike any teacher they'd ever encountered before.

Shelby once told me that nobody ever got into trouble in his class, because nobody ever misbehaved. I'd asked her why, and she looked at me like I'd grown horns and said, "Because then you'd let him down." It was such a simple answer, but said so much about those kids, but especially about the man teaching the class.

Literature and writing were Shelby's "things," so she smoothly sailed through Advanced English. At the end of her junior year, I was diagnosed with Colon Cancer. The news, the diagnosis, everything was too much for Shelby to bear. She neglected her studies, her friends, everything. She'd just been told by a horrible doctor that her mother, her last living parent, had three months to live. Shelby couldn't focus on school, on anything really. The news was too devastating for her to endure.

On the last day of class, Mr. Hannity, the God of all things English, distributed their final exam questions. He handed the essay question to each student personally. Shelby received her question, from the bottom of the pile in his hand, and all the little slip of paper said was "Tell me what you're going through." That's it. Nothing more. Nothing less.

Shelby said that she looked at that little slip of paper, took out her notebook and pen, and began to write. With that writing, her emotions poured out of her, flooding the paper with tears and words. At that moment, she realized three things: (1.) Writing was therapeutic and cathartic; she was going to write whenever her life was too difficult to face. (2.) The good teachers, the ones that mattered the most, cared more about the student sitting in the seat than the book on the desk. (3.) She was going to be a teacher.

It's probably shocking that I know this story so well. But the truth is, Shelby told it a lot...and I mean a lot. Actually, she wrote the story so well in her personal college essay that she was awarded quite a few scholarships. I never really had the heart to tell her that it probably wasn't the "teacher story" or her particular writing ability that won her the scholarships, but that it probably had more to do with the few lines within the story about her dead father and dying mother that sealed the deal on her scholarship awards. Seriously, no evaluator in his right mind would grant the scholarship to someone other than the soon-to-be orphan. Even I knew that, and I never went to college.

"I can't believe my daughter's a teacher, a teacher!" Carl said, excitedly. "Me, I hated school; you couldn't pay enough to go back in one." He was laughing.

"Oh Carl, she went back and back and back..." Lila said happily. "She's even got her Master's Degree."

"What? Are you serious?" I asked, incredulously.

"Yep, first one in all our family to get one." Lila said. I couldn't believe it. My baby girl, the daughter who I left when she was only 20-years-old, had a Master's Degree. Wow. She'd made it. She'd succeeded when I worried that she'd be too broken, too devastated to make something of herself. Granted, I knew she was a spitfire, a feisty little thing, but I worried that the loss and pain would change her, harden her. It hadn't. Oh thank you.

"Is Shelby married, does she have kids too?" Carl asked eagerly.

"Ummm...nah...not yet," Lila answered. "She's focused right now on work and her students."

"But does she have a boyfriend, something like that?" I asked.

"Not at the moment; they broke up." Lila said. I saw a grimace quickly cross her face. "About a year ago."

"A year? Hasn't she met someone else?" I asked; this seemed peculiar. Feeling guilty, I had to do some math, which made me feel even worse. I should be able to rattle off my children's ages quickly, but time didn't pass normally here.

"She's what? Uh.....almost 30 now?" I inquired, looking for confirmation.

Lila just nodded.

"Well, what the—Why isn't she with someone?" Again, Lila looked away and a little pained at the mention of this. "Lila, what is it?"

"I don't know really. Shelby...well...she..." Lila was stalling, and I hated it.

"Shelby what? Damn it! What?" I yelled, feeling all the muscles in my body tense with worry for Shelby and anger again for Lila. Carl began rubbing my back, trying to calm me down.

"I don't know. Every time she gets close to someone, like, starts falling in love, she just ends it." Lila said.

"That's stupid. She must not really like him then. She'll meet Mr. Right and be fine." I said, feeling the tension and fear start to flood back out of me. Why was it a big deal that she hadn't found "The One" yet? Lots of women focused on their careers first and then worried about finding a husband and having children later in their thirties. Lila was making it seem like it was a tragedy that she wasn't married yet.

"I don't know Betheny; it seems more than that. Shelby doesn't let anyone in; nobody gets close to her. Ever since...you...ever since..."

"Ever since what?" I asked.

"Well, ever since you died, Shelby keeps everyone at a distance. Almost like she's too afraid of getting hurt or getting too close or falling in love." Lila came over to me, grabbed my hands and said, "I really think Chance was 'Mr. Right.' We all did...Do."

This did not make any sense. If he was "The One," then he'd be the one, right? Fate always stepped in and took over when you were too stupid to see things for what they were. "Nah Lila, you're crazy." I said. "You just said that she's a great teacher. She loves those kids right? She must be letting them in if she connects with them so much." I argued. Lila missed the target on this one. I was sure of it.

"It's different; she's teaching them, preparing them. She knows at the end of the year, they're gonna leave her." Lila explained. "But it's not them she's preparing. She's put herself in a career where they have to leave her, and she never expects them to stay." Lila looked at Carl, hoping that he understood her. "She knows that they can't get too close, because soon they have to leave anyway. Betheny, she's closed herself off. We're all worried about her."

Did she just say, "we're?" I knew Lila was talking about Vaughn, Darby, and her, but I hated that she knew a world of "we" without me. I know that I wanted her to be with them, but the jealousy was killing me. (No pun intended.) Moments ago, I thought I'd reconciled these feelings of envy and resentment, but now, I just wanted my sister to shut her mouth. My daughter, my Shelby Lynn, wasn't "closed off." I knew her better than anyone; she loved with every ounce of her being. Closed off? Impossible.

"Beth, listen to me--"

"No, you listen to me," I said, pointing at Lila. "I saw her fall for Nate, her high school sweetheart. You cannot turn off that kind of love and passion. She has it in her. Your kid, this new guy that you think is so perfect, must not be right for her." I knew my daughter. Lila couldn't tell me my daughter had lost the ability to love. Bullshit.

"Carl, will you listen to me? They were perfect for each other." Lila said. Then, looking at me, she said, "Beth, it's like she met her match. Remember how she used to walk all over Nate in high school? She tried that crap with Chance. He wouldn't hear of it."

"Oh, so he's an ass?" I didn't understand why Lila was so against Shelby and against me for that matter.

"No, he was teaching her how to fall in love. How to hold people close—not push them away. Chance wouldn't take all of her hot and cold feelings. He just held on tighter when she'd go cold and afraid. They were perfect together." Lila explained, looking between Carl and me, hoping that we'd understand. "Chance even golfed and went to games with Vaughn. Darby loved having Mallory over to play with Becca. They were part of the family." Lila claimed.

"Mallory? Who's Mallory?" I asked.

"Mallory is Chance's daughter; you should've seen Shelby with her. I didn't know she had so much maternal instinct in her. She was selfless, but firm, consistent, but loving and kind. Remarkable." Lila never really spoke with such pride and awe for Shelby; there always seemed to be a wedge between them for some reason.

"Alright fine, what happened?' I couldn't deny that she was making me awfully curious.

"We don't know. One day, Chance called Vaughn beside himself in tears. Shelby broke up with him and said that she never wanted to see him again. He kept trying, pulled out all the stops." Lila said, shaking her head in wonder. "We all knew he'd been shopping for engagement rings and then she just pulled the rug out from under him. Even cut herself off from Mallory. Poor little girl. First her mom up and left her and then Shelby left her."

"What did Shelby say? Why'd she do it?" Alright she got me; I was fully invested in this saga.

"We don't know. We've been....or...ummm...we'd been trying to figure it out for the last year. Darby and Chance even planned this surprise dinner for Shelby and Chance to talk." Lila said. I eyed her, urging her to go on. "Shelby walked in, took one look at Chance, and walked right back out. We all know she's head over heels in love with him." Lila explained.

"Maybe he did something. Maybe he cheated on her or something like that." I couldn't believe that Shelby would throw away something that everyone deemed perfect if it weren't flawed in some way. I couldn't believe that for one minute. Wouldn't believe it.

"Vaughn took Chance out, golfing and to dinner; he grilled him on it. Nothing. Shelby blindsided him. They didn't have any problems. They were perfect Beth, I tell ya." Lila got up and started pacing. "Vaughn even asked Chance straight out why he put up with all of Shelby's crap and kept going back for more. Do you know what Chance told Vaughn?"

"No, what?" I asked, needing to more about this man, the man that everyone believed my daughter should be with.

Teary-eyed and smiling, Lila said, "Chance said that when he looked at Shelby, all he could see was forever. When she wasn't around, it felt like there wasn't even a tomorrow. If that isn't true love worth fighting for, then I don't know what is."

Agreeing, I said, "Alright, that's a good line. A great line actually." This Chance seemed like the real deal; what was my daughter thinking?

Lila continued, "I'm worried about her. It just doesn't seem like she feels anything anymore." Lila admitted.

I didn't understand this at all. I remembered seeing Shelby and Nate together; they were so lovey-dovey. Her face would just light up when he walked into the room. My girls were filled with love. They always opened their hearts to those who deserved their love. Darby was quick to give it—even to those who didn't quite deserve it. But Shelby, she was more reserved with her heart, but shared it when someone proved worthy or needy. Granted, when she and Nate broke up, it shattered her. She was broken and quite gruff for some time, but after a while, she began bouncing back. None of this made any sense.

"Lila, Shelby is soft, loving, kind-hearted. None of this makes any sense." I said, deciding that she must have had strong, valid reasons for breaking up with him.

"She's not anymore Betheny. Ever since you left, she's been an isolated island. Nothing gets on that island anymore." Lila said with tears in her eyes. "She's broken; I'm afraid she's gonna end up alone." Then, Lila took a deep breath and let the tears flood. "....and I think I could've made it a hundred times worse..."

There

"Hey sleepy head, wake up," I hated that I'd given Nina a key to my house. I put the pillow over my head, blocking out the sun and her high-pitched annoying voice. Normally, I found it endearing. Today, I wanted to reach in and rip out her larynx. Chance was right; my head was throbbing. Shaking me a bit, Nina said, "I brought you a Chai Tea Latte."

"Just shove it under the pillow," I grumbled. "I'm not getting up. Go away...need more sleep."

"Wake up, I brought Advil too." Nina came armed and awfully prepared. I needed something to dull the pain, and not my headache pain. I needed something much stronger than Advil to dull the pain of my aunt's letter and what transpired with Chance and me last night. Why had I allowed myself to kiss him? I knew better. It was so unfair of me. "Come on cranky pants, let's go. We're gonna talk about kissing Chance and your aunt's letter. Up and at 'em!" she said, pulling the pillow from my head.

"What the---? How the f--"

"Chance called me when he left here last night. He was worried about you." She took off her shoes and got into the blankets with me. "I came by last night after my date with Evan and checked on you. You were out cold. So, I figured I'd let you sleep it off and come back this morning. So SURPRISE! Here I am." Nina was way too bubbly for so early in the morning.

"God, he told you about...oh God." This just sucked more and more. I knew I'd eventually tell Nina and possibly Amy about everything, but I certainly wasn't ready just yet. Christ.

"Listen to me, when are ya gonna get it in your thick skull that he isn't going anywhere and that everything that freaking boy does is for you?" She was audibly annoyed.

"You just don't get it." Nobody got it. Frankly, nobody got it, because I'd never told anybody. Nobody.

"And that shit with your aunt." She shoved me over, so I'd look at her. "She didn't mean any of that. I knew her. I know you. I saw you two together. That woman loved you. She was pissed that her sister died and so she looked for someone to blame." Nina took a long drink of whatever was in her cup. Obviously, it was something cold, because Nina hated hot liquid. She chugged it effortlessly and painlessly, proving it wasn't a scorching hot beverage.

"Here's the deal. You gotta stop beating your crap up about your mom's death. Isn't it clear that you couldn't have stopped that cancer? Every single one of her sisters died from cancer. You didn't give it to her. You couldn't stop it," she said, pulling the pillow out from under me, and smacking me with it. "The doctors couldn't stop it. It's just one of those assy things that you get to be pissed off about, but have to accept it as just an assy thing you can't do one damn thing about." She ranted breathlessly with anger in her voice. I hoped the anger was for the cancer and not for me.

When I wasn't having a "woe is me" party, I did allow my head to go that way. All of my aunts died from cancer—every single one. It was quite apparent that I wouldn't have been able to stop it—no matter how much I wished I could have. I had so many regrets. That first night that I came home from being out with Nate, and my mom was doubled over in pain, vomiting in the toilet, I should've taken her to the hospital. I was smart enough to know that what I was witnessing didn't seem so normal. But being 17 and ready to get on the phone for an after-our-date phone marathon with Nate, I took my mom's word for it that she just had a stomach bug, would drink some Pepto and go to bed. However, I really should've caught on after a few months of this "horrible stomach bug." When I finally did call Vaughn and Darby, it was too late; I'd let it go on too long. The guilt trip was round trip and went full circle.

"Now, what's this Chance shit? I'm done accepting that you 'don't wanna talk about it' Shelby, because I do. You're gonna sit here right now and tell me why you two broke up, or better yet, why you broke that scrumptious Chance Charming's heart." She said, glaring at me. I'd seen that look before; she wasn't going to take "No" for an answer this time. I supposed it was about time. It'd been almost 14 months since we'd broken up. I was surprised that Nina and my brother and sister had waited this long for the truth. I looked at Nina and decided to tell her the whole story.

"Tell me you're kidding! Tell me this is just some convoluted story to shut me the Hell up!" Nina was staring at me like I'd just told her I was an alien from Mars.

"That's the story. I don't even understand why you're looking at me like that." I just spilled my guts to her, and she was treating me like a child, a child deserving admonishment.

"You need therapy, chick. Deep, deep, get to the heart of it therapy." She got up from the bed and started fiddling with her hair in the mirror. She was using my brush; I hated when people used my brush. Nina knew it too.

"Please don't tell Chance." I begged.

"Oh Hell no, I'm not making that promise." She turned and looked at me, still brushing her hair with my brush. "Actually, I'll probably tell him today, and it'll be one of those things that you thank me for on your wedding day....to Chance....when I'm fixing your veil....as the maid-of-honor, eh matron-of-honor. Evan better propose soon," she whined. I really wished we were talking about her and Evan and not about Chance and me. Chance and me? There was no "Chance and me." It was over.

"Nina, seriously--"

"No Shelby, this is ridiculous; you're ridiculous. How long do you expect me to sit around and watch my best friend suffer and let something, someone, so wonderful slip through her fingers? I'm not gonna do it anymore. I wanna see you happy; I need to see you happy." She explained.

"I just can't do it anymore." I said.

"Oh, you're going to and it's about time," Nina said. She walked over to the bed, hugged me quickly, kissed the top of my head, and said, "...and another thing, don't ever go through that shit again without me. We're best friends. We're always there for each other, always, the good, and the bad. It's Friendship 101, duh." She picked up the brush, brushed her hair a few more times, and said that she needed to meet Evan and his family for brunch. She left after stealing three shirts and a pair of pants. Leaving the house, she was singing "Take a Chance on Me" by Abba; I supposed that was her way of reminding me of what she wanted out of my future. Nina always sang that particular song when I finalized our conversations about Chance and refused to speak any more about him.

Last year, Chance, Mallory, and I went to the drive-in movie theater in Chance's pickup truck. He made an event of it. He packed enough food for the entire audience; we actually did end up sharing quite a bit of it with our neighboring cars, turning it into a drive-in movie, tailgating event before the two movies started. That was how things always were with Chance; he turned everything into a party. People flocked to him; he was lively, fun, and so outgoing and personable, as long as people agreed with his conservative political views and loved belting out choruses of country songs at random, inopportune times.

When the first movie began, the three of us climbed into the bed of his truck, snuggling on a pile of cozy blankets Chance brought with us. About halfway through the second movie, Mallory was sound asleep on my lap. Chance and I were getting tired too and hadn't really wanted to sit through the rest of the Disney cartoon while Mallory slept. I eased myself out from under Mallory and started to pick her up. She reached up, put her arms around my neck, and fell back to sleep with her head on my shoulder. As she was laying her head down, she looked up with those adorable, glassy, sleepy eyes, and said, "I love you, Mommy."

My heart melted and turned to goo. I glanced at Chance and his eyes were watery as he smiled at me with the happiest grin I'd ever seen. It was a magical moment, one I'd never expected. The moment meant everything to me, still does. I could see a future with these two. I wanted a future with them, needed a future with them. I think Chance sensed it too. We'd made love that night in a way that said forever. I'd never experienced such a connection with anyone like that before; it was all-consuming and passionate. Each kiss, every caress, every tender moment whispered, "forever," and I couldn't have been happier.

The next morning, Chance and I were both still floating from knowing that we'd both found the one. We were more amorous and affectionate with each other than ever before in front of Mallory. Mallory noticed and seemed to be even more blissful than the two of us. We'd made heart-shaped pancakes like a real family, a happy family. As I was making the pancakes, I even allowed my mind to drift to how much I liked the name "Shelby Michaels." It flowed so well.

Growing up, I never thought "Shelby LeeMaster" sounded that great together; I was one of the few women in this day and age who looked forward to changing her last name. I was completely on board with finally becoming "Shelby Michaels," if Chance ever proposed. But after the previous night, I was certain we were well on our way to that step together. Everything was falling into place, and I loved every second of it. Unfortunately, I'd had to cut our fun short, because I had an appointment with my doctor for my yearly exam.

At the exam, my doctor felt something on my left breast. I heard the words, and then suddenly felt like I was under water. I could hear his words, but they were muffled and strange, out of place. How could he be saying these words when an hour ago, I was happier than I knew was humanly possible? Obviously, I wasn't meant for such happiness. His receptionist scheduled a mammogram for three weeks away. I decided that nobody needed to know about this test until I knew what the results were. I'd face this courageously and alone. During those three weeks, I distanced myself from Chance more and more. I was terrified and didn't want to bring him with me on my road to terror and doom.

The mammogram revealed a mass that the doctor decided needed to be removed with a biopsy. At that point, terror consumed me. Anger suffocated me. Chance believed that the closeness of the perfect pancake breakfast spooked me, which was why I was pulling away. I allowed him to continue to believe that. I didn't want to worry him, or Vaughn, or Darby, or anyone. I was going at it alone.

The problem came when I realized that I needed to have a driver for the biopsy; I wasn't permitted to drive myself home. Finally, I asked Janessa, my student, to take me home. I knew it seemed strange, but with all the secrets I had on her, I knew she'd keep mine. Janessa wasn't just my student; she was my friend. However, I did lie to her. I told her that I was getting a "boob lift." She loved being a part of the "scandalous secret." To this day, she still comments on how perfect my "enhancements" look. After the procedure, she picked me up at the hospital, took me home, and stayed with me the first night, eating ice cream and watching movies. The procedure was easy; the waiting for the results was the hard part.

Thankfully, the mass was benign, harmless they said. They didn't know the half of it. The whole thing, the exam, the mammogram, and the procedure more than "harmed" me. It destroyed me. I knew at that moment I'd been given a sign. I wasn't meant to be happy; it was obviously not in my destiny. I knew I wasn't supposed to experience that sort of bliss. At that moment, I accepted it. The last thing that I was ever going to do was put Chance and Mallory through similar agony.

I received a sign that fateful day, maybe not right then, but someday, I was going to die a long, horrifying death after a long, losing battle with cancer, just as all of my aunts had. There was no way that I was going to make Mallory (or Chance) sit back and watch that. They would never have to experience such heartbreak and pain; I was sure of that. Sure, they both felt sadness when I ended the relationship, but it would've been so much worse after years of being a family. I was certain that a broken family was worse than never being a family at all. It was already excruciating after having only one morning as a "family."

Vaughn and Darby were my family; I'd never have another. I even tried to keep my nephews and Becca at a distance. With the boys, it was easy; they're toddler boys. But Becca, she was harder. I loved her with every fiber of my being. I just tried to make sure that she didn't feel similarly. I never told Vaughn or Darby about the tests or why I'd broken up with Chance. Chance recently stopped asking. He still showed up from time to time. He actually did stop completely for a while, but when my aunt died, he walked right back in my life as if he'd never gone. I just wished he'd find someone, someone perfect for his sake, and for Mallory's. Chance needed to let me go, move on, and stop always being there.

Chapter 13

Here

Not wanting to hear what more Lila had to say, I stormed away from her, Carl still close on my heels. Lila knew better than to follow me when I was in this state of mind. I'd needed a breather after all the drama over Shelby. I didn't want to hear how terribly flawed my daughter was. What mother would ever want to hear that her daughter was anything other than perfect? What did Lila know? She'd never had children; she wouldn't be able to tell if there was something wrong with my daughter. What experience did she have with being a mother? Shelby and I were close; I knew her well enough to know that she'd never be dumb enough to shut love out. Would she? Shelby was smarter than that, stronger than that. Wasn't she?

Truthfully, I'd always wanted to believe that Shelby and I were more like friends than mother and daughter. After Carl died and Vaughn and Darby moved out shortly after, it was only Shelby and I living in the house together. We'd grown closer than I'd ever been with Vaughn or Darby; we shared everything, no topic was ever off limits. She confided in me about everything. I knew if there was alcohol at a party she went to, which of her friends were sexually active, and what boy caught her eye and made her swoon. She sought my advice over boys, hair, friendship, and clothes. Shelby never made me feel "out of it" or uncool; I was part of her life. She'd have her friends over, and they'd all sit and talk with me, never stealing off to the basement to be alone. I always thought it was strange that they'd enjoyed wholesome board game nights with a parent and weren't looking for a secluded spot to sample liquor and make out. Shelby was infinitely tamer and more reserved than I was when I was in high school.

Even when Shelby's relationship with Nate became more serious, and they declared themselves an "exclusive item," our time together didn't diminish. In all actuality, it increased. Nate relished in spending time at the house, being a part of our family. Oftentimes, I cringed whenever I witnessed Shelby walking all over Nate's feelings and ego. On numerous occasions, I begged her to soften her tone and her mood with him. He was so love-struck; he never stuck up for himself or put his foot down. I knew it was only a matter of time until she realized that she needed a stronger man or until he realized that she treated him like dog poo on her shoe. Unfortunately, for her, he realized it before she did.

Their breakup was the first time I ever realized that Shelby and I weren't as close as I'd thought we were. When Nate broke up with her "to date other people," Shelby was shattered. I'd never seen her so broken and hurt, not when Carl died, nor when I was diagnosed with cancer. When Nate chose to walk away from her, Shelby realized how disposable love could be and how disposable a person could feel. I knew she was in love with him, but she was thoroughly shredded, and I couldn't quite understand why she was letting a man tear her up like that. It was unlike her.

Vaughn and Darby clarified the hazy picture for me. Vaughn was baffled that I didn't see it for what it was; he'd said that I was always able to read people and situations so easily. Darby was certain that Shelby had confided me, but still I remained in the dark. Basically, Vaughn and Darby had to spell it out for me. Shelby and Nate were not only each other's first loves, but their first....everything.

As a mother, it was gut-wrenching and maternally-defeating to hear. I'd thought I'd raised her "better than that." But then, it all did make perfect sense. Shelby gave herself completely to Nate, something that she'd never done before, and he regarded so lightly, so carelessly, and trampled all over it. Once this news was revealed, my heart broke for Shelby; I understood in a way that I really didn't want to how much she loved Nate. I felt horribly for her and disappointed as well. Shelby probably never realized that ultimately there was a price to pay in the end—her innocence.

I hated that my daughter had chosen to take that step, long before getting married, a decision that I never made. Carl and I waited for each other, gave all of ourselves to each other on our wedding night. I wanted that for my children. I wanted them to feel how true love and true passion were destined to be. My husband will have a piece of me that no other person would ever have. And Nate, he had that piece of Shelby, and it hadn't meant everything to him. It had meant "for the time-being" for him. I hated that. But truly, I hated that I hadn't recognized the change in my daughter and the intimate connection she had with Nate. I'd thought mothers were just instinctively supposed "to know." I didn't know, had no clue really. But even more than that, I hated that Shelby couldn't trust me, trust the closeness between us and tell me the truth. I had failed her, yet again.

I wasn't surprised that she kept her distance from boys after that; she'd gotten burned. People didn't want to go anywhere near a flame once they experienced the pain of being seared. Then, my cancer came back with a vengeance and I got sick, terribly sick. Shelby didn't have time to date or worry about men during that fun-filled time of chemotherapy and vomi-arrhea. I assumed she'd put love on the back burner, away from her fragile skin and heart, and revisit it again in the future. Apparently, according to Lila, I was wrong, yet again.

"Please talk to me," Carl pleaded. I hadn't heard him approach.

"I'm not avoiding you; I'm just thinking." I admitted, turning around to look at him. "Maybe Lila's right, maybe I don't know...didn't know her like I thought I did."

"Betheny, Lila never said that," Carl countered. "You're just blaming yourself for something that isn't your fault."

"I hurt her...many times." I cried. "I should've been better..."

"Not the football game story again, Beth," Carl consoled. "I thought we'd reconciled that regret a hundred times over."

"I don't know why you always have to be so nonchalant and dismissive about this when I bring it up," I argued. "If I could just get one 'do over' parenting day--"

"You don't Beth; you've got to let it go," Carl begged.

"I can't; I'm...it was horrible."

When Shelby was a senior in high school, she started gaining weight. Being overweight myself, and feeling miserable about it, I wanted to do everything in my power to deter Shelby from my gluttonous fate. I'd thought that her cheerleading skirt was getting a little too snug and her butt a little too large. Therefore, I'd told her that she needed to drop 15 pounds by Parent Night at the football game, otherwise, I wasn't going to go to the football game to escort her across the field. As if that ultimatum wasn't tragic enough, on the day of the game, we'd both gotten ready for the game. Minutes before we left, I told her to get on the scale to see if she'd accomplished her weight-loss goal. She was 4.5 pounds shy of her goal. Shrugging it off, she said that she'd lose those last few unwanted pounds at some point. Shelby was so unconcerned with her weight; it bothered me. I hated that she disregarded my threat and didn't heed my warning. I didn't want her to miss out on glorious parts of her life, because she felt too heavy to partake, like I'd done so many times before.

I looked at her, and with a heavy heart, I told her that I wasn't going to the game. She was "on her own." She sized me up and down, staring at me in disbelief. With glassy, teary eyes, she nodded, walked out of the house, got into her car, and drove off. My attempt at making her stay home and think about how to change her eating habits and health failed. Shelby was confident in her own skin; she didn't need me to support and guide her. She was strong, stronger than I. I trembled as the tears flowed down my face. My lesson in "tough love" suffocated me.

Finally realizing that I couldn't make my daughter, my baby, walk across the field on her final Parent Night as a senior alone, I jumped in the car and sped off to the high school stadium. I illegally parked my car by the ambulance entrance and ran up to the end zone, only to hear the following words, echoing over the loudspeaker: "Shelby Lynn LeeMaster, escorted tonight by....by....Shelby Lynn LeeMaster is a senior, the president of student council, a member of pep club, and drama club. She's been a cheerleader and gymnast for nine years. Next fall, she plans to attend The Ohio State University. Her life goal is to get married, have children, and be a high school English teacher. She wants to be remembered here as 'The Girl who could handle anything.' And next up is Dana Rosenbaugh, escorted by Mr. and Mrs. Denny Rosenbaugh. Dana is..."

The words droned on; I blocked them out. I'd missed my baby's final Parent Night. I'd tried to tear her down. I failed. Oh thank God I failed. My Shelby had held her head high and solely walked across that field with aplomb, not letting a few negative and ego-shattering words destroy her big night as a senior. "The girl who could handle anything." Boy was she ever. I felt more pride and self-loathing at that moment, standing on the track staring at the field than I knew was humanly possible. Simultaneously, my daughter achieved the ultimate success, whereas I was nothing more than a flailing failure.

When she got home from the game that night, she was ecstatic; during halftime of the game, Nate asked her to the upcoming Homecoming dance. She was bubbling with excitement and determined to find a yellow dress for the dance, even though all of her friends wanted short, little black dresses. She was floating, talking a mile a minute.

I'd wanted to talk about how I'd let her down and apologize for how badly I'd treated her. When I told her so, she crinkled her face, rolled her eyes and said, "You can make it up to me at the mall tomorrow...with your credit card." She'd been unfazed by my actions; the same actions that proved how little I knew about parenting, but also proved how tenacious my daughter was.

If I hadn't broken Shelby's will and confidence that night, then I was pretty convinced that nothing could. But Lila's words were making me doubt myself once again. I'd let her down; I'd made her feel inferior to her peers when she was in no way inferior to anyone.

"Betheny, you told me yourself that she didn't even think twice about that incident," Carl argued.

"Yes, but I did. I regret everything about that night; I need a do over." I whined, wanting to show Shelby how truly remarkable she was. I didn't have the energy to shoo Lila away when she came back, standing close to Carl and me. She stood there, waiting to speak. Carl and I ignored her, finishing the conversation we needed to have.

"We don't get do-overs, you know that. Beth, you were a wonderful mother. Our kids adored you, worshipped the very ground that you walked on." Carl pulled me into him. "You have nothing to feel guilty about. We made mistakes; we're only human. You taught Shelby that night how sorry you were by apologizing," he said. Brushing my hair out of my eyes, he said, "I know she blew you off, but you taught her that it's okay to be wrong, just as long you admit your mistakes. She held no animosity or grudge against you. You taught her the importance of forgiveness."

Carl was always big on apologies. He used to preach that love, honesty, and trust weren't "the big three" in relationships. He always said that it didn't matter how much you loved someone, how honest you were, or how much trust you had, if you couldn't find forgiveness in your heart and within yourself, then the relationship was doomed. Without forgiveness no relationship or friendship could ever last, because inevitably at some point, someone was going to screw up. Shelby had forgiven me, but I still couldn't find it within me to forgive myself. I'd hurt her; I'd let her down. I hated myself for it.

Lila sat back and listened to this entire conversation, letting Carl and I ramble on with our innermost thoughts and fears without ever letting on that she was listening or even comprehending what we were saying. "Ummmm....while we're on the topic of forgiveness, there's something pretty important that I think I need to tell you both."

There

I'd spent the afternoon with my niece, Becca, while Darby volunteered at the elementary school. The school was sponsoring an evening blood drive. Leave it to Darby to volunteer for everything under the sun for Becca's preschool. It was so her. You couldn't pay me enough to work at one of those blood mobiles, all that blood and needles. No thank you.

Darby has a crazy sort of blood disorder, called I.T.P. It's some big word that I never cared to really learn. I heard "blood disorder" and checked out. As long as it wouldn't kill my sister, then I was good. Apparently, this blood disorder, disease, ailment, or whatever it is, makes little red spots on the body and blood takes longer to clot. Sounded scary to me, but all the doctors said that it really wasn't something to worry about. I think that since her blood "is tainted" as she likes to call it, and she cannot donate her blood to needy bloodless people, she feels compelled to volunteer at the drives. That way, she can feel like she's doing something, giving back. I find it ironic and strange; she finds it worthwhile and important. Tomato Tomahto. Sisters don't always see eye-to-eye, but their blood certainly runs thick and deep.

Since I got a freebie night with my niece, we went to the mall, to dinner, and to see a movie, a movie that I knew Darby'd never let her see. I figured Darby was going to be mad about the movie, so I decided to lessen the blow of the movie and let Darby choose which battle to fight. Therefore, I'd gotten Becca's ears pierced too.

Isn't that so sweet of me? That's me, always thinking of my sister. Don't judge me. An aunt has to get to do some of the fun stuff, otherwise, we're just old, boring adults, like their dumb parents. And nobody wants that, especially not me or Becca.

I could honestly say that the day Becca was born was one of the happiest days of my life. She was so gorgeous and perfect. Of course, she was a stubborn little nugget from the get-go. I'm sure all mothers argued that their newborns were stubborn and "wouldn't come out." However, Becca really wouldn't. Since Darby has that blood issue, the doctors wanted to be vigilant, careful, and proactive with Becca's birth by inducing Darby's labor a week early.

On a Monday night, we all assembled at the hospital for the big event. Darby was induced, pumped with Pitocin and Cervidil, and we waited. Nothing. After about six hours of nothing, we were all sent home, including Darby. Then on Tuesday night, they did it again. Nothing. By Wednesday night, everyone was pissed; Darby, her douchebag ex, the doctors, the hospital staff, and Vaughn and I were all ready to bounce on Darby's stomach until that little brat shot right out into the bassinet.

So again on Wednesday night, they did the induction, and contractions finally started, but they were slow going and barely registered on the monitor. I couldn't wait it out another day; I'd already missed three straight days of work, so I left to get some sleep, deciding that I must go to work on Thursday. I was worried about missing so much work already. I was a new teacher; my administrators didn't know much about my family history. The school could not thoroughly understand how the birth of my niece was such a monumental event. I guess they didn't realize that my family was more accustomed to "getting rid" of family members than adding little itty bitty new ones. It was a monumental event, no doubt about it.

That monumental event occurred right before I left for work on Thursday morning by C-section, of course. People can say that their babies were stubborn and "wouldn't come out," but seriously, who in the world has ever heard of three failed inductions? Damn little pumpkin had to be ripped out before she agreed to come see us. Who'd blame her though? The world is a scary place, full of heartbreak and disappointment; I think I'd want to hide away in a safe, warm, protective sanctuary too.

I had to wait to meet my brand new niece, the first baby to bless our family and change our lives, for an entire school day as the day dragged on and on. By the end of the day when the last period's bell rang, I was ready to internally combust with excitement. Vaughn and Darby had been emailing me pictures of Becca all day long. I was already swooning. I couldn't wait to get my hands on her and kiss her sweet little face off. From the pictures, her lips looked perfect, flawless; I'd never seen baby lips look so downright kissable. I couldn't wait to see them in person.

When I arrived at the hospital, the room's lights were dimmed, and Darby was sound asleep. I looked up to the head of the hospital bed and to the right was the smallest little bundle swaddled up snugly in the clear, plastic hospital bassinet. Little baby Becca was staring around the room, not making a sound. I was shocked to see her awake and alert as Darby snored peacefully in the bed next to her daughter. Tip-toeing as not to startle or wake my sister, I walked over to the little crib and stared in awe at the most beautiful baby I'd ever seen. She was gorgeous. I'd never believed in love-at-first sight until that moment. I looked at her and immediately filled with wonder and unconditional love. I picked her up quietly and snuggled her to my chest, feeling my heart warm and beat a little faster. She fit so perfectly against me. Tears poured down my face as I tried to steady my breathing and imminent sobs, not wanting to disturb Darby's rest. I already loved Becca so much. All I could think at that moment was if I felt like this with my niece, what would it feel like to hold my own baby snugly against my beating heart?

For the first time in a long, long time, I believed that maybe I'd been wrong all these years and that life could be beautiful and perfect, filled with moments of true bliss, beauty, and magic. My niece and her perfectly plump and pink little lips brought out the romantic in me, kicking my biological clock into full tick-tock, scaring the ever-loving shit out of me at the same time.

It was shortly after that epiphany that I allowed Chance and Mallory into my life and heart, with full-force and no looking back, or so I'd thought at the time. Everyone noticed a change in me, a full 180-turn, especially the way that I gave myself so completely to Chance and to Mallory. I saw a glimpse of the magic of motherhood, and I wanted more than a quick peek. I wanted forever. I did...up until that doctor's appointment extinguished that spark, forcing me to remember that fairy tales are only just fantasies for naïve little girls and nothing more.

But man, I loved Becca; I couldn't help myself. As a six-year-old, she was already just so smart, beautiful, and so thoughtful of others. She was the perfect combination of my sister and my mom, the two most important women in the world to me. I couldn't get enough of her fun sense of humor and her gorgeous dark brown hair, big brown eyes, and chubby little cheeks. She was spunky and determined, but yet loving and generous. She was both of them in one perfect package. I wanted to steal her for myself. For the past six years, I'd tried to deny my feelings for her, but I just couldn't help it. I was head over heels in love with that little girl. Truthfully, I'd started to feel similarly for Mallory as well, but... but it just wasn't in the cards.

"Alright, she's in bed now," Darby said coming down the stairs, glaring at me.

"I know you're mad, but did I really have to wait through the bath, the blow-drying, and the bedtime story to just get yelled at?" I complained, flipping through a magazine.

"It gave me time to think. I'm not gonna yell at you, but I am going to punish you." My sister smiled smugly.

"Punish me? You can't..."

"You put holes in my daughter's ears and let her see a movie that had the "S" word in it." She said through gritted teeth.

"Now, let's get this on record, Becca's six-years-old. She wanted to get her ears pierced; she didn't cry or flinch. They look cute," I argued, trying to lighten the air around us.

Continuing to argue my case, I said, "And....another thing...the 's word" is shit. They did not say 'shit,' it was 'sucks,' which isn't really a---"

"Don't start, that's your punishment, you're not allowed to talk. I'm talking. I've had a lot to say for a long time now. And you, missy, are gonna listen." My sister said, pointing at me, emphasizing the word "missy." It was the term my mom and aunt used when we were in trouble and about to be scolded. Darby was obviously pissed, but I didn't say so. I knew better than to use the "p-word" in her house.

"Alright, but do you have any wine? Beer? Tequila? Anything? Crack? Something to numb whatever you're about to drone on about?" I asked, trying to be funny, but only getting a bone-chilling glare from Darby. "Okay, okay, I'm listening." I said, admitting my defeat.

Darby wanted to tell me that it wasn't fair that I'd gotten Becca's ears pierced and taken her to a movie. When I tried to explain myself more, she cut me off. She wasn't mad that I'd done those activities with Becca and made those memories with my niece; she was mad that she wasn't given the opportunity to do them herself. I'd felt badly for taking that away from her and told her so, but apparently, I'd completely misunderstood her. She was mad that she wasn't going to get the opportunity to do them with her niece. Vaughn and Rachel had boys; I had no idea what she was talking about. Darby didn't have a niece.

"Shelby, you're gonna be alone forever if you don't do something about all of this business with Chance." She screamed, exasperated with me.

"Chance? What does he have to do with Becca's ears?" I paused, looking at her with confusion. Then it hit me, full out smacked me in the face. "Ahhh, this isn't about Becca's ears, or even about my non-existent baby's earrings; this is about Chance and nothing else."

Was she kidding me? She tried to link Becca's ears being pierced to breaking up with Chance. Now that was a stretch—even for her. No wonder she took so long to dry Becca's hair; she had to come up with something to turn the tables around and connect Becca's bejeweled little lobes to my life of pending doom, full of isolation and despair. It was not a clever or creative parallel at all.

She was usually much better at being sly than that; it was almost embarrassing.

"Seriously Darb," I joked, "You should've rewashed Becca's hair and dried it again,

searching harder for a better connection, because this one's tres lame-o."

"Don't...you're not turning this into a joke, like you always do." She said.

"I don't..."

"Shut up, you're not talking, remember your punishment?" She said using her "mom" voice on me.

Pantomiming the zipping of my lip, I sat back on the couch, folded my arms across my chest, and gave her the go-ahead nod. Darby went on a 15-minute straight tirade, lecture, monologue, soliloquy, whatever you wanted to call it, about how my life was going to lack meaning if I didn't allow myself to fall in love, completely and totally, swimming in blissful love and matrimony. Blah. Blah. Blah. I ignored the burning desire to interrupt her to point out that she wasn't currently dating anyone either, but I knew she'd tell me that she was "working on herself" at the moment and that she occasionally went out with that bald dude, whatever his name was, from work.

"Chance was perfect...no...is perfect for you." Darby said. "I just don't understand what happened."

"I've told you all a thousand million trillion times, nothing happened. I just wasn't into it." I said. "I can't understand why everyone still harps on this. Can't a girl decide whom she wants to be with?" I argued, filling with exasperation. "What freaking year is it anyway? Was this supposed to be some arranged marriage or something that nobody ever bothered to tell me about?" I added, feeling my face start heating up and my blood boil. Why couldn't my friends and family just mind their own damn business? Chance and I were over. Why couldn't anyone, other than me, accept that?

"Yes Shelby, a girl can choose who she wants to be with, but everyone who has ever been in the same room with the two of you knows how much he loves you and how much you love him. You can't hide that when it's as plain as day to everyone effing around you." Darby said, shaking her head at me in full disgust and disappointment. Oh, and she said "effing" too; God forbid her drop an "f-bomb" in a moment of heated verbal Blitzkrieg.

"I'm sorry Darb, but you said the same thing about Nate. Hell, you even said it about Rob." I screamed as quietly as I could, not wanting to wake Becca, but needing to prove how wrong she could be about other people's love affairs.

"Rob? Who the heck is Rob?" she yelled, exasperated. However, without me even answering, she said, "Oh, Rob, Navy Chicago Rob, yeah him. Okay...I was really wrong about him....and wrong about Nate. But, I'm not wrong about Chance. Not at all." She said determinedly.

For a long time, I thought that Nate was "the one who got away," and that I had ignored my destiny by treating him so badly and regarding his feelings and our relationship so lightly. I did love him; I loved him the same way all girls love their first love. Nate showed me what I wanted in a relationship, in a boyfriend. He believed the world revolved around me and did everything in his power to show me. Sadly, but importantly, I learned how wrong I really was about Nate and that he was just a "stepping stone" to Mr. Right. When Nate didn't show up, make any sort of appearance or effort at my mom's funeral, I knew without a shadow of a doubt that he was definitely not "the one who got away." When you're truly meant to be with someone, they would never make you suffer those horrific tragedies alone.

Nate additionally showed me what else I did not want in a man. Nate didn't have any ambition, no drive to speak of. Education and intelligence weren't important to him. Going to college to be a teacher at the time, I didn't, couldn't respect or accept that. However at that age, I'd ignored it, thinking that we'd work it out. If he hadn't broken my heart back when it was so unguarded and fragile, then I may have never figured it out. Oh, it would've been disastrous if the two of us actually stayed together. A woman needs more than a man who just loves her; she needs a man who loves her, shares her same values, and does all he can to protect her and those values.

But then...then, I met Chance. He loved me like Nate did, more so than Nate, because he even loved my awe and excitement for education. Our values were the same, written in stone and meant the world to both of us. Chance loved me, but didn't think the world revolved around me. He's more evolved than that. The world doesn't revolve around one person; it revolves around true, unconditional love, a love that no matter what, lives on. According to Chance, the world revolves around love, and love revolves around the relationship.

Okay, he's probably the sappiest, most romantic man on the planet, but nobody really got to see that side of him. I always liked knowing that little secret about him. I especially liked knowing that it was saved and special only for me. If someone were to ask him what his favorite movie was, he'd tell them Young Guns, but I know the truth. It's The Sound of Music, that movie gets him every time.

But Chance is also ambitious, smart, oh so smart, and witty. But most importantly, he knows that relationships are delicate and need to be regarded with care and held close to the heart and soul. He was shredded when he saw Mallory's mom with another man, wounded. I promised him that I'd never hurt him like that. I'd never hurt him in a way that it'd take time to mend all those little pieces of his heart. I was hurting him now, just so I wouldn't have to shatter him and Mallory further on down the line. Everyone figured I fell out of love with him; I didn't. I couldn't. He's perfect, but I had to remember that it's not about me. It's about him and how I love him so much that I had to let him go, so be could be perfect for someone else.

Darby was pissing me off. I hated thinking about Chance, missing Chance, justifying my break up with him to myself over and over again. It got old, fast. I just wanted to close it off, shut it down.

"Actually Darby, your track record for picking men for me...or even for yourself for that matter isn't so great, so why don't you just let it go and leave me the 'f-word' alone," I snapped, grabbed my coat, snatched my keys off the counter, and walked out.

I didn't butt into other people's lives. Why did they all butt into mine? Nina was different than Darby. Nina wouldn't tell Chance about my breast cancer scare, even though she threatened to do so. Nina wasn't intrusive like that. Darby and Vaughn, they wouldn't last one second with that knowledge without beating the crap out of me for not telling them about the lump and without calling Chance a millisecond later. I vowed on that day to never tell

Chance, Darby or Vaughn about my biopsy; it was a vow I was never going to break.

Chance would find someone, and probably fairly soon. He needed to anyway. He had so much love and devotion to give that it was crucial that he find someone to share it with. Also, Chance needed to make sure that he found someone for Mallory to love. She needed a mother-figure, someone to do her hair, buy her clothes, talk to her about boys, and all that teenage girl drama. It was important for her to have someone to take her to get her ears pierced and do girlie things like that. She needed someone. But unfortunately, I was not going to be that someone for either one of them.

Chapter 14

Here

"Get...Away....From...Me!!!" I screamed.

Lila moved closer to me, "No, let me explain!" she yelled, igniting the interest in my other four sisters, who'd been on their way to come sit with us. "You need to hear me out, Beth!"

"What the fuck is going on here?" Anna asked, coming between the two of us. Being the oldest and the scariest of my five sisters, she was always able to stop an argument in seconds.

"None of your damn business, Anna, this is between that big-mouth bitch and me." I yelled, trying to get around Anna, so I could claw Lila's eyes out. If Lila didn't go through the experience soon and rid me of my "earthly emotions," then it was quite possible that I could kill her here, which was impossible. But I was seriously considering it. The urge was definitely within me. How could she? She had no right to blame my daughter for my death. Who the Hell did she think she was?

Then, without warning or rationality, the strangest thing happened. All anger and feelings of hatred and destruction disappeared. All I felt was a deep, empty sadness. I looked around at Carl and my sisters; all eyes were on me, staring at me suspiciously and fearfully. I tried to regain my anger, thinking about Lila blaming my Shelby Lynn for my death. I tried to restore the rage in me. Nothing—just sadness. I felt robbed; I wanted to get angry over that too. I focused—nothing. Interesting. Maddening, actually.

"Uh Betheny," Anna broke my train of thought. "Are you okay? What's going on?" I looked at all of them; worry was on each and every one of their faces.

"I...I'm not...I don't know." I confessed, shaking my head, looking at all of them. "I wanted to be mad, to kill Lila, then all my anger just sort of vanished, like 'poof,' gone!" I had no idea what was going on; this was obviously new to all of us. We all looked around at each other, hoping someone could shed some light on this.

"Honey, why don't we take a break and clear our minds a bit?" Carl offered, putting his arm around me for support.

"No Carl," the voice behind us declared, startling everyone. "Betheny needs to listen to Lila tell her story, and then she needs to come with me." We all turned around to see Julian staring at me with a look of regret and sadness in his eyes. Julian normally looked like that, so I was hopeful that it didn't have anything to do with what just happened here with me and the uncontrollable rage I'd just experienced.

"Julian, what do you...what's..."

Julian held up his hand, shook his head, and silenced me. "Betheny, please just listen to what Lila has to say," he said.

All of us sat down, giving Lila our undivided attention. Back in the day, this sort of attention would have pleased Lila thoroughly. Lila loved basking in the limelight, drawing all eyes on her. But, she seemed terribly uncomfortable right now. She cleared her throat and looked pleadingly at Julian, "Ummm, Jerian sir..." she said.

"It's Julian, Lila, what is it" he asked softly.

"I'm sorry Julian, may I just talk to Beth alone?" she asked.

"Unfortunately, no. Everyone needs to hear what you have to say, all of your sisters and Carl too," he said with finality and authority, an authority that I was pretty certain he didn't actually have. It was odd, because nobody was questioning him on it either.

Lila cleared her throat and nervously began to speak, "When Betheny died, I felt like I'd lost a limb. People aren't supposed to bury their sisters. It's just not right, it's unbearable really. A sister is a continuation of yourself, a different version, a 'what if' I'd chosen a different path version." Lila explained.

When did Lila get so philosophical and insightful? I'd never thought of that before. My sisters were definitely a different version of me; they'd chosen different lives, different avenues, but we'd all come from the same starting point, the same beginning. How we lived our lives, what we'd chosen to do, that was all individual and separate. Despite those choices, we'd all remained close, together, choosing to share our lives and deaths with one another. All sisters, all the same, but different versions of each other.

Lila continued, "Watching you die," she stared at me with pain in her eyes, "was the most devastating thing I've ever endured, still, to this day." My other sisters looked at me and nodded in agreement. Patricia scooted nearer to me, so that our sides were melded together as she laid her head on my shoulder.

"It's hard to admit this, but with each one of you, it got easier to say 'goodbye,' because I knew you'd all be here together, the way we'd always intended it to be," Lila admitted, wiping the tears away from her eyes and taking a moment to collect herself. "Patti, you'd think that losing you, my last sister, would've been the worst, because I was alone after that. It wasn't. I was so jealous of you. You got to leave me and be here with all of them." Lila confessed. Ha! I knew it. I knew she'd be jealous of all of us being here without her. Lila was so competitive.

"I understand, honey, I would've felt horribly without all of you," Patricia consoled her. Then Patti looked at me and said, "But she's right, Beth, losing you, our baby sister, was the hardest. The first 'goodbye' is always the most painful" she confirmed. The rest of my sisters nodded, looking slightly guilty, but relieved that the truth was finally revealed.

Lila kept going, purging herself of a decade's worth of thoughts and regrets, of words never spoken or heard. "I know Beth that it was horrifying to leave your children, and I'd never say otherwise, because it was hard for me to leave them, too. And I was just their dumb ol' aunt." She paused, gathering her thoughts. "But believe me, please believe me, the way that you look at me as the lucky one is the exact same way that I look at you," she said, shaking her head guiltily.

Knowing that I wasn't supposed to interrupt her, I tried to stay silent, but I couldn't help myself. "Lucky? Me? For what? I'd lost my husband, left my children, and died before any one of you even started to fear cancer or what it could do! How am I the lucky one?" I marveled.

Lila smiled, "Oh Beth, don't you get it? You found true love, true love found you. You were blessed with three perfect children, yes you left them entirely too early, but you had them, enjoyed them, experienced them. Oh my God, you loved them and they loved...no...love you...they still do," she said, her voice cracking with emotion.

I knew it was wrong for me to keep making her relive and remember how ultimately unfilled her life really was. She'd never experienced the kind of love Carl and I had; she'd never looked into the eyes of her own child, filling with unconditional and devotional love. She'd missed so much in her life. It was wrong of me to keep harping on all that I'd lost, when she'd never found it in the first place.

Continuing with her explanation, she said, "But mostly, I'm referring to the deaths. You didn't have to watch as each one of your sisters suffered in unimaginable ways, with agonizing pain, as you sat back not being able to do a damn thing to help them." At that, she broke, sobbing into Virginia's shoulder. Virginia wasn't the lovey-dovey type, but she held Lila as if her life depended upon it, knowing that her own discomfort didn't matter right now. That's what sisters did; they held on, mainly because it never felt right to let go.

I knew Lila was right; I knew that I'd dodged a shattering experience. I just couldn't grasp how that gave her the right to blame my daughter for my death. We all died from the same terminal disease. Shelby certainly didn't inject us with it or wish it upon us. And yet, Lila found her to be the scapegoat, the scapegoat for cancer. That was absurd.

"So after I left your house that morning," Lila continued once she was done composing herself. "I was angry and so terribly distraught. I sat down in my lonely condo, put pen to paper and just started writing and writing and writing. I wrote to Allen Hart and mailed five different letters to his old address, blaming him for all the woes in my life, knowing he'd obviously never read them," she recalled. Lila was referring to her "husband," who died long before Carl and I did.

"When those letters didn't ease my suffering, I started to look for someone to blame. I decided on Shelby, because she'd let you be so sick for so long without ever telling anyone. I knew it was a stretch and ridiculous, but I was reaching," she said. The rest of my sisters nodded. Were they agreeing with her? Had they also concluded that my daughter was the one to blame for my sickness, my death?

I started to interrupt, when Julian shook his head slightly, silencing me. I closed my mouth reluctantly, allowing Lila to go on.

"I was filled with such anger and sadness. I never even addressed that letter, never planned to give it to her, but yet, I'll admit, I did feel that sense of anger toward her at the time, for a long time afterward actually. I just wanted to blame someone, anyone," she lamented.

I didn't quite understand this. How do you blame a person for someone's death when cancer was the villain? Shelby couldn't have saved me. The doctors couldn't either. I couldn't comprehend how Lila's mind worked, or my other sisters' minds for that matter.

"Even though in my rational brain, I knew it wasn't her fault, or anyone's fault. The letter centered my anger, gave me an outlet," Lila admitted. "I'm not saying that I didn't carry a grudge with me for a long time, even all the way up until my final moments, but I truly never believed it. I just wanted someone to be at fault...that's all." The reality was that there was nobody to blame. Death happens, ultimately there is no rhyme or reason to any of it.

Everyone always wants to know why, but the truth is, there is no answer. It all comes down to luck, the draw of the shortest straw. You can't fight death, cheat death, or hide from it. When your straw is drawn, then that's it.

Certainly, people can cure illnesses, take care of their bodies, and try to live a healthier lifestyle. But those lifestyles, they really don't prolong lives. Those lifestyles, changes, and choices just make your body more able to enjoy those lifestyles. That's why it's always so common to hear about a young man, who only ate healthy meals and ran four miles a day, who killed over from a heart attack on his 44th birthday. It was his time. It didn't matter what he did or didn't do. It was just time.

I thought I'd beaten cancer and put that bitch right back into remission, which I did for the most part. However, my overeating, my incessant smoking (up until Carl's poor physical), and my lack of exercise probably wore my body down, destroyed my immune system, initially allowing cancer to come in and make a nice little home for itself in my colon. But the positive attitude, the changing of my eating habits, the chemotherapy, didn't truly prolong my life. Those things just helped my body try to evict that damn cancer-dwelling squatter. But in the end, it wasn't the cancer, it was in fact that my card was pulled, plain and simple. It was my time.

People still continue to question it all. Why would that boat sink with all those children on it? Why would that man shoot innocent people? Where was God when that psycho blew up that building? Unfortunately, there's no answer; it's all in the cards. With my family and the choices we made throughout our lives, it was easy. Cancer was the easiest choice, the most practical villain, moving our cards closer to the top, one-by-one.

"My final words were to Shelby Lynn; I told her that I forgave her. But the truth is, I never really blamed her, I just wanted to blame her. I finally saw the truth in those final moments of pure clarity," Lila said. She looked weighed down by remorse, feelings I knew all too well. "I'm just worried, so worried, that she'll find that old, meaningless letter, and it will confirm all of her darkest fears," Lila cried.

Agreeing with Lila, I said, "That's exactly what's gonna happen. The only way that it won't happen is if Darby, my nosy little Darby, finds it first, reads the letter, and destroys it before Shelby can lay eyes on it." I looked to Carl and my sisters, who were all nodding in agreement. We all knew Darby so well. She'd read that letter for sure, if she found it first. But she'd never let Shelby read it if she knew what it said. Darby was a protective older sister; she'd never do something that would hurt Shelby.

We all turned when we heard Julian clear his throat, "Unfortunately, Shelby did find and read that letter, which is why I need to speak with you, Beth, privately." He said, confirming all of our fears.

Walking away, I couldn't calm my terror. This was new territory for all of us. Julian didn't really talk to anyone; people went to him from time to time. But he never, ever, went to find people to talk to them. He was a loner; he stayed away, kept to himself. I also didn't know how he'd known that Shelby'd read that letter. That didn't make any sense. We just didn't know things that happened there.

Cutting my thoughts off and surprising me with his words, Julian said, "Oftentimes, a person's card is pulled, and he or she still has unfinished business there." I knew exactly what he'd meant; I'd had unfinished business. I needed to finish raising and loving my children. Carl did too. Carl was literally in the middle of a project of painting our house on the weekends when he died. Our house remained ½ blue and ½ white on the outside aluminum siding for over three years until I found the monetary means to hire someone to paint the remaining sides of our house. Yeah, there was a lot of unfinished business there. Everyone I knew had unfinished business. Wrongs to right. People to love. Chores to finish. Promises to keep. A lot of meaningful and not-so-meaningful business went unfinished.

"Most of the time, that unfinished business sorts itself out, dissolves into someone else's business, or works out with time and healing," he continued. "But sometimes, rarely even, that unfinished business festers, grows, and turns into something more, something bigger, which is what I wanted to talk to you about." Julian said.

"I don't....I'm not sure..." I started speaking, when Julian put up his hand again to ask me to wait.

"Basically, you're being given a chance to go back and talk to Shelby, show her, tell her, prove to her that love is a natural, integral, crucial part of life, and needs to be...must be... part of her life too," he said.

What? Was this some joke? Go back? Julian was the only person we'd known who'd ever gone back, and he told me to my face that it was Hell. I didn't understand any of this; was Shelby really as damaged as Lila believed? I didn't know enough about her, well the adult her, or anything about that boy to fix this. What if I made it worse?

"Beth, I know you're scared, but you have to trust me on this. It's important for Shelby to open her heart to love, to Chance's love." he said. Did he mean open her heart to take chances or to actually Chance, the man?

"Shelby needs to be with him," he said, answering my question before I could even ask it. "I can't tell you anymore than that. I've already said too much."

"Then answer this, why would you tell me 'it's Hell' to go back, and then try to convince me to do the same thing you said was so awful?" I asked, terrified of the answer.

Chuckling, despite his morose and sad demeanor, he said, "That's easy, it was Hell for me, because my 'unfinished business' never got resolved, never finished, even after my return." He looked away, shaking his head, running his fingers through his thin hair. "I got to see once again how much damage my poor choices had on those I loved. But, I'm not gonna tell you any more of my private life though. I'd like to keep it as such," he stated definitively.

Then with that same authority, that I wasn't certain he actually had, he said, "But with you, yours is gonna work. You're gonna save Shelby."

There

"Thanks for meeting me for breakfast," I said for the hundredth time.

"It's not you I care about. I wanted a Skillet Scramble; cubed cheesy ham is the bomb," Darby said.

"Nobody says, 'the bomb' anymore, Darb," I said, laughing at her complete and total lack of with-it-ness. Poor Becca.

"Did you invite me here to put me down and insult me or to apologize for last week?" she said, taking a bite of her cheesy ham and egg deliciousness.

"Neither, I just missed you is all." I admitted. We'd gone a week without talking and that was just unacceptable. I talked to Darby every morning when I drove to school and every afternoon when I drove back home again. I didn't call her on Monday, because I was still pissed about the "Chance" ambush. Then out of spite and pride, I ended up not calling all week. Finally, last night, I asked if she wanted to meet for breakfast today, knowing that she never turned down the Skillet Scramble.

"I'm gonna have to run this afternoon and again this evening after eating all of this," she said, looking down at all the food on her plate. "Wanna come with?" she asked innocently.

"Nah, I think I'll just eat a little more and then crash on the couch for the rest of the day," I admitted. Luckily, she thought I was kidding; I wasn't.

Darby spent the next 20 minutes talking about Dane, a new guy in her Running From Problems club. He was younger than her, older than me she said. Apparently, he was extremely good-looking, but had never been married. He'd spent the last twelve years or so waiting hand and foot on his invalid mother, until she died last month. Dane then realized that he'd given everything, his energy, his soul, his time, to his mother, and now, she was gone, and he had nothing to show for the past decade. So Dane, the-new-and-improved, started running, got his hair cut, bought some new clothes and reinvented himself. Darby was visibly impressed with the new guy.

"What's he do?" I asked, humoring her, taking interest in her new man.

"He's a family therapist," she laughed, "pretty, ironic, huh?'

"Well good, I'm happy for you," I said. "Is he any good in bed?"

Darby'd spit her coffee out, "Shelby!"

"What? Obviously, you're into him, I just thought I'd ask." I said.

I knew she wasn't sleeping with this new dude; I just liked ruffling her feathers. Darby wasn't the "sleeping around" type. Neither of us was, really. She'd obviously been with her ex-husband, but that was it. Me, I'd only been with Nate and Chance. My mom raised us well. At least I thought so, anyway. If she'd ever found out that I'd had premarital sex, she would've disowned me and dismembered Nate. (And I do mean that particular "member" too.)

As for Chance, she wouldn't have touched him. He's such a persuasive charmer, he'd have talked her out of the dismemberment. Then, they'd probably sit back and laugh about the whole incident. It was a shame that they never had the opportunity to meet each other. She'd have liked him. He'd have loved her.

"I'm not into him, you fool. I'm telling you this, because you're going out with him next week," she declared. "On a date. A real live blind date....with a man."

"Excuse me?" I questioned with heightened annoyance and increasing anger.

"I already told him about my beautiful sister," Darby explained. "He's intrigued by my 'exotic-looking' sister with the big blue eyes and dark hair. He even said that he had 'a thing' for tiny girls. So, when are ya gonna go out with him?"

Darby must've undergone a lobotomy, because there was no way in the world that I was going to date her new friend, especially after she described me like that. Yeah, I was five foot and pretty tiny, but there was nothing "exotic" about me. I had long, light brown hair that looked drab and mousy, so I colored it a dark cocoa color. I had friend in elementary school that I idolized. She had the darkest hair and really light blue eyes. I wanted to look like her. (She, however, was a statuesque ballerina that I could never emulate.) But, once dark hair became the "it" color, I jumped on that hair-dying bandwagon and never looked back. My friends and family seem to prefer my lighter hair, but I'm a big fan of dark hair and blue eyes. My brother and sister got all of my mom's dark features; I got my dad's side of the family's lighter features.

"Hey Shelb, when do ya wanna meet him?" she asked.

"Uh... I'm not. You've lost your freaking mind if you think I'm letting you fix me up with Running from Problems, Mama's boy, Dane." I said, incredulously.

"Here's how I see it, you either tell me what went down with you and Chance or you go out with Dane. Those are your options. It's up to you," she said, matter-of-factly.

"Ummmm, let's see....how about...option C! None of the above." I said, feeling my anger start to boil.

"Option C is: I don't forgive you, and Becca and I aren't going to be a part of your life ever again," she said, trying to up the ante.

"I call BS, you're bluffing," I said.

"You're right; I'd never do that. I couldn't do that," she admitted. Then, she thought for a minute and said, "How about this, if you go on one, just one, date with Dane, then I'll never, and I mean never, bring up Chance or Mallory again?"

"Seriously?" I asked, not believing my ears.

"Swear to God, scout's honor," she said, crossing her heart.

"Done!" I said. "Tell him to pick me up at my house next Saturday at 6:00 p.m." This was too easy. One date and I never had to hear about how I screwed up my life for letting Chance slip through my fingers ever again! This was a no brainer. I'd take this deal in a heartbeat, plus, I'd probably get a free meal out of it. Nice.

The rest of our breakfast went well. She texted Dane and gave him my number to set up our date for the following Saturday. I paid for breakfast; I figured I did owe it to her. I had allowed someone to make holes in her daughter's ears, which by the way, Darby caved and eventually admitted that they looked cute on her. As I was leaving, Darby gave one last ditch effort to get me to go running with her later that afternoon, which I quickly and easily declined.

Getting into my car, my cell phone dinged, alerting me to a new text message. I got in, buckled up, started the car, and slid the bar over on my touchscreen to read the message. It was a message from Chance, a long message from Chance, a three-scroller message from Chance.

Shelby, I just met Nina for coffee. I think you and me need to talk. I'm so angry with you right now I can't see straight. Shelby, how could you? How could you shut me out like that and choose to go through all that shit alone? We were in this together. I was in it for the long haul. If something had been wrong with you, I woulda been there, no questions asked. You had no right to take my decisions away from me. So you got scared? Who doesn't? For a long time, I was afraid I'd walk in on you with some jackass, like I did with Mallory's mom, but I still went for it. I learned to trust, to trust you, Shelby. Why couldn't you see that everything I ever did and ever wanted was you? Still is. I'm sick without you. It's been over a year and I still cannot imagine my life without you. My life doesn't exist, can't exist without you. I don't want it to. Please at least talk to me. Come back to me. Come back to us, Shelby. We miss you. I miss you. I love you, Shelby.

Oh my God, I was going to kill Nina; she promised! I'd repeatedly made her swear at work this week that she'd never tell Chance the truth. She swore. She swore on our friendship. Before I lost my nerve and succumbed to what my heart was begging me to do, I texted a response to Chance.

I'm sorry Chance. I've done a lot of thinking over the last year. It was more than the health scare. I just don't love you that way. I don't see a future with us. I'm sorry. Please move on. I think it'd be best if you deleted my number from your phone and me from your memory. Goodbye Chance.

Really Shelby? "Me from your memory?" What is that about? God, I was so freaking cheesy and stupid sometimes. I wouldn't hurt him, not now, not ever, and I certainly wouldn't hurt Mallory. I couldn't let them get close to me, knowing that someday we'd have to say a horrifying and tearful goodbye when there was so much more on the line. It was better this way. My phone dinged again.

Shelby, please, DON'T do this. Talk to me.

This was all Nina's fault. I couldn't trust her. She always claimed to care about Chance and his feelings. But this, this made everything worse. She'd given him false hope. It wasn't fair to shatter his hopes when he'd already given up and lost hope once before. Chance was too good of a man to keep doing this to him. Sadly, I had to hit reply and end it once again.

I already did it, Chance. It's over.

I turned off my phone as I drove to Nina's house. I needed to see her, let her see how much pain she'd just caused me, which in turn caused even more pain for Chance. I couldn't understand why everyone was so involved in my life. Nina wasn't married; she'd been dating Evan for a while now. Darby wasn't married. Why did everyone care if I was with someone or not? Darby cared so much that I'd just been bribed and threatened into a blind date next weekend. Why was my love life or nonexistent love life suddenly everyone's concern?

Chapter 15

Here

"Julian, I think you're gonna need to tell me more. What's so wrong with my baby that I have to go fix her?" I asked him, pleaded with him

"Lila was right; she's closed herself off. She needs to open her heart, completely to Chance, and allow herself to fall deeply in love with him as she's destined to do," he stated.

"But what if she won't, refuses to?" I questioned again, pushing for whatever it was he wasn't telling me.

"You have to convince her, Betheny; it's important."

I could tell that he wanted to tell me something, but was struggling with admitting it to me. "Julian, I need all of the information, before I agree to do this." I calmly said.

"Beth, I don't know why you're even trying to play hardball here; we both know you're gonna do it. You'd do anything that would benefit your daughter," he countered correctly.

"Okay, you're right, I would. But, you've never interrupted people's lives here to ask them to go back, something you, yourself said was Hell," I argued, wondering just what it was that he wasn't telling me. "Please forgive me if I would like a little more information or reasoning than 'it's important,' Julian. We're talking about Shelby; shouldn't I have all the knowledge in order to get her to do what you need her to do?" I asked.

"That's the catch-22, we need you to convince her to let down her guard, but you can't just tell her to love him, to be with him, and take away her free will. She has to love him, because she loves him."

"But why? Why is this so important? Tell me." I begged.

"Alright, the most, the very most I can tell you is that Shelby is denying her destiny, and if she does, it will skew the course of her life and many other people's lives too. And she doesn't realize it," he explained.

I nodded, feeling scared and unsure.

"So Beth, you'll do it? You'll go back?" He asked again.

"Of course, anything for her; you already knew that," I said. "But Julian, how? How do I go back?"

"We'll go over all that. There's a lot to learn. First of all, you'll get to have your experience again when you return, so that's something to look forward to," he said.

He was right; I did enjoy seeing how much of an impact my life made on so many people, even strangers that I'd never met. Life was truly a precious gift, one that should never be taken for granted or regarded lightly. I would look forward to going through my experience again. The serenity that follows is meaningful and spectacular. I'd certainly be glad to rid myself of the angst and animosity I had toward my sister and toward myself.

"Secondly, and don't freak out or get too excited, but before you go back to see her, you'll be allowed to go through Shelby's experience. You'll see her past, her present, and even her future.

That way, you'll have all the knowledge you need to succeed." Julian revealed.

Oh my God. I was going to go through Shelby's experience. I would get to know every aspect of my daughter's life. She'd no longer be a mystery, a stranger to me. Shelby's heart, her feelings, her fears, everything, would get to be mine for a moment. I would see her happiness, her sadness, all aspects of who she was, who she is, and what she'll become.

"But, and Beth this is important, you cannot reveal anything." He stated firmly. He grabbed my shoulders and looked at me deeply with seriousness. "There's no giving away the secrets. When you return here, you can share Shelby's experience with Carl and the others. You can even tell them about your visit with Shelby, but you mustn't tell Shelby anything, anything of here or her experience."

"But what if she won't listen, what if I can't fix this and need to say something that I shouldn't?" I asked, feeling nervous and uncertain that I could be the answer to Shelby's issues. "Julian, what if I should fail?"

"You won't, just be her mom, you'll know what to do." He seemed so sure of himself, of me. I wasn't so sure. I'd failed her before. Who was to say I wouldn't do it again.

"Julian, you really are a wonderful man. I'm sure what you did, what you saw isn't nearly as bad as you think or believe it was," I said, trying to console an awfully troubled man.

"Betheny, believe me, it was Hell," he confirmed again.

Hell. People use the word so casually, and yet it means so much. I know a secret, a secret that only we know here. There is no Hell. As children, and basically all throughout our lives, we're taught a story, a myth, a legend about Hell, an underworld run by a diabolical man, who punishes and destroys, searching for those who'll do his bidding. No such person or demonic being exists, or ever has. No fiery depths of torture and punishment exist. All people, good and bad, evil and infinitely good, all exist here, coming together in afterlife, complete with retribution, forgiveness, and then finally acceptance.

There is a Hell here, but it's more of a feeling, not necessarily a place. It's a punishment of sorts for those who shattered and destroyed the lives, the hearts, and the innocence of others in their earthly lives. The punishment isn't eternal or everlasting, but it is severe, effective and mind-altering. People aren't born cruel, evil, and with a notion to crush the will and life of others. That spark of darkness is ignited by incidents of their pasts, creating an evil within that grows and festers through more heinous events and happenings.

The Hell that these people must endure is in fact hellish and dastardly, but in turn, it extinguishes that flicker of evil, that spark of hatred. Once a person endures the Hell here, his evil thoughts diminish entirely without residual feelings of resentment or anger. He learns, no, he endures and experiences, the errors of his diabolical actions and horrendous deeds.

Those people who were wronged, hurt beyond their wildest nightmares don't carry that agony here; their particular experience is even more profound and integral to the whole cycle of life and the hereafter. Their experience creates a vicissitude that ignites a feeling of everlasting euphoria and enlightenment, releasing them of their anger and feelings of vengeance, allowing them to find forgiveness in their heart and soul.

Personally, once I understood the real Hell, I found it to be genius and creative, an idea much more superior to the burning fire and horned little man. Ultimately when a murderer dies, he is immediately removed of all of his angry and vicious feelings, his evil thoughts and desires, but the memories of his actions remain. Then, he must endure the emotional pain of those family members who've experienced similar tragedies. His heart must feel their pain and fully experience the loss and the agony that they've encountered. But the truly amazing part is that it really is the pain and agony of the people there. Those people who committed beyond-repulsive actions have to actually take the innocent people's pain away.

I remember it vividly after Carl died, I would have moments, usually in the early morning hours when I woke up, when I felt no pain. I'd have a split second of a painless heart, forgetting for just a moment of the loss I'd had. I'd wake up feeling refreshed, carefree, and light-hearted. Then, like a bolt of lightning, it'd all come back, the pain, the sadness, and overwhelming sense of guilt and loss. Those moments of pain-free forget were because a villain here took away my pain, granting me a restful night's sleep, a peaceful calm. But when the pain returned to me, a new pain, someone else's agony would then enter that villain's heart. This cycle would repeat itself, easing the suffering of those of us there, and revealing the damage to those individuals who'd chosen the evil way of life. They would have to endure the excruciating pain of the aftermaths of dealing with death, abuse, molestation, and any other despicable act they may have inflicted upon another. They never had to experience the physical pain, because the emotional pain they'd caused was always that much worse. Emotional pain always trumped physical pain. I'd take a body full of broken bones over a broken heart and broken spirit any day.

People don't realize that when they have those fleeting moments of a pain-free heart that the pain is in reality punishing and ultimately educating someone who'd chosen the worst paths in life. And dealing with all the emotional pain in the world certainly is Hell. When you coupled the real Hell with that evil individual's experience, then that person comes out changed and enlightened, but remorseful and understanding of the crimes committed on a level unlike any that any of us have ever experienced. Then, after undergoing an unbearable Hell, that person is changed, changed for the better with a fresh and untainted outlook. Who's to tell us that we cannot forgive them or accept them? Nobody. It's just part of the big picture; we're only human and deserving of a break.

Actually, for the most part, forgiveness comes easy here. Certainly, when we are given our "earthly emotions" back to facilitate a new arrival's acclimation, we get a little feisty, some would say, "neurotic" at times. But eventually, a sense of forgiveness and peace overcomes us, creating a place of true lightness, lightness from the burden of hate, anger, guilt, and vengeance. Those feelings pop up from time-to-time, but they never linger or inhibit our happiness. Carl was right all those years ago; forgiveness is truly one of the most profound aspects of life, and even in the afterlife. It is easy to carry a grudge, to fester in anger and hatred. It's easy to say, "I hate you; I'm done." And act as such. What's truly hard, truly excruciating, is saying, "I forgive you." It takes a strong, tenacious person to forgive, to forgive someone who has hurt you or to even forgive yourself for mistakes you've made and opportunities missed.

There

I was kicking myself for agreeing to this date with Dane, the Running from Problems mama's boy, when the doorbell rang. I knew it couldn't be him, because he wasn't supposed to be here for another hour and a half. I'd just finished showering and hadn't yet gotten dressed. I threw on my white fluffy robe, and shook my hair out of the towel. The doorbell rang again.

"Coming," I yelled, stomping through the house. "I said I'm coming," I screamed louder after it rang a third time. Looking through the peephole of the door, I could make out the back of Chance's head, as he stood on the porch facing the road. Sighing, I unlatched the door and reluctantly opened it. "Hey Chance."

"Tell me she's kidding!" he said, storming past me.

"Hi Chance! Hi Shelby! Good to see you; good to see you too," I said, role-playing a civil, normal greeting for Chance's educational benefit.

"Tell me that when I talked to Nina today and when she said that you were going out with some guy tonight that your sister...your sister...fixed you up with, tell me that she was pulling my leg. Tell me that Shelby; tell me it's a freaking joke." He said, pacing back and forth across my living room floor.

"You guys sure do spend a lot of time talking about me....Actually, come to think of it, you two have been spending quite a bit of time together, lately. Does Evan care that you spend so much time with his girlfriend?" I asked snidely, trying to divert Chance's attention to another topic.

"I'm serious Shelby, do you have a date tonight?" He questioned, ignoring my insinuation.

"Chance...it's..... it's not really a date." I said, dropping my gaze from his face, terrified to actually look him in the eyes and admit the truth.

"So, you didn't choose to go out with some dude, simply so you wouldn't have to admit to Darby why you'd broken up with me?" he asked, already knowing the answer.

Oh for God's sake! I was going to kill Nina. It was bad enough that she'd told Chance last week why'd I broken up with him. When I confronted her about it, she just smiled and said that it was for "my own good." Then, thinking that I would finally get everyone off my back about being alone, I'd told Nina and Amy about my "ultimatum" date with Dane, swearing them both to secrecy.

"Well...hmmm...seems like you've got all the facts," I responded. "Why'd you even bother stopping by? Don't let the door hit you in the a--."

Before I could finish my sentence, Chance's arms were around me and his lips were on mine. I held my lips together, refusing his kiss. However, the feel of his body against mine, the heat from my desire, and...and...the love in my heart couldn't resist him. I welcomed the sensation his tongue erupted on my lips.

Parting my lips, he slipped his tongue further into my mouth. My breath caught and a slight whimper escaped my breath. I reached up, tangling my hands into the back of his hair, pulling him closer. He moved back slightly, dropping his mouth to my jaw, and beginning to kiss my neck, traveling to my ear. The heat from his breath ignited me, making me tremble and weak. It felt so wonderful, so right. Another moan betrayed me, and Chance stepped away, taking four steps backwards, leaving me breathless and distraught. He stared at me as he ran his hands through his hair. His eyes were on fire with desire and longing.

"Chance..."

"I know you feel that Shelby, and not just physically either; you feel it in your heart, in your soul. Why are you denying it? Denying us?" he asked, searching my face for honesty and truth.

"I can't--"

"Shelby, right here, right now, admit the truth, admit it," he said, begging me to lay it all out on the line.

"The truth? The truth is....Chance...I fell out of love with you a long time ago." I said, lying through my teeth. "I didn't...I don't feel anything; I'm sorry."

"Shelby! Grrrrr...God! Damn it!" He yelled, closing his eyes and shaking his head. Throwing up his hands in defeat, he finally caved, "Fine! I'm done then; I'm walking away. It's been almost a year and a half. I'm never gonna get through to you." He headed for the door, angry and hurt, determined to rid himself of me.

"Chance wait! Where are ya going?" I asked, afraid to watch him walk away.

"Columbus," he said with defeat, his shoulders sagging.

"Columbus? Whattya mean? Why?' I asked, feeling myself start to panic. Chance always said that he wanted to move back to Columbus, so he could be closer to his family. He thought that it would be best for Mallory to be closer and more connected to her grandparents.

"It's Doug's bachelor party tonight, in Columbus. I'll be back in town tomorrow morning... in case...in case you change your mind," he said, looking away, refusing to look me in the eye.

He opened the door and started to leave. Then without turning to look at me, he said, "Oh yeah, have a great time on your date tonight Shelby. Take care."

And he walked out the door. I stood staring at the door, wanting to run after him, to tell him that I was wrong, and he was right. I did love him. I do love him. And Oh God, yes, yes I absolutely feel it. I feel so much love and warmth for him that it scares me every minute of my life. I'm terrified by how strongly I feel for him. I wanted to do and say all of that, but I didn't. Instead, I did what I always do. I grabbed a glass of wine, and went and sat on the back deck, staring out at my back yard.

I loved my backyard and all the memories it held. I came home one time from elementary school, and my dad had painted my swing set. He'd always paint things in our house when we were least expecting it or even wanting it, actually. It drove my mom crazy. My dad painted buildings for an inner city school district, so he always had extra paint laying around, ready to change the color of something, making it fresh and new. There was a time when I'd gone to school with pink bedroom walls and came home to a bright yellow bedroom. It was so bizarre; he was so bizarre. We were the only people on the block who had a lavender garage. Lavender! Luckily that was the garage's inside wall colors and not the actual color of the outside of the garage doors. But with my dad, you never knew.

Our school colors were orange and black. One day, he painted his old "junker" car orange and black. My brother thought it was awesome, maybe at the time it was "totally rad." My sister, however, was mortified and would only sit scrunched down as to not be seen by the public eye. Darby even forced my dad to drop her off a block from each of her destinations, due to her overwhelming sense of humiliation.

My rainbow-striped play-set that was in the backyard was vibrant and fun, and then one day, I came home to a jet black swing set. It was hideous, dark, and repulsive. Why would someone paint a child's swing set black? As an eight-year-old, I was beside myself with fury. My dad had even painted the metal slide black, rendering the slide nearly worthless, since the slipperiness had been coated with a matte heavy paint. It was ridiculous. But after I got over my initial shock and everyone in the neighborhood began referring to it as the "Black Fort of Fun," I allowed my anger to subside and took pride in my new and improved swing set. Since the slide had lost its smooth and slippery exterior, it was easier to run up without fear of sliding backwards. Therefore, the slide then became a ramp to ascend and then jump off into a small kiddie pool. My little friend down the street and I got hours and summers of enjoyment from that swing set, even with its ridiculous appearance.

Despite stripping the colorful exterior, that play-set remained the source of many of my childhood memories. Although I didn't know what happened to it, there was still evidence of its existence, the place where it would always be in my memory. The grass was still worn and the earth unleveled where we used to swing and drag our feet as we flew back and forth, back and forth through the air. Sometimes, even though things seemed old, worn out and useless, they could still provide a lifetime of fond memories. But sometimes, after time had worn on, it was time to let go and move on as well.

The swing set was gone, but in my mind, it was there, as bright as the sun and then as black as the night. I wouldn't find amusement from having it in the yard right now, but I did find enjoyment thinking about those hours, those days, even those summers spent swinging, sliding, and climbing. That play-set was just as much a part of me as my house was a part of me—even though it had been gone a long, long time.

Looking at the yard and finishing my wine, it hit me, I was struck with a realization that I couldn't deny. My house, my yard, that swing-set, they were my past. I'd survived my mom getting rid of the swing-set; I didn't crumble and die, because a hunk of metal was removed from my backyard. I wouldn't shatter if I moved on and got a place of my own, starting new memories. My memories of this house, this life, would always be paramount and with me forever.

It was settled; I'd made my decision. This June, when I was on summer vacation, I would finally put the house on the market. I'd spend the rest of this school year painting and getting the house ready for a new family, a family to enjoy the large backyard, creating a memorable childhood of their own. It was time. Maybe letting Chance go for real this time was the push I'd needed to start a new life. Maybe this was the beginning of something wonderful.

"I love the feeling of knowing I'm making a difference in someone's life," Dane said, as he buttered a roll and handed it to me. Darby was right; he was a great guy. He was kind and sensitive, ready to save the world. It was refreshing to talk and spend time with someone who cared about the same things I cared about. We'd found that we had all the same interests. We listened to the same type of music and even voted for the same candidate in the last election. Now that was a first, but it was refreshing to say the least. It got old and tiring arguing about politics on a regular, oh God help me, so regular basis.

Nodding, I said, "But it also sucks when you can't convince someone that the choices they're making are all gonna blow back up in their face." I took a drink of my iced tea and then continued as he waited for me to go on. "I have a student who couldn't make the right choice if her life depended upon it," I said, chuckling as I thought about Janessa's latest debacle.

On Thursday morning, I'd gotten a text from her to hurry up and get to my classroom. When I arrived at the classroom, she was antsy to tell me what she'd done and get my opinion on her newest financial endeavor. She wanted to help her mom with the expenses of college and room and board, so she'd gotten "a job." She signed up to sell silverware, knives to be exact. She was certain that this would be "an onslaught of earnings, because everyone had to cut their steak." Those were Janessa exact words.

Sure, it was important for young people to find jobs and help whenever they could financially. But, she'd spent nearly $1,000 of her own money to buy the knives for her marketing presentations. I told her that she should've talked to me first, and I would've gotten her a part-time job at my brother's company. I felt badly for deflating her enthusiasm, but really, she hadn't thought this through at all. She jumped before checking if she had a parachute, something a lot of adolescents did these days.

Dane was choking on laughter as I told him the story and many other stories of Janessa's life choices. "You're never gonna believe this," he said, still laughing and wiping his eyes. "I sold those knives one summer when I was in college. Never made a penny."

Surprisingly, I was enjoying my time with him. He was funny and humble. I'd only found myself thinking about Chance once during the dinner. Okay, maybe twice. Three times at the most.

Dane and I were talking about movies and neither of us could remember who starred in a movie we both liked. We sat for a moment trying to recall the actor's name, but both of us were drawing a blank. Then he said, "Ah, doesn't matter any way. Who cares?" and he went on to a new topic. I grinned, because I cared. Not recalling stuff like that drove me crazy, nearly to the point of neurosis. Those things could send me off the crazy-train edge. Dane obviously didn't know that about me. Chance did. Chance would've pulled out his phone immediately to Google the movie, before I'd lost my mind trying to figure out the actor's name.

When I got out my phone to look it up, Dane put his hand on mine, and simply said, "Not during dinner." I'd never eaten a meal with Chance without one of us, or both of us, checking something on our phones. This was different. Maybe different was good. But it was definitely different.

After dinner, Dane wanted to skip the movie, so we could talk and get to know one another more. I was fine with that as long as it involved ice cream in some way.

Smiling, Dane said, "Ooooh, a woman after my own heart. I know just the place." He leaned in front of me to open my car door, and said, "I'm sorry, but I just have to do this. I can't help myself." Then he kissed me, lightly and ever so slightly. I stood motionless and shocked, not expecting such a forward and blind-siding advance.

Stepping back, he stared at me, trying to gauge my response. When I didn't move or say anything, he said, "I'm sorry, I shouldn't have--"

Finally shaking myself out of my surprise, I said, "No...no really it's fine. I was just a little caught off guard."

"No, I shouldn't have. It was too abrupt, too soon. I just think that damn first kiss is always so awkward and strange," he explained as he closed the door. The first kiss was awkward and strange? Now that was the first thing that I disagreed with him about all night.

The first kiss said it all. It was magical and a prologue of moments to come, memories to be made. I loved first kisses. Granted, he'd just blown it; that first kiss wasn't spectacular in the least. But normally, first kisses set the stage for the rest of the play. It was a prelude to what was to come.

Getting in on his side of the car he said, "But the second one, the second one says it all." Then, he leaned over, kissing me harder with more force and intention.

Pulling back and maneuvering out of his reach, but not wanting to make a scene, I said, "Down boy, I haven't even had my chocolate dipped cone yet." I didn't know why he'd felt so compelled to come at me like that. I didn't think I'd been sending off signals, green lights.

Laughing, he said, "Alright, alright, ice cream first and who knows, maybe after--"

"After? What? Uhh...Dane, I think maybe--"

"Relax, I'm just kidding. Just trying to make ya laugh. Lighten up," he said, slapping me on the knee as he turned the radio on. He scrolled through his iPod until he found a song that he knew we both liked based on our conversation during dinner, and let the sound and lyrics reverberate through his car. He sang at the top of his lungs and pointed to me when the girl part came on. He was fun, light and airy.

Dane was right; I was probably a little too uptight. Three hours ago, I'd been kissing Chance; it was weird to have someone else's lips on mine so soon after, especially out of the blue when I wasn't expecting it....at all. I needed to relax. Dane was turning out to be a pretty fun and good guy. Admittedly, Dane was also pretty hot, almost the physical antithesis of Chance. Not that Chance wasn't attractive and sexy as all get out, oh, he was. But, Dane had those movie star looks, pretty and polished. Where Chance was dark and brawny, Dane was light and slight. Chance was tall and broad. Dane was probably a little taller, but much more lithe and sculpted. Chance's look was more my type, but Dane's was every young girl's dream. Yes, Dane was a dream. Darby was right.

Chapter 16

Here

Julian wanted me to talk to Carl and my sisters before I finalized my decision, but he knew as well as I did, I'd already decided what I was going to do. Not only did I want to help my daughter, get her through this terrible time in her life, I wanted to hold my daughter, see my daughter, take in the scent of the child I missed and left so many years ago. But I agreed; I'd talk to Carl and the girls.

"I don't think I've ever been more jealous of anyone ever before in my entire life," Anna said, hugging me. "This couldn't be any more exciting. You deserve this; Shelb deserves this."

"I think it sucks," Rosemary said. We all turned, not believing what we'd heard. "It's a bad, bad idea."

Carl squeezed my hand and said, "Ro, why? Why do you think so? I'm thrilled that Beth has been given this opportunity to help our daughter."

"Because so much could go wrong and because of how hard the last ten years have been for her," she explained. "Beth, don't you realize that if you mess something up, you could make Shelby's life, her heart, more screwed up than it already is? And what if it doesn't work? What if that stubborn little girl still does what she wants? Then what?" Rosemary was yelling now, and her veins were starting to show on her forehead. Looking around at all of us, waiting to hear what we had to say, how we'd respond. Then she finally gave up and said, "I'll tell you what! You're gonna go back to sulking and blaming yourself for every problem in the world today...just like you always do!"

"Oh shut up Rosemary! Her daughter needs her. You'd be there faster than shit on a shingle if your kids needed you. You're just jealous that you don't get to go back." Anna said. Anna and Rosemary had a long history of heated arguments; they were the closest in age, Anna being the oldest with Ro close on her heels, only 11.5 months younger.

"What're ya gonna do if I don't, stab me again?" Rosemary said. Oh no, here we go again. Anna would never live, or beyond live, that down.

"Guys....guys...just stop! I love you, Rosemary; I love how worried you are about me, but I'm going back. I'm gonna go see my baby." I said, extinguishing the fire before more fuel ignited an all out holocaust between my sisters. "Wild horses couldn't keep me away. They wouldn't keep any of you away either, because whether we ever decide to believe it or not, we were great moms. We'd all do anything for our kids...anything."

I felt Carl's arms wrap around me, as he pulled me back against his chest. "Ladies, can I have a moment alone with my wife, the most amazing woman of all eternity" he asked, as he nuzzled my neck.

After all of my sisters walked away, Carl snickered knowingly and asked, "You're not gonna break any of those rules are you?" He knew me all too well.

Giggling, I said, "Not if I don't have to--"

There was a time about six years after Shelby was born that I wasn't sure if Carl and I were going to make it. I was worried that we'd become a statistic, a member of the exclusive "divorced society." We never talked about those days any longer; once we closed that horrific chapter of our lives, we never looked back on it. We closed and sealed it for good.

Carl was working second shift, the evening hours, like always, and my sisters and I were all struggling for money. We decided to start an Italian catering business, The DiBellini Sisters' Catering. We used Virginia's basement kitchen as our home base for preparation and cooking. The business took off; apparently everyone wanted authentic homemade Italian food for their weddings, parties, and ironically, even for their Bar Mitzvahs. The DiBellini Sisters were in high demand. I spent my weekdays working 9:00 a.m. – 5:00 p.m. (except for Thursdays) at my job as a head cook and nutritionist at a drug and rehabilitation center and spent my weekends catering with my sisters for weddings and other events. We did all the prep work on Friday nights, cooked all afternoon on Saturdays, and hosted and served on Saturday nights, leaving Sundays to count money and clean.

I was working all the time; Carl worked nights. Darby was practically raising Shelby. Our lives were chaotic. The kids fared well, learning the ropes of independence and fending for themselves, preparing them unfortunately for what the future had in store for them. Carl and I were drifting apart, never finding the time or energy to reconnect. We'd both become complacent, neglecting to do the little things for each other, forgetting to make the other a priority. Eventually, the distance between us became too great. When I would see him for brief intervals of time, I felt like I was talking to a stranger, making idle chit chat. The spark, the mystery, the fun, and even the love had vanished from our marriage. We were just going through the motions, but just barely, because we never saw one another, so even going through the motions was minimal.

Then, the hall that we catered most of our events at was bought by a new owner, a younger, divorced, extremely flirtatious and good-looking man, who had charm and sophistication oozing out of every ounce of his being. Whenever my sisters and I were at the hall, handling an event, Greg was there to lend a hand, make us laugh, or charm the other guests in the hall. Many nights, he offered to stay and clean up with us, talking and laughing with us the whole time. He was new, different, and refreshing.

One night after a particularly tiring event, my sisters and I were exhausted, thoroughly whipped. We sat down, ate some leftovers, and had a few drinks. Being tired, but also wired from the event, we decided to play a few hands of cards. After the night wore on, each sister left one by one. Finally, it was just Patti, Greg, and me. Patti had drunk a few too many Screwdrivers, so Frank, her husband, had to come pick her up. I offered to drive her home, but she insisted on making him get out of bed to come get her, since she'd been forced to do the same for him many times before. I didn't want to leave her alone with Greg since she was more than a little tipsy. Drunk women and newly divorced good-looking men were a volatile combination.

Once Patti was safely in Frank's car and on her way home, I started packing up the last of the leftovers and cooking utensils. Greg charmingly convinced me to have another drink with him and play another hand of cards. I agreed, feeling too guilty to decline his offer since we worked so closely together. We drank and laughed over cards, enjoying each other's company. We only played one hand and had one drink. Greg packed the rest of the stuff into my car and started it up for me, while I put the chairs up on the tables, making it easier for the cleaning crew to vacuum the following morning. When I went out to my car, Greg was leaning against it, leisurely waiting for me. I thanked him for his help and for a nice evening. Then suddenly, he moved in to kiss me, bracing me against the car. The second his lips met mine; I reacted, kneeing him directly in the groin.

The whole incident was disastrous. He'd called me a "tease," and left me alone in the parking lot, only after telling me that our catering company would no longer be hosting events at his hall. I was terrified. I didn't know what I was going to tell my sisters, and I certainly didn't know what to tell Carl. The bottom line was: I didn't do anything physical with this man. The problem was: I enjoyed the company of another man when I hadn't enjoyed my husband's company in over a year. The issue was bigger than a sleazy drunk man trying to kiss me. The issue was that I hadn't given my husband the opportunity to do so in a long, long time.

The second I walked in the door to my house, I ascended the stairs and walked straight into the bedroom. I woke up Carl and confessed the whole ordeal, sobbing throughout the entire story of my contrition. He took me in his arms, held me against him, as we both cried ourselves to sleep, promising to never drift from one another ever again. That night, our bond, our marriage strengthened, because we saw how easily it could all slip away, slip away to a place neither of us ever wanted to go. Carl and I were meant for one another. We were bound and determined to never let anyone or anything ever come between us...until death took him from me, four short years later.

Shortly after the incident with Greg, my sisters and I dissolved our catering partnership. Apparently, Virginia and Raymond were having problems too, due to the hours away from one another. Our business just wasn't worth the price of our marriages. There was nothing in life that was worth the price of our marriage.

Additionally, rumor had it that one night as Greg was getting into his car, a man came out of nowhere and punched him right the face, shattering his nose. The man left as quickly and quietly as he arrived. Carl never admitted to the incident, but would just grin and rub his bloody, scabbed-over knuckles. Apparently, only one thing could turn a lover into a fighter, and that was true, unconditional love.

People take marriage and their vows entirely too lightly, believing that marriage is disposable and meaningless. On the contrary, marriage is meaningful and absolutely worthwhile. To share a connection, a love that lasts forever is the second most important thing in life to ever experience, next to becoming a devoted and loving parent. Nobody would ever be foolish enough to call marriage easy. It's not. It's hard to stay connected and utterly devoted to another human being when you're being pulled in a zillion different directions. But the truth is, eventually, you're going to retire, quit, or move on from that job. Your kids will graduate, move out, and start lives of their own. Then what you'll be left with is a stranger staring back at you, if you don't take the time to cater to your marriage and hold on to it with all your might. Otherwise, the hustle and bustle of life could whisk him (or her) into the arms of someone else or into the clutches of his (or her) career, either way, destroying the marriage. It's too easy to give up and throw in the towel; it takes strength and courage to hold on tighter even when the grasp is slipping and coming loose.

The reality had just struck me, tumbling down on me like a pile of broken, misplaced hearts. I'd never once told Shelby how important, how crucial marriage was. I'd never even told her or shown her how much I truly loved her father and that he took a piece of me when he died. Since I died when she was only 20 years old, there were so many things that I didn't tell her or teach her. Shelby entered adulthood, and I never told her the secrets to surviving it. She needed to know that even though my heart broke a million times over when her father died, I'd never change one thing about giving him my heart, completely and totally. And it was definitely time to finally tell her.

There

"A chocolate and vanilla twist dipped in hard chocolate? That's it?" Dane asked, staring disappointedly at me.

"Yep. That's what I like, this girl knows what she likes," I grinned and batted my eyelashes at him, flirtatiously.

"Nah, I got this. I bet I know what you need more than you do," Dane said, planting a quick kiss on my nose. He was being awfully forward, maybe a little too much so. As we approached the counter, he smiled at the girl in the window and put his arm around me. "This girl here, she wants a hot fudge sundae with mint chocolate chip ice cream...oh yeah...and pile on the cherries and whipped cream," he said to the perky blonde teenage girl. The girl just stared, blushing at him as he talked.

"Wait...that's not even close to what I--" I said, interrupting the order he placed for himself.

"Oh you'll love this...now go get us some napkins and meet me at the picnic table," he commanded. I stared at him in disbelief and shock. I couldn't even order the ice cream flavor I wanted? That's just bizarre. As I started to walk away, he slapped my butt, and said, "Atta girl!"

Walking away, I felt extremely uncomfortable. Dane was coming on a little too strong and forcefully. Darby said that he'd pretty much been secluded with his ailing mom for nearly the last decade. He certainly wasn't coming across as some recluse. I started feeling a bit leery toward his aggressive demeanor, although he attempted to hide it behind humor and charm.

Pull it together Shelby, he wanted you to try something new. He's just being fun. It's a first date. Let it go. I always did this. I always overanalyzed things. I needed to just go with the flow and enjoy my date with this good-looking, incredibly good-looking guy. Don't forget that he didn't let you Google D.B. Sweeney's name. D.B. Sweeney! Yes! That was it. He was great in Cutting Edge and Roommates. Alright, give the guy a break, the benefit of the doubt. He's just trying to impress you, make you swoon.

When he got back to the picnic table, he had a root beer float for himself and the sundae for me. He also had a vanilla and chocolate twist cone dipped in hard chocolate. "Alright, first try the mint sundae, if you hate it, then I'll give you the cone you think you want," he said, smirking. Okay, so he was being fun and playful. I could handle that. What I couldn't handle was someone who tried to make my decisions for me and who thought he knew what was best for me, like I couldn't formulate my own opinions.

Dane nailed it; I had to admit. The sundae was good, but honestly, I didn't particularly care for mint-flavored food. Mallory loved mint chocolate chip ice cream cones, especially dipped in hard chocolate. She used to order the twist cone dipped in the hard-coated chocolate, because she wanted to have what I had. But then, Chance told her that she could get her favorite ice cream dipped in the hard coating too, then she switched over. She said it was the "best of both worlds." She ate Chance's favorite ice cream with my favorite coating.

"Hey Babe, where'd you go?" Dane asked. I'd evidently missed his last question.

"I'm sorry, I was just thinking about ice cream. Tends to make me lose all other focus," I joked, refusing to admit that I was thinking about Chance and his daughter while Dane talked about something else.

Dane grabbed our trash and threw it all away in the garbage while I started walking toward his sleek black sports car. We arrived at the car at the same time. His eyes were a deep blue and his blond hair was styled into spiky casual perfection. He was very pretty, prettier than I was. Dane was exactly what Chance would call a "pretty boy." Shelby! Focus!

The look in Dane's eyes changed. There was desire in the smoldering look he gave me. He'd just gone from "pretty" to "smoking hot" in a blink of an eye, weakening my knees. Dane put his hand on my waist, and pulled me against him. This time, I didn't pull away or even flinch. I was ready to have our first kiss, what I was going to consider our first kiss anyway. Those first two were ridiculous and didn't count. He leaned in and kissed me. His lips were soft, but the kiss was hard and hungry. My arms were pinned against his chest, so I couldn't wrap them around him. We stood in the parking lot, kissing for longer than I felt comfortable doing in the public eye. Finally, he pulled back, breaking our kiss, and whispered, "Where to now?"

Feeling awkward, but breathless, I said, "Home, I guess." I really wasn't sure what else to say. I wasn't going to tell him to take me somewhere if he didn't want to go out, and I certainly wasn't going to tell him to take me to his place.

"That's my girl. Now, you're thinking. Mine or yours?" he asked. Holy Hell. That was not what I'd meant.

"Uh...Dane?" I started to say, when he interrupted me with an exasperated scream.

"Fuuuuucccck!" he bellowed, slamming his fist down on the roof of his car.

"What? What happened?" I asked, totally confused and out of the loop.

"I locked my god damn keys in the car, that's what." he said, kicking his tire.

"Niiiice, real smooth," I said, joking as I looked for my cell phone in my purse.

"Shut up, Shelby, I don't wanna hear it right now," he snapped at me. "I can't fucking believe I did this."

"Calm down, it's fine. I'll just call--"

"I said, 'shut the fuck up!' I don't wanna hear your yapping," he said, through gritted teeth. Jeez. Holy erratic and inconsistent behavior! Moody much?

"Dane! Seriously, I--"

I'd wanted to tell him that I'd call roadside service and it'd be fine, but he grabbed me by the shoulders, and shoved me back, against the car, bellowing, "What'd I just tell you?"

With his hands still clutching my upper arms, squeezing me, I raged, "Holy Hell, get your fucking hands off--"

He let me go and said, "I said, 'shut the fuck up," and hauled off and swung at me. Seeing his fist coming at me, I dodged and fell to the ground, dropping my phone and spilling the contents of my purse. His fist landed on the side of the car, denting the spot he connected with. Seeing the dent, he screamed, "Bitch" and glared at me.

Staring at him in horror and disbelief, I grabbed what spilled out of my purse and phone and ran to the front of the ice cream stand. Crying and hysterical, I asked the perky blond girl if I could come inside and make a call. She looked confused, so I scurried around to the door, walked in, and closed it behind me.

All the counter girls were staring at me, so I just wiped my eyes and said, "Boy troubles." They all nodded and went back to what they were doing. I could speak teen-girl talk fluently. But what I really needed to do was get the Hell out of there. Before realizing whom I called, I heard Chance's greeting on his voicemail on the other line. I hung up as fast as I could, before the beep went off. The last thing I needed was to talk to him right now. I couldn't believe I actually dialed his number. I knew he was in Columbus, two hours away, probably at some game or strip club with all the guys at the bachelor party. Plus, I couldn't call him every time something went wrong in my life. I'd made my decision.

Needing to have someone come get me far away from this psychopath, I called Darby, knowing that she owed it to me. It was the least she could do. Darby thought this guy and I were a perfect match. Yeah, thanks for that, Darbs! Of course, she didn't answer. It went straight to voicemail too. I called Nina, no answer. Where the Hell was everyone?

Knowing Vaughn would be pissed and annoyed, but at home, I called him. He said that he'd be right there and not to leave the inside of the ice cream store. I ended up sitting with the girls and listening to their "guy-drama." Teenage girls loved talking to me. Couldn't they see that I didn't have a clue as to what to do with a dude? I was failing miserably in that subject.

Once Vaughn arrived, I'd calmed down a bit and looked a little better. I didn't want Vaughn to cause a scene when he saw Dane in the parking lot, waiting for someone to come get his keys out of the car. I was pretty certain that Vaughn wouldn't do anything; he's a pretty small guy and doesn't go around starting crap with other guys. I got into the car, but Vaughn didn't pull out of the parking lot.

Curiously, I asked, "What...what're ya doing? Let's go."

"Hold on Shelb, let me take care of this," he said. Men and their desire to handle everything drove me crazy. I didn't want my big brother fighting my battles and doing anything. I just wanted to leave.

When the tow truck pulled in and the guy got out with his tool, Vaughn drove over to him and got out of the car. I could see Dane yelling at him, but Vaughn put up his hand, silencing him as he spoke to the driver of the tow truck. Vaughn reached in his wallet and gave the tow truck man a handful of bills. Dane lunged at Vaughn, but the tow truck guy pulled him back. Vaughn walked quickly to the car, jumped in, and drove off.

"What the hell?" I asked. "Vaughn did you just pay that guy to get Dane's keys out."

"No Shelby, I paid him not to get his keys out," he said, matter-of-factly, grinning triumphantly. Who said money didn't buy happiness? I was pretty darn happy right now. I turned around in the car, just in time to see the tow truck leaving the parking lot, as Dane kicked the dirt and punched the air.

"Thanks big brother," I said, smiling at him. He really was the greatest brother, always taking care of me when I needed him. "You really are Vaughn-derful, ya know that?"

"Any time little sis," he replied, smiling.

We drove in silence for a while, when I said, "Remember when Nate and I broke up, and I went to you for help?"

"Not really, why?" He looked at me, confused.

"Because! It was the jerkiest thing a brother could do!" I said, laughing and feigning anger.

"Why? What'd I do?" he asked, seeming actually interested.

"Well, Nate and I had just broken up and I was in hysterics, bawling my eyes out." I explained.

"I remember that," he said. "You were whacked."

Slapping his arm, I said, "Do you remember what you told me to do...so I'd feel better?"

"Uh....nope."

"Vaughn, you ass, you told me to listen to that song from Prince of Tides, the one by Barbra Streisand." I reminded him.

"Ha ha ha, oh yeah, that's funny, brutal, but funny." He said, laughing as he remembered.

There was a song that Vaughn liked when he had just gotten out of high school or something. It was a slow, sappy song. He told me that if I listened to it after Nate and I broke up, that I'd feel better and everything would make sense. I'd never heard it; it was before my time. Believing him, I went to my room, put the CD in the player, and started the song. What I'd learned from that incident and that song was that my brother was a heartless ass.

The song was the ultimate break up song, about a couple that wasn't meant to be together, and their breakup was for the better. I sat in my room, listening to that song for days and just bawled my eyes out. That song, "Places That Belong to You," will forever be the song that I go to when I need a good cry. Just the instrumental part now can shred me into a crying mess. I hear the first few notes, like Pavlov's dog, and I'm watering up.

"Was I right though?" he asked

"Right about what?" I didn't know what he'd meant.

"Didn't it help?" he explained. "Listening to that song, didn't it help?"

"Help what? Make me cry like a baby? Yeah. Helped a lot. Thanks for that!" I responded sarcastically.

"No, didn't it make you get all your feelings out, flood them right out?" he asked. But not waiting for an answer, he said, "Sometimes Shelby, you have to let it all out, just cry it out. Everyone has to. You can't bottle all that crap up." I nodded, knowing what he meant. I often tried to pretend everything was okay. "And plus, I knew Nate wasn't the guy for you, so I knew you just needed to cry it all out and move on."

I nodded, knowing he was right. Laughing, I said, "Yeah, Nate wasn't the guy for me and neither was Dane. What a douche!"

"Dude, where'd you find that guy?" he asked.

"Uh....your sister fixed us up," I said, refusing to claim her as my own sister right now. I was going to kill her. She owed me big time.

"Oooh man, yeah that was not the guy for you," he said. Finally, after a few moments of silence, Vaughn said, "Notice how I never told you to listen to that song when you and Chance broke up."

"Oh yeah, that's true. Did you forget about it's magic?" I joked.

"Oh no, not at all," he said, shaking his head. "That's the song people need to listen to when they break up with the person they're not meant to be with," he said, glancing over at me with sadness in his eyes.

Oh God, not Vaughn too! Seriously, how many more people were going to tell me that Chance was the one who got away? First Darby, then Nina, and now Vaughn was in on it too. Good thing I didn't have any more friends or family members to harp on and on about how I should get back together with Chance. Geez, this was getting old.

"Nice try Vaughn, nice try," I said, sitting back as I tuned the radio to a different station and tuned him out.

Chapter 17

Here

"Remember when we took Shelby to Disney World when she was going into eighth grade?" Lila asked after all of my sisters and Carl were gone.

"Oh yeah, it was the greatest vacation ever," I recalled. "Spending all that time alone with you and Shelb is up there as one of my fondest memories." Darby and Vaughn had moved out; Carl had been gone over two years. It was time for Shelby and I to start making some memories of our own. She'd never been to Disney, and Lila had been dying to take her. I finally relented and agreed to start saving money; we didn't have disposable income at all.

When Carl and Raymond, Virginia's husband, had passed, my sisters and I resurrected the catering business, looking for ways to supplement our incomes and kill time without our husbands. I saved money for over a year, so I could take Shelby and Lila to Florida for nearly three weeks. We visited Orlando, Tampa, Jacksonville, and St. Augustine. It was the time that Shelby and I needed to connect and learn how to live and exist as a "twosome." We started forming a bond that summer on that vacation that lasted until my final days. She wasn't just my daughter. In those seven years, she became my best friend too. Of course, we had our mother/daughter quarrels and all-out battles, but she was my "other half" when I never could feel quite whole.

"We were so worried about taking a teenage girl to Disney...worried she was gonna be cranky and just a bratty teenager, remember?" Lila asked.

"We talked about canceling that trip so many times, thinking she was just going to be a grump." Shelby was a typical teenager; she slammed doors, sighed and groaned at louder than necessary decibels, and rolled her eyes as if she was trying to see the inside of her own skull. "But wow, she was wonderful on that trip."

"It was like we got to push a 'rewind' button and make her 7-years-old again," Lila said, smiling. "She was so happy, so full of life and adventure. She stared at everything with wonder and awe—the whole time too—not just in Disney."

"That's when she started that whole 'dancing in public thing' whenever we wanted to get in the car." I laughed, shaking my head at my daughter's goofy behavior. Shelby was crazy at times, just a blast to be around. Every time we would go anywhere, I mean anywhere, she wouldn't let me get back in the car to leave until I slow-danced with her in the parking lot. We'd have to do three full circles around, slowly humming and swaying to our own music, before she'd let go and let me get in the car. She started that in Disney with Lila and me. I'd feign disgust and embarrassment, but I loved it. I loved that side of her. She was so spontaneous and fun, never cared about what anyone thought of her, especially strangers that she'd never see again.

Stilling thinking about it, I said, "She still continued to do that when she was a freshman in college...in front of her college friends...outside of her dorm. She didn't care who saw us."

Man, she was a goofy girl. Whenever we would go to the grocery store, she'd fall to her knees and beg for a quarter in the checkout line, screaming and pretending to cry for "just one quarter, Mama." She'd embarrass the bejeezus out of me as I stood there rummaging through my purse for a quarter, which inevitably was never there. I learned later that while we were shopping, and I wasn't looking, she'd rid my purse of quarters before her little stunt. And her little stunt, it never failed. Someone, some sap who felt badly for her, always, and I mean always, gave her a quarter. I'm pretty sure they thought she had "problems" of some sort and took pity on her and even on me for having to publicly deal with her.

"Beth..." Lila looked at me, concerned.

"Yeah, what is it?' I asked with worry, reading her face.

"She doesn't do anything like that anymore. That spark, the fun, it's all gone. I think Julian's right. She needs you...needs help...something." Lila said, beginning to cry. "She bounced back after Carl died. She was too young to be crushed by his death. But my God, Beth...something happened to her...in her... when you died. You need to save our girl, fix what I broke."

Finally realizing it, I said, "You're not taking this blame, Lila. I'm not letting you...and...I'm done blaming you." This wasn't Lila's fault; I just wanted to blame someone. Just like Lila wanted to blame Shelby for something that wasn't her fault. We always look for people to blame when sometimes there isn't anyone to blame. The blame sometimes just lies within the tragedy itself. I continued, "She was young; she saw a lot. And grieved more than anyone should have to mourn....all before her twenty-first birthday."

"Oh thank you, thank you for saying that," Lila cried, hugging me tightly. "I love her so much. I love you Beth. I missed you, missed my baby sister."

Crying and holding her, "Lila, you know I've never gone one minute without thanking my lucky stars for you and for the time that you were spending with my kids. I love you."

Trying to compose herself, Lila said, "Beth, I'm scared she's going to end up like me, hurt and broken, hating the world, hating life." Lila shook uncontrollably now, crying and shattered.

"You, Lila DiBellini, are not broken. You do not hate the world," I said. "What you have is pain....and regret. Once you go through your experience you'll be able to see it all, understand it all....and eventually forgive him." I consoled her, as she cried in my arms.

"How can I understand? How can I ever forgive what I can't forget?" She asked, innocently and full of trepidation.

"You'll never forget, but you will forgive, and you'll understand so much more.... Lila, you just have to trust me on this," I said, holding her tightly.

Lila's story isn't of epic torture and pain, but it was torturous and painful for her. It was even painful for us, those who loved her, to watch Lila hurt without being able to help her. When Lila was young, in her 20s, she worked at a tavern, much like the one where I met Carl. She loved that job; she loved be-bopping around and making friends, flirting with men, just having a ball as she worked, while making money the whole time. Most people thought that waitressing was grueling and "lowly" work. Not Lila. She loved it— never wanting anything else. It was exciting and worthwhile to her as she met new people and heard the stories of their lives.

One night, she picked up an extra shift; a friend of hers needed the night off. To this day, I wish we could all go back in time and Lila would've chosen to stay home with me by the fire, drinking hot cocoa. But we can't, that's the problem with life. There are never any do-overs. Just moving "forwards." The tavern was particularly slow that night, as there was a horrible blizzard in northeast Ohio. Shocking. It was February. A lone man sat in Lila's section; she didn't have any other tables to tend to. Therefore, she spent a large portion of the night talking with the man, learning his life story.

Allen Hart was a traveling salesman, who was in Ohio on business, hence why he was alone. His office was located in Boston, Massachusetts. His thick Bostonian accent was like a lure for Lila, reeling her in, closer and closer. The company that he worked for was expanding to the Cleveland area. Allen was chosen to help get the ball rolling. Currently though, his car was having difficulty in the Ohio wintery elements, and he was having difficulty finding a cheap apartment to sublet on a month-to-month lease as he traveled to and from Boston on a regular basis.

Knowing so many people in town since we came from such a large close-knit Italian family and from being so friendly with the clientele, Lila gave Allen a list of names and numbers. Lila was certain one of the names on the list would be able to help him with his car and with finding a place to live. They talked at his table until the restaurant closed. After her side-work was completed, napkins rolled, and she was cashed out at the register, Lila agreed to go to an all-night diner for coffee. From that moment on, they were inseparable. She was smitten and soaring with elation. Allen Hart had my sister Lila's heart.

My sisters and I found him charming and lively enough, but we weren't as equally as smitten. There was just something about Allen that rubbed us the wrong way. Carl despised him and didn't trust one thing he did or said. Carl thought he was smarmy and "too slick to be anything other than a dick." (Those were my eloquent husband's words.) My sister's southern- educated and intellectual husband, John-Mitchell, said that Allen Hart was a bombastic megalomaniac. None of us really knew those words. I just knew that I thought that everyone was overreacting, even though I agreed that he wasn't as spectacular as Lila believed.

It wasn't long before Allen Hart had a ring on Lila's finger. Once they were engaged, Lila didn't see any reason for two cars or two apartments. Allen moved in and they settled in to a cozy little life together. They never fought or found ill words to say about the other. They were turning into one of the cutest couples I'd ever met. Carl wasn't convinced. Carl was a great judge of character, and he despised Allen. However, I did hate that my sister was "living in sin." We were not brought up that way; it was wrong to do...those things...before getting married. But, she didn't care; she was in love...and in lust. Allen and Lila couldn't keep their hands off of each other.

I spent the majority of what little alone time I had with Lila trying to convince her to start planning the wedding, to get the ball rolling. She was adamant that she didn't want to push it. Allen wanted to wait until he was completely settled and established in Ohio, because he "couldn't imagine leaving his wife every other week to travel to Boston." Allen didn't want to marry Lila until he was permanently located in Ohio and no longer required to travel. So they waited; we waited.

Finally, after a year of being engaged, Lila's biological clock was rocking around the clock at loud, thumping tickety-tocks. Allen agreed to start making a family, but still refused to meet her at the altar until he was residing only in Ohio. He wouldn't hear of being a man who had to leave his bride every week. Carl flipped at this. Carl confronted Allen, demanding to know why it was okay to leave a child, but not a woman. Allen simply told Carl to "butt out" and worry about his own life. It was the first time in our lives that Lila and I struggled with our relationship. We had to sneak around to spend time together, because our men hated each other.

Carl wouldn't let it go. He and his friend decided that they needed to do some dirt digging on Allen. Carl's friend was on the police force, and Allen's background check came up crystal clear, not one blemish. Carl wasn't satisfied. I started to worry about Carl's interest in this; he'd never cared who Lila dated prior to this. But he was determined to uncover the secrets behind Allen Hart. Carl just admitted that when he fell in love with me that he fell in love with my family too. That meant he would do whatever he could to protect me...and therefore my family too. Carl felt strongly that Lila needed protection from Allen Hart.

Meanwhile, Lila spent month after month, trying to get pregnant. Her spirits were diminishing. After nearly eight months of trying to conceive a baby (out of wedlock, I might add), she decided to go to my doctor. Sitting in the office with her, I was very uncomfortable about being there with her since she was unmarried; her lifestyle and behavior were against my moral-upbringing. However, she was my sister, so I bit down and through my tongue as I sat beside her for support. Allen was in Boston at the time; he hadn't realized that she'd made the appointment. I was prepared to hear that she was counting the days incorrectly and wasn't truly aware of her exact ovulation cycle. The words, the diagnosis that I heard, was and still is unbelievable to me.

Lila crumbled in sobs as the words "upside down uterus" were uttered from the stern and baffled doctor's mouth. Lila learned that due to a reproductive malformation, an oddity, a rarity, that she'd never be able to conceive a child. Lila would never have children of her own. I didn't have the words to comfort her. Allen was not there to ease her worry that he would never want her again. My sisters and I gathered around her night after night as she cried over babies never held, never loved.

The week seemed interminable, but finally, Allen arrived home to his devastated fiancé. He was shredded by her news and immediately began packing her bags; his were still packed. Allen wanted to take her away, whisk her away for a memorable, romantic getaway. Reluctantly, she agreed, despite the pain in her heart. Allen said that he'd have her back by her Tuesday evening shift at the tavern.

Upon their return, Lila was a changed woman, as well as a married woman. They'd eloped on the beach and had a quick, but yet romantic little honeymoon. Allen convinced her that the minute they were settled permanently in Ohio that they'd start the adoption proceedings. He promised that she'd be holding her very own baby within the next two years. She was ecstatic, ready to be a mother, now that she was officially a wife. Lila was made for domestication. She loved hosting parties, cooking meals, serving Allen in every way. Being a mother would be the finishing touch on her happy little life.

All lives are happy and perfect until they're not, until that fateful day when everything you dreamed of, worked for, wanted, all comes crumbling down around you. Lila's day of devastation came the day before Valentine's Day, nearly two years after they'd first met. She was planning a romantic and sexy night filled with surprises for Allen. The events were almost too much for my ears to handle. While the cookies were in the oven, there was a loud, demanding knock at the Harts' small apartment door. Lila was confused when she opened it to find a woman, with two small children, glaring at her. The woman began yelling obscenities and accusations at Lila, never allowing Lila to get in one word of defense.

Suddenly, Allen came running up the walkway, screaming and waving his hands in defeated surrender. Lila was being berated by none other than Allen Hartman's wife, as his two children stood nearby in fright. Carl was right. Allen Hart (aka Allen Hartman) was a slimeball, scumbag, a worthless piece of crap. The only truth he ever told my sister was that he worked in Boston as well as Cleveland. He'd been married for nine years and had two little kids. Lila and Allen were not married on the beach; the papers were doctored and fake. He'd never intended on adopting children with her, or even staying in Ohio. He was a liar, a phony, and the worst thing that ever happened to my sister.

Lila never recovered. Allen Hart destroyed her heart and her faith in love. Lila never dated another man, never even came close. The hurt turned to hate, and with that, Lila found strength. Granted, it was a painful strength, but it helped her move on, move forward. She fueled herself on fire and anger, never forgiving or forgetting. We tried to help her, convince her to let the pain and anger go, but it was to no avail. She held on to that anger as if it was the husband she'd never have or the baby she'd never raise. That anger, that pain, was hers, and she was going to carry it with her "until death do them part."

"Beth, I'm ready; I'm done being so angry. I want to be free of the pain he caused me...and...and from the agony I felt from not being able to have a baby of my own. I wanna let it go," she confessed, crying harder into my shoulder.

I was so proud of her, so amazed by her. She'd come to this on her own, even before her experience. Lila's experience was going to be monumental for her, for everyone. We'd all watched her internal suffering for ages. It would be wonderful to see her free of that regret. But first, I had to take care of my own. It was time to rid myself of my regret and my fear. It was time to help my daughter find a lifetime of love and happiness.

There

When Vaughn pulled into the driveway, he asked, "Ya ever gonna move out of this place, Shelb?"

"Funny you should ask," I responded. "I decided earlier today that I'd start getting it ready to sell this summer." Vaughn didn't say anything; he just looked at me and smiled. I leaned over and hugged him. "Thanks for picking me up V, always coming to the rescue," I kidded, knowing it was the truth. I got out of the car and started up the walkway.

"Hey Shelb!" Vaughn called, as he put his window down. "Remember when I took you to that party my senior year?" I stopped and walked back to the driver's window to talk to him.

When Vaughn was in twelfth grade, my mom had recently started her catering business back up. Normally, being in sixth grade and pretty responsible, I was allowed to stay home alone. However, on nights that my mom had to do a wedding, she insisted that Darby or Vaughn watch me for the night since she wouldn't get home well into the wee hours of the night. Darby was typically the person chosen for the job. Heck, she may have even volunteered; I wasn't sure. Darby and I have always enjoyed spending time together. Anyway, on one particular night, when Darby had plans, Vaughn got stuck with me. He was less than thrilled, as he had intentions of going to some upperclassman party that night.

After Darby left for the evening, Vaughn told me to get ready that he was taking me with him. Thrilled, I changed clothes and got ready. Mind you, I was almost 12-years-old and was just informed that I was going to a high school senior's party. I piled on the makeup and wore my most scandalous outfit, a cardigan and a ruffle skirt with boat shoes. I teased my hair and was ready to go. Vaughn and his buddies just laughed and shook their head at me when I came down the hallway. I didn't know what I was more excited about: (1.) going to the party (2.) bragging about it at middle school on Monday. Either way, I was beyond hyped.

When we got to the party, Vaughn and his friends filed quickly out of the car. As I started to get out, Vaughn stopped me. He wasn't letting me out. He was going to the party...alone. I was instructed to stay in the car and not get out...for the whole night. Vaughn was serious too. Being the obedient child that I was, I stayed put. I didn't step one foot out of that car. I even stayed inside when a rather wobbly guy stumbled in front of the car, took his penis out of his pants, and peed directly on the hood of my brother's car. I did, however, honk the horn and wave at him while he was in mid-stream. He quickly zipped up and walked away.

When Vaughn and his friends came back, three hours later, I was asleep in the backseat, livid with my brother for the first time in my life, definitely not the last time either. The whole drive home I was sworn to secrecy about the evening's events. I crossed my heart; I hoped to die. I promised that I'd never say a word about going to a party with my brother. I kept that promise too, for about 14 hours, right up until I relayed the entire story to my beyond-furious mother. I stood back and took great joy in the tongue-lashing Vaughn received for corrupting his baby sister.

Vaughn didn't speak to me for weeks while he was grounded, but I didn't care. He locked me in a car while he went to a party. He deserved it. At the time, I couldn't figure out why he'd chosen his dumb friends and some stupid party over me in the first place. I was his little sister; we could've spent the evening together playing games and watching TV. Over the years, Vaughn and I grew closer and closer. Once my mom got sick, we weren't just brother and sister anymore. We were friends, confidantes, support for each other. I loved him. He was the man in my life when there was nobody else.

I never realized how much that story would come in handy over the next seventeen years. The night that he took me to the party was probably the only bad or poor decision Vaughn ever made. Whenever Vaughn's company had a work function or gathering, it was up to me to tell the story of Vaughn's bad judgment, filling the room with laughter. Nobody could believe that strait-laced, goody-two-shoes, Vaughn had brought his 12-year-old sister to a high school, alcohol-induced party or that he'd even made an appearance at a soiree that had underage individuals consuming alcohol. Inevitably, I always had to add on, "No Vaughn hadn't had anything to drink that night." Vaughn never drank, never contaminated his body with toxins. He was a certified teetotaler.

"Of course, I still talk about it all the time, you know that though," I said, looking at him as if he'd lost his mind.

"Oh right. Ummm....Shelb, I never shoulda taken ya there," he said sincerely.

Laughing at his sincerity and regret, "Ummm V, why is this coming up now?" I asked.

"I'm not sure. It's just that sometimes, when I look at you, I can still see that 12-year-old little girl. I still want to introduce you to all that life has to offer, but protect you from how much life can hurt you." Was this for real? Was I on Candid Camera? Was I being Punk'd?

"Vaughn..." I started to question his words, but he cut me off.

"Shelby, I'm afraid that you're trying too hard to protect yourself from pain and suffering, but you're gonna end up hurting more in the long run." He confessed.

"You're a great big brother, Vaughn, but I'm good. I promise you." I said, quickly turning to run up to the house, away from this mushy conversation. I couldn't handle "deep" with Vaughn. He and I didn't do "deep." That was more Darby's jurisdiction. Vaughn and I did jokes, laughter, cynicism, definitely not profound statements about life. Hell no.

"Shelb--"

"Thanks for picking me up V! Good night," I yelled as I unlocked the front door. I ran inside, closing it quickly behind me, shutting Vaughn and his sentiment out.

Leaning against the door, I lost it. The day's events all slapped me in the face. First my third and final "official" break up with Chance, then Dane, and then finally that strange and weepy conversation with Vaughn was enough to send me right over the edge. I slid to the floor, letting my emotions and tears overcome me. I wasn't certain how long I sat there crying on the floor of my foyer. I must have dozed off sitting against the door, when the ringing of my cell phone woke me or snapped me back to reality.

I looked down and saw Chance's name and his grin smirking back at me. I considered hitting "ignore," but that wouldn't stop him from calling back. And calling back. And calling back. I knew Chance well enough to know that the only way to get him to stop calling was to answer the phone. It really wasn't rocket science. Plus, I knew he was in Columbus for that bachelor party; he wouldn't want to talk long.

Touching the screen and then taking a deep breath, I said, "Hey Chance!" as cheerily as possible.

"Shelb? Are you okay? I saw you called." Called? Oh right! Damn it! I'd forgotten that I called him. Damn that stupid Dane.

"Uh yeah, sorry. I butt-dialed ya!" I claimed, knowing that "butt-dialing" was pretty rare nowadays with the passcode and lock on the iPhone. "Sorry to interrupt the bachelor party. Ya having fun?"

"Good times. Good times." He said with an air of sarcasm to his voice.

"Where are you?" Why was I talking to him, keeping in on the phone? Just let him go Shelby! Tell him you'll talk to him later.

"Losin' It... it's a strip club," he admitted.

"Oh, I know how ya love those! Did you bring a rainfall of ones with ya?" I asked, laughing. Chance always claimed to hate strip clubs. He said that strip clubs were like going to an all-you-can-eat ice cream sundae bar when you were on a strict water diet and couldn't even have one lick. Chance considered it complete and total self-induced torture for no apparent reason.

"Oh yeah, you know me...actually, a few of us were in the back playing Golden Tee, but I came out here to call you," he confessed. "I'm up $20.00; this is so my jam."

"That means a 'song,' Chance," I chuckled. He always tried out some "high school" slang to fit in to my life. But he always pulverized it—intentionally—for a good giggle.

"Oh believe me, I'm singing as I take these guys' money," he said. I could hear the smile in his voice. Playful, light Chance was my favorite Chance. "So...uh...Shelby, it's pretty early; what happened to your date?" Damn. I was hoping that he'd just let it go.

"Ahh, we just called it an early night," I lied.

"Nice try, now tell me the truth Shelby. What happened? You know you can tell me anything," he coaxed.

"Chance, nothing. It's fine. Go enjoy your naked chicks and video golf," I said.

"No...not nothing...tell me," he said.

Knowing that he'd never give up, I caved. Ultimately, I wanted to tell him anyway. Breaking down, crying between the words, I told him the whole sordid story, complete with the kisses, the mint chocolate chip ice cream, and finally finishing with the keys, the thrown punch, and Vaughn picking me up. When he didn't respond, I'd thought that he'd hung up or that we'd gotten disconnected. I waited a little longer. Nothing.

After a few more moments of silence, I said, "Hey Chance, I know you're busy; I'll just talk to ya later."

Honestly surprising me, he said, "Yeah Shelb, I'll talk to ya."

I looked down at my phone and Chance was gone. Just like that. I couldn't believe it. Maybe, I didn't want to believe it. He was never gone, but this time he was. I'd told him something, something that made him finally come to the conclusion that we were over. Knowing that I'd kissed Dane and started to enjoy an evening with another man must have put him over the edge. Chance must've listened and actually heard it this time. I knew I should be relieved, happy even. But...but...I wasn't. We were both moving on, separately, but forward.

Chapter 18

Here

Carl was holding my hand as Julian looked at me and asked, "You're sure you're ready?"

Not finding my voice, I just nodded and glanced at Carl. He smiled, squeezed my hand, and kissed my cheek. "You're gonna be great, babe. I love you."

"Love you too," I said, feeling my voice catch. I was a nervous wreck, not of going back, but of failing my daughter once again.

Julian put his hands on my shoulders, looked me in the eyes, and said, "Remember the rules and why you're there." I took a deep breath and nodded. "Just relax, close your eyes, and concentrate." I nodded again, closing my eyes, feeling Carl's hands lightly rubbing my back. "Now Beth, think about Shelby, remember all you can about her, every second that you can recall."

Immediately, I was taken to a moment when Vaughn was screaming, crying hysterically, as he came running across the lawn with a bloody, banged-up Shelby in his arms. Terror swept through me as I realized that she wasn't crying; she was out cold. She was covered in blood, and in ROAD. There were particles of the road imbedded into her forehead; blood coated her face and hair. Screaming, I asked if she'd been hit by a car. Luckily though,

Vaughn had said that she'd only been hit by a ten-speed bicycle. Then, Vaughn cried louder, saying that it was a game he'd made up, and it was all his fault. I had him call Carl at work and tell him to meet us at Children's Hospital. In the car, rushing to the hospital, she finally woke up and smiled at me. Relief flooded through me as I realized that she was okay. She smiled.

Another memory hit within seconds of that smile, she'd just come home from her last basketball game as a high school cheerleader. I was prepared for a forlorn teenager, lamenting the years gone by, but what I got was an ecstatic and thrilled girl instead. Before the game, she'd gotten the mail and had received her acceptance letter to Ohio State. Crying, she told me that she couldn't have done it without me.

Then, it happened. I was in her experience. I saw Shelby. I felt her past, her present, and glimpsed her future. Every moment, every second. I felt her happiness. I was shredded by her pain and fear; I could feel it all. I saw his face, his eyes, felt his love. Chance. Then I saw it all. Saw how it should play out; how it wouldn't if I failed. Again, I felt her fear, was crushed by it all. My heart weighed heavy; my soul ached. I felt alone. All alone and empty. So alone. Oh Shelby. My baby.

Then, all at once we were dancing, in the parking lot of the bank, swirling around and around, laughing while our bellies ached. That sparkle in her eye was shining and glistening. She dipped me backwards and kissed me on the nose. When she propped me back up, I was standing in my living room, the living room of the house that I lived in with my husband and three kids for the best twenty-one years of my life. Oh my God, my home. It hadn't changed. Every piece of furniture, every picture, every knickknack was exactly as I had left it, remembered it. I looked around, taking it all in, breathing it all in. This was my house, my home, my life. My life.

I'd sat in that same chair, night after night, reading books, watching TV, waiting for my kids to come home. I looked closer. There were a few books on the end table, none that I recognized. I touched one, ran my fingers over the letters. This was Shelby's book, a book she'd share with me if I were here. We'd read it together, rip it apart if we hated it, cry together if we loved it, but it would be our book. Taking a second, I read the jacket, hoping to get more insight on my baby, even though I knew it all. Maybe, I was just stalling. Maybe, I was just as nosy and as curious as Darby. Either way, I read it, and it gave me more purpose, a sense of why I was here. It was a typical romance novel; Shelby still believed in the fairy tale. There was still hope.

I walked down the hallway, back toward the bedroom, not knowing if she was home or not. But the pull, the yank from my heart, told me she was home. I followed my instinct and walked to my bedroom, the room I shared with Carl, the place I took my final "earthly" breath. The door was slightly ajar; I pushed it open. Oh Shelby. My heart pulled; tears stung my eyes. She was sleeping just as she always slept, curled up on her stomach, a bit to the side, one hand under her pillow, but braced against the headboard. Her other hand was under her chin; she looked angelic, my little cherub. She was stunning, the most beautiful girl, no, not a girl, a woman, the most beautiful woman I'd ever seen. My baby was a gorgeous woman.

I sat down on the bed, soaking in the sight of the one person I was worried about and missed the most; the one person I feared

246

needed me more than I could ever deliver. Quietly and softly, I brushed her hair away from her face. Shelby stirred. I smiled at how familiar her movements and sounds were; they hadn't changed since she was just a tiny infant in my arms. I leaned over, breathing in her scent before placing the lightest kiss on her cheek. She stirred again, shifting position.

"Honey? Shelby Lynn? ...I need to talk to you baby," I whispered. Shelby rolled toward me, smiling slightly in her sleep. "Come on honey, wake up for me."

Slowly, Shelby opened her eyes and closed them again, moaning a bit before falling back to sleep. I placed my hand on her shoulder, shaking her ever so gently. Again, she opened her eyes, but this time, she focused them on me. She rubbed her eyes, scooting slowly up in the bed.

Realization hit, and he questioned, "Mom?"

Terror spread across Shelby's face, exactly what I was afraid of. Shelby did not like anything unknown. She'd always been afraid of stories of inexplicable happenings. This was not going to be easy for her.

"It's okay baby; we're just gonna talk...talk like we always used to," I consoled her.

"But...how...what? Mom?" she said, staring incredulously at me, still rubbing her eyes looking around the room for some sense of reality.

"Yes baby, it's me. It's fine...just fine." I knew I was treating her like a child, but she was. She was my child, my baby. I reached for her; she shied back. Afraid of me? Afraid of this? "Shelby, it's okay," I said, reaching for her again. She brought her arms out of the blankets and slowly reached back for me, hesitantly. Our hands met and my heart melted. I held her hand, felt her warmth.

Shelby smiled and whispered, "I don't understand..."

"There's nothing to understand; I just missed my girl and wanted to talk," I explained.

"I...I missed you too," the words seemed to open a floodgate and tears soaked her face as she scooted across the bed, wrapping her arms around me, burying her head in my shoulder.

Oh my, the feeling of holding her again knocked the wind out of me. I'd dreamed of this, wanted this. My daughter was in my arms again; where she was meant to be. Suddenly, I was sent back to reality, remembering my purpose, reminded of why I was there.

"Shelby--"

"Mom? Your locket....how...I don't get it." She said, confused. She had my locket, my gold locket that my children had gotten me years ago for Mother's Day, in her hands, inspecting it as it dangled from my neck. It never left my neck.

Remembering the rules, I just shrugged my shoulders, and said, "You know I always wear this."

"But....how...Darby....Darby wears it every day?" she said, staring with wonder at the locket, opening it. "Our picture is in this one too? Mom?"

Okay, this may be a little harder than I initially thought. There were secrets, secrets that weren't supposed to be revealed. But what was I supposed to say when she was holding evidence of a secret right now between her thumb and forefinger? I guess some of those secrets weren't meant to be kept, especially right now.

"Honey, you kept what was special and meaningful to us, but it wouldn't be fair to take them, to keep what meant so much to us.

We get to have them, too," I said, showing her my wedding ring, the same ring that I saw dangling from the chain on her neck. She held the ring against her chest, smiling at the realization. We were closer and more connected than she really knew.

Seeing how much I pleased her with that, I said, "Do you know what your father keeps in his chest pocket?" At the mention of her father, Shelby's eyes widened as tears filled them again. "The letter you wrote him....the one you left on the kitchen table the night he died. Remember?"

Shelby and Carl had a little spat the day before he died. It was horrible to Shelby, but I'd talked to Carl about that incident nearly a thousand times, and he hadn't even registered it on his radar as an argument. Sometimes, what one person thinks is so significant and monumental means absolutely nothing to another. People fret over the simplest things without realizing how insignificant those things really are. This was just the case. It was unfortunate that poor Shelby had never known that Carl hadn't even thought twice about their scuffle.

Anyway, that Thursday evening, Shelby left Carl a note on the kitchen table. One of her classmates, a boy classmate, was having a boy-girl party that Friday night. It was going to be Shelby's first boy-girl party. She was so excited to be spending a Friday night at a party with boys, since her older brother and sister often spent their Friday nights out at parties and having fun. She was just thrilled. Her little fifth grade boyfriend was attending the party as well. It was a birthday party, so the note requested that Carl stop at the store on Friday while he was home to get a "boy" birthday present and a card. Carl was always our "task man," since he was home all morning and afternoon. Those little errands were his contributions to our family life. Well, the errands and his income, of course.

I read the note over before Shelby went to bed. I thought the note was written rather rudely and selfishly. I told her that she wasn't going to be rude to her father in a note requesting him to do something for her. She wasn't some entitled little brat who got everything she wanted. Shelby needed to be nice, respectful, and appreciative. He was her father. She didn't change the wording or the letter itself. But, she decorated the note with a colorful border, emphasizing the words "thank you" and "I love you" with hearts and flowers surrounding the note.

The next morning, the letter was no longer on the kitchen table where she left it, but next to Carl on the end table where he was sitting when he died. That letter, the letter that she decorated and told her father she loved him over and over again has remained in his breast pocket ever since he got here. Shelby was relieved to know that he saw the letter, read the words "I love you" before he died. It gave her comfort to know that even though the words "I hope you never get up with me again" were the last words ever spoken to him, that he at least saw the written words "I love you" before he died.

Shelby jumped up, "But how? It's right here!" She asked, rummaging through the bottom drawer of her dresser. She produced the same note, yellowed, crinkled, and worn now, but still complete with all the colorful wording and letters. "I've always had it, knowing that he touched it and saw that I still loved him."

"I know that sweetheart," I said, turning to face her. "It's one of our special mysteries. Something small can mean so much to two different people, but it doesn't seem fair that only one person gets to cherish it." I smiled. Back when I first realized and understood this "sharing" of intimate tokens, I regretted that Shelby had insisted on putting her First Holy Communion necklace in Carl's casket when he died. Knowing what I know now, nobody should ever secure their loved ones with "goodies" or family mementos when they die. If those little trinkets, little gifts mean enough to us, then we get to have them too. No sense in burying them in the ground.

"Mom, does he...does he....hate me?" she asked, tears filling her eyes once again.

"Are you kidding? Shelb, he loves you so much. We talk about you and tell stories about how funny and vivacious you are all the time," I explained. "Your father loves you. Talks about his little 'Mutt' constantly." Shelby laughed when I used his old nickname for her. Shelby used to get so jealous of Darby, because Carl called Darby "Pumpkin," but Carl didn't have a pet name for Shelby. Pretending to think long and hard about it, he then decided on "Mutt," just to be funny and make her laugh. Meeting the challenge, Shelby accepted her horrible nickname. So, "Mutt' it was, and it stuck.

"Really? Oh my...I miss him....you...oh Mom," and then the floodgate broke once again. Sobbing, with shoulders shaking, she choked out, "Are you really here? Is this real? I've dreamt about this moment forever." Her arms wrapped around me, holding me tightly, squeezing as if she were holding on for dear life.

"Right here."

"I have so much to tell you, so many things to show you. Oh Mom, wait 'til you see Becca. You're gonna fall in love with her. Darby and Vaughn...Oh my God, they're gonna--"

"Whoa...whoa...hold on Honey...I'm here to see you....to talk to you," I admitted. Shelby looked at me confused. "I'm sorry, but I'm not sure how long I can stay."

"But...you just got here! Whattya mean?" she asked looking bewildered, searching my face for answers, but not wanting the truth.

"I'm here to talk to you, spend time with you. But I don't get to stay long," I said. "Need to get back to your dad and your aunts." She smiled. Her face really brightened; it must have made her feel comfort to know that they were with me, or that I was with them.

"But how long--"

"I'm not sure...let's not waste time talking about time, let's just spend time talking," I said. I looked at her; she really didn't look much different than she did ten years ago. Shelby's hair was longer and certainly not as "big" as it once was. I was pleased that she'd stopped highlighting it; her natural dark hair was so much prettier than the fake blonde she'd insisted on in high school. Her eyes were the most magnificent shade of blue, such a stark contrast from Vaughn and Darby's dark eyes. But right now, they were puffy and red; she must've been crying when she fell asleep. "Shelby, how're you?"

"Mom, I'm great...perfect now," she said, staring at me.

"But, how is your life? How are you?" I asked, trying to find answers without really prying, but really needing to pry.

"Great! I'm a teacher....I'm.....I'm an aunt. Mom, Becca is--" she said, changing the subject to her niece, my granddaughter instead.

"I know all about Becca and even Vaughn's boys. Lila filled me all in. I need to know about you." I said.

Looking pained, finding difficulty in what she wanted to say, she finally took a deep breath and said, "Mom...I'm...I'm so sorry for not calling Vaughn and Darby the second you got sick. I'm sorry that I wasn't there--"

Interrupting her, cutting her off before she could say anymore, I said, "Shelby Lynn stop that right now. I was a grown woman; I knew something wasn't right. I was too afraid, too worried about what it was. My health, my cancer is not your burden to bear," I pleaded as I held her hand. "Nobody...nobody blames you. No one—not me, not your brother and sister, and not Lila. You need to stop right now, stop blaming yourself." I admonished.

"But--"

"No! No 'buts'—this topic of conversation is over. You need to stop blaming yourself....and stop arguing with a dead woman, you'll never win," I joked, hoping to get a reactive giggle from her.

"Mom!" she laughed. "You can't say that!"

"Sure, I can! Who's gonna stop me?" Instantly, I felt a pull within me, something yanking on my heart, maybe on my soul. I understood the message. My time was running out. I was here for a purpose—not for fun. I could stay forever. It felt so right being with her, laughing with my daughter. It'd felt like I'd never left.

"Honey, tell me what you're afraid of?" I figured that I'd just lay it all on the line. I was her mom; I'd confronted her with much worse in my lifetime.

Shaking her head, she said, "Afraid? ...I'm...I'm not..."

"Shelby, I'm your mother. You can't hide anything from me. I'm here, right here, right now, for you. This is your only shot to talk to your mom about whatever it is." I explained.

She stared at me, not speaking. She opened her mouth, then closed it quickly, shaking her head. When did she get so close-lipped? Shelby used to talk about everything with me, except Nate. We were so close, so connected. It was hard for Shelby to keep anything inside. I certainly did not know this side of her.

"Talk to me," I coaxed, rubbing her arm.

After an interminable long pause, she nodded slightly, "Everything....Mom, I'm afraid of everything," she admitted. I pulled her to me, wrapping her in my arms.

"Just talk, please just tell me what's on your mind," I begged.

"I'm ... I'm so afraid ... afraid of being alone ... but then... I'm ... I'm also so afraid of leaving people to make them alone too. I never want anyone to feel like I feel right now," she confessed.

"Oh baby," I said, holding her tighter, stroking the back of her hair. "Look at me," I pulled her away, staring at her face. "Listen, you can't....no matter how hard you try....can't protect people from pain." She was crying harder, sobbing as I spoke. "Pain is a part of life."

"It just hurts too much. I don't wanna feel--"

"But that's just it! You have to feel....pain hurts, but you have to feel it. You have to feel everything. Love, joy, pride, those are feelings worth feeling. If you shut down, then you don't get to feel the good things too. Things that matter," I explained.

"I just don't think I can do it. I'm not strong enough, brave enough," she said.

"That's absurd; you're the most courageous person I've ever known," I replied. "Shelby, when your father died, my world crumbled. I felt like someone shoved a knife in my heart and chopped it into a thousand pieces." Shelby wiped her eyes and blew her hose, still holding on to my every word as she stared at me over the tissue. "But if someone said to me that I would never have to feel pain like that, but in turn, I'd have to forfeit meeting him, falling in love with him, and having my three kids, then I would've told them to forget it."

"But, you don't understand--"

"I understand more than you could ever realize. I had some horrible, terrifying nights after your dad died. Even more when I found out that I'd be leaving my kids...all alone," I said, trying to get through to her. "But Shelby, I wouldn't trade them for anything in the world. Those moments of magic are worth every single ache and tear in the heart. The heart is strong. It can hold a lot of pain, but it can hold even more love."

"I don't want to...I don't wanna hurt....anymore," she cried.

"Honey, you have to let go of that pain. You're holding onto it like a shield, to protect you from future pain. But you can't do that. There is no protection. Pain is a part of life, but you must experience loss to truly understand the importance of love." I could tell that she was listening, giving it her best to understand and accept what I was saying. Continuing, I said, "Shelby, you are such a caring, strong, and loving woman. Please give that strength and love to someone else. It would be such a tragedy if someone missed out on all that you have to give."

Suddenly, my heart felt full. I'd never felt such completion, such love and pride in one person. My burden lifted. My sense of worry was gone. Did this mean I was getting through to her? Was I saying the right things or was my time just running out? I didn't know; I just knew that I felt infinitely lighter, more sure of myself as a mother, as Shelby Lynn's mother.

"Mom?" Shelby's voice was full of fear. "No...not yet...please..."

Looking around, I realized that things seemed blurry; I knew what this meant. My time was running out. Wow. That was fast. Julian hadn't warned me how quickly this was going to go. I wanted more time, felt that I deserved more time. How would I know if I changed her mind? I needed to make sure, needed to know that she understood, believed what I was saying. "Shelby..."

"Mom...what? No..." she said, holding my hand, squeezing it, pulling me toward her.

"Honey listen...listen to me," I commanded holding her head in my hands, looking at her, taking her all in. "You need to love Chance, give your whole heart to him. No more holding back. You have to. No more fear."

With wide quizzical eyes, she asked, "Chance? But how? How do you--"

"Because I'm your mother; I know everything," I smiled. I had to make her truly understand. "Shelby, I....I...I also know that he's the father of my grandkids." Screw it. I'd deal with the consequences when I got back. If they let me come back...

Shelby's eyes sparkled at the mention of her future kids. I wiped a tear from her face and smiled, nodding knowingly at my beautiful daughter. "Now wake up honey, he's calling you." She smiled, glancing at her phone. I leaned in and kissed her, the last time I'd ever kiss my baby, my Shelby Lynn. "Goodbye my love," I kissed her hand and started to go.

"Mom... Mom, I love you too," she sobbed. "Thank you. Goodbye. I love--" Those were the last words I ever heard my daughter speak. But they were also the best words that I ever heard my daughter say.

There

"They read you Cinderella

You hoped it would come true

That one day your Prince Charming

Would come rescue you..."

My cell? It was ringing? Okay, so shoot me. In 14 months, I never bothered to change my ringtone. Not a big deal. It's just such a nice song. I missed Chance's call; it was probably for the best anyway. He'd basically hung up on me when I was bawling about Dane and our disastrous first and only date. Glancing at the clock, I realized that I'd been asleep for a little over two hours. My head was pounding. Suddenly, all the day's events came flooding back: Chance, Dane, Chance again, even Vaughn. No wonder I conked out; that was too much for any one person to endure.

I went to the bathroom and decided to wash my face and brush my teeth before getting back into bed for the rest of the night. Heck, maybe even the rest of the weekend. As I was rinsing off my face, something caught my eye. My necklace. My mom's wedding band dangled from my neck, sparkling in the light. My mom. What a dream. That was...that felt so real.

In my dream, my mom said that he, that Chance, was calling me. I ran back to my phone and checked the callers' list. He'd called twice, two times in the last ten minutes. Ten minutes. Wow. My subconscious was a sick son of a gun. I must have registered that his ringtone was going off and let it become a part of my dream. There was really no other explanation. It had seemed so real though, so natural. Shaking my head, I tried to put the dream out of my mind. It'd felt so perfect having her with me, made me feel complete in a way I hadn't felt in ages.

I glanced over to the dresser and there it was, the letter I'd written my father. It was no longer in the bottom drawer, buried under the mementos of my childhood. It was on the dresser, unfolded and visible, just as I'd left it in my dream. Oh my God, it wasn't a dream. She was here. My mom was here with me, holding me, talking to me, guiding me. My mom, the woman I longed to see for the last decade, was here. My mom told me she loved me and didn't blame me. My dad still loved me. She came for a reason; she needed to share something important, needed me to listen. My mom wanted me to take a chance. Chance.

As the realization hit me and my emotions were unleashed, my doorbell rang. It was nearly midnight on a Saturday night. I knew Chance was in Columbus; Nina was out with Evan. Fear enveloped me. I prayed that Dane hadn't come to apologize, or worse, finish what he'd started. I certainly did not want to be alone with Dane. I was afraid of him. Before I'd passed out, I'd forgotten to set my new alarm system.

My phone rang again, making me jump, scaring me. Luckily, it was just Chance. Must be a pretty boring bachelor party. But oh good, I'd answer the door while I was on the phone with him. "Hello?"

"Shelby, open up! I'm on your front porch," he said, as two thoughts filled my head: Prince Charming always comes back and He's the father of my grandkids.

I opened the door, and he started talking immediately, "Listen, Shelby, I can't just--"

I cut him off midsentence as I wrapped my arms around him and kissed him with all the passion and love I had in me. He didn't move his arms, or even his lips for that matter. After a few moments, he put his hands on my upper arms and yanked me off of him.

"Shelby, no! I'm not drunk. I came here to check on you. I didn't come for some midnight...ummm... hookup," he explained. "I couldn't function thinking about that guy, that asshole, trying to hurt you. I needed to see if you were okay."

"Chance, I'm okay. I'm better than okay," I admitted excitedly.

I reached for him again, but he grabbed my hands, holding them to his lips. "Okay, now that I know you're okay, there is nothing that I want more than to pick you up and take you back to that bedroom....but...I'm not gonna Shelby," he said.

"So you drove two hours home to see if I was still alive, knowing that I was, because you just talked to me?" I asked smugly, grinning at him.

"I guess...I mean...I couldn't be there...away from you... when you were still here...hurting," he confessed. "I guess it kinda sounds dumb now though, huh?"

"And...you're...you're not looking for....ya know?" I said, batting my eyelashes at him as flirtatiously as possible, as I ran my finger along the buttons of his shirt.

"Girl, you're insatiable!" he laughed, grabbing my hand, shaking his head. "No! I'm not looking for that. I told you before that until you can say--"

"Right! Ya don't need to remind me," I said, cutting him off. "There's no 'bad boy' in Chance Michaels....Just a Prince Charming...ready to swoop in and rescue me, right?" I laughed, reaching for his hand.

Taking his hand back, he said, "Shelby, I didn't come here for you to make fun of me. I'm sorry...I shouldn't...I just shouldn't have come," he said, sadly as he turned and opened the front door.

Watching him walk out the door, I smiled, knowing exactly what I wanted and needed to say. "Hey Chance!"

He stopped, but didn't turn around.

"Turn around, you're gonna wanna see my face when I say this," I said. He turned and stared at the ground. "Will you look at me, Chance?" I asked.

He lifted his head; his eyes looked directly at me, into me. "Shelby--"

Cutting him off again, I walked out onto the porch and placed my finger over his mouth, "Shhh," I whispered as I traced my finger over his lips. Chance James Michaels was truly the most wonderful man, no, not man, person, most wonderful person I'd ever met. How could I have been so stupid, so blind and stubborn, to not see it all before? My love for him wasn't something to fear, but was something to cherish and protect.

"Always," I said. He looked at me, confused. I nodded, and repeated myself. "Chance, I mean it. Always."

Chapter 19

Here

"Oh Betheny, you were brilliant, just brilliant," Carl beamed, enveloping me in his arms. I felt weak and very wobbly; I allowed him to hold me, support me. "I got to watch the whole thing. You were amazing, honey."

"They did? You got to watch?" I asked, surprised and pleased that he was able to share in such a miraculous event.

"Every last second, your memories, her experience, everything you said, she said. It was magical," he said with elation and wonder.

"Ya done good, girl," Julian said, slugging me lightly on the upper arm. "We'll go ahead and let a few things slide," he said, winking at me.

"But...how...how do you...will we know if it worked?" I asked, worrying again about Shelby.

"Well, how do you feel? Describe yourself in one word," he commanded.

"Ummm...one word? Okay.... I feel..." I thought about it for a moment and realized that I understood what he meant. "Light."

"Exactly. There's no worry, no burden of regret. Shelby's gonna be fine," he said smiling, leaving Carl and me alone. It was the first time that I'd ever seen Julian smile. I knew we'd never be friends, that he'd never open up to me about his life, his past, his pain, but I hoped that one day he could feel as serene and as "light" as I did right now.

"Oh Carl, our kids..." I said, tearing up. "They're...they're just wonderful."

Carl hugged me and I could feel all the love he had for me and for our kids in his embrace. Parenting was a hard, trying task, filled with worry and second-guesses. But in the end, all that ever really matters is how much you love your children and how you remember to show them your love each and every opportunity you have. It's not about what you can give them or even about how much time you get to have with them; it's about loving them and showing them how important love really is. That's parenting. That's love. That's life.

There

I stood at the doorway, terrified. I was so scared of what all was in store for me on the other side. I'd feared this moment for so long, tried to hide from it, run from it really. But like all inevitable things in life, it found me. I couldn't hide. I stood there alone, worrying. What if I'd forgotten something? What if I still had something to do? I hated being alone like this. I always thought that I'd feel such peace and comfort when this time came. I should be excited, curious about what comes next. But this, this was frightful; I shouldn't have to be standing here alone. I felt so alone.

"Sorry Shelby! I had to pee. Took longer than I thought," Vaughn said, still tucking in his shirt and adjusting his jacket. Almost on cue, the music started. "It's Go Time!" He leaned in and kissed me, and said, "Don't tell Darby or Rachel, but you really are the most beautiful bride I've ever seen," he complimented me, as I wrapped my arm around his, ready for his escort.

The doors opened and I saw him. His smile lit up the aisle as tears fell down his cheeks. I started crying immediately. It took us so long, such a long, scary journey to get us here, but we eventually made it. Today, I was going to marry my best friend, my Prince Charming. And I really couldn't be happier or more at ease with this decision. Even though I'd been too blind to see, he'd had my heart ever since that fateful day I visited the Chance Encounters chat room. Chance Encounters? Chance. Oh man, it was right in front of me the whole time, and I was too dumb and too scared to see it.

As I walked down the aisle, I glanced at how full the church was, filled with members of my extended family. Looking around, I realized something, something that I'd also failed to see before. My parents and all of their brothers and sisters may be gone, here only in spirit and love, but as I looked at the people in the pews, I saw them all. I saw them still, in my cousins, in my niece and nephews, and in the friends I'd cherished for so long. The church was filled with love, love for me and my soon-to-be husband, the father of my future kids. Love was everywhere.

Chance met Vaughn and me by the first pew. Vaughn was wiping his eyes as he "handed me off" to Chance. I heard Vaughn whisper, "Take care of her," as Chance nodded his silent promise.

Chance and I decided to write our own vows, words that came from the heart and meant more than someone else's idea of what we should be saying on our wedding day. It was Chance's idea originally; I agreed only on one condition. He had to go first. I knew protocol was that the woman said her vows first, but I needed him to go first. I needed to be the closer, not the opener.

But now, I was regretting my obstinate decision. There wasn't a dry eye in the church as Chance vowed to love me unconditionally for the rest of his life. He even promised my parents that he'd take care of me and respect me for all of his days. It was heartfelt, emotional, and just perfect. Damn it. I should've gone first. But now, now it was my turn.

I took a deep breath, and glanced at Darby and Becca, at Vaughn and his family, and then at Mallory, as she stared up at me in awe, holding my bouquet. Then, I looked at Chance, the chance that I almost missed.

"Chance James Michaels, I love you with all that I am," I said, tears welling in my eyes. He smiled, wiping a tear from my cheek. "I've loved you for so long—even when I didn't want to believe that you had my heart." My voice was beginning to quiver. Chance just nodded and squeezed my hands, urging me to continue. "I love you because you're kind; you're giving, and you're so incredibly intelligent. I love your passion for me, for Mallory, for everything that you value." I took another breath, pausing before I finished the final words of my vows. "But I realized recently what sets you apart from all others, what makes you such a part of me, a part of my family, and ultimately the most important part of my life. You're just like the rest of the people in my life that I cherish and love. Because when I' m with you, I know that no matter what happens, no matter where we are, it's going to be you. You are my family. You, Chance, are the one who's Always There."

Chapter 20

Always

I grabbed Chance's hand, holding tightly. I knew he was afraid, but he'd never admit it. These were scary times, not knowing what was ahead, strange and unknown. Squeezing his hand, I winked at him, to let him know that it was going to be okay. We were all going to be okay. Chance didn't have to worry.

Smiling, I glanced at Darby as she inched closer. Darby's face was filled with worry, worry for us, worry for what was to come. Then, all at once, the brightness flashed, vibrant colors illuminated us and in one shining moment, Shelby stood before us. Smiling she ran to Chance, embracing him as her blue hospital gown clung to her sides.

With tears in her eyes, Darby leaned over and whispered, "The hospital gown from Jerry Carl's birth." I smiled as my heart filled with love and joy for my grandchildren, all of them.

Looking at Chance, my heart warmed even more. For the last two years, I'd loved that Chance was in the hospital scrubs he'd worn during Shelby's C-section with their son. Seeing that they both shared the same "perfect day," ignited my heart. That kind of love, the truest form of love, was rare and extraordinary. They'd found it in each other, with each other. Chance and Shelby had forever.

Seeing me over Chance's shoulder, Shelby let go of him and came to me. It had been forty-five years since I last saw my baby girl, since that visit in our old bedroom, and she was still as beautiful as that day. Crying, Shelby hugged me, fully enveloping me in her arms. Wiping her tears and smiling, she said, "Even after you were gone, I still knew that you were there, felt that you were there." And that is the purest, simplest truth about love. It doesn't matter how far apart you are or how many lifetimes away you are, the people you love, those who mean the most, their love for you is Always There.

The End

About the Author

Carol Ann Albright-Eastman is a wife and mother of four, crazy, adorable, incorrigible, intelligent, kind, and athletic children. She's taught high school English for fifteen years. She earned a Bachelor's Degree in English from The Ohio State University, a teaching license and a communications minor from the University of Akron, and holds a Master's in Education from the University of Akron.

Eastman spends the majority of her time grading papers, reading, but not as voraciously as other "Indie" authors and their devout followers, watching her sons play baseball (or whatever seasonal sport they're in at the time), negotiating futilely with a toddler, and falling deeper in love with her husband every day. Eastman is a motherless and fatherless daughter, but a day doesn't go by that she doesn't think of them. She misses her mother and is grateful to her mother for teaching her about the importance of true love and lasting friendships. If you'd like to contact Eastman, then please feel free to email her at: eastmancarolann@gmail.com

Acknowledgements

I would like to thank the following people for helping me make this book, my 20-year dream, a fantasy come true:

My family

Michael James Eastman

Thank you for being so strong and supportive, especially when writing didn't seem to be "the best idea" for me and for our family. You never gave up on me or faulted me for striving to reach my goals and dreams. You are the perfect husband. I am so lucky that I took a "chance" on you and agreed to go out with my crazy online stalker. Pie, I loved you then, and I love you more and more every day. Always.

Carla Ann Albright Grasso

You are the sister all girls should get to have. You've been my best friend and biggest support my entire life. I would not be the person I am today without you. After all of these years, I finally understand what Aunt Footo meant when she said, "What about us? She was our sister." Losing you would be like trying to live without a limb. You're a part of me and always will be.

Carlee Lorraine Northup

I love you, Wog. You make me want to be an "Aunt Mary," someone who gives everything to her nieces and nephews. The moment that I held you against my chest, I knew what true, unconditional, maternal love was. (And you weren't even mine!) I've loved you and your gorgeous pink little lips since the moment I laid eyes on you. Honestly, I've loved you since the day your mom told me she was pregnant with you. I will forever be indebted to you for kick-starting my biological clock.

Carl Anthony Albright

You take care of me. You've been my father-figure, the man I look up to, my entire life. You've never faltered in your role as "big brother." I am so lucky to have you in my life. There is nothing you wouldn't do for me. You bring me laughter and confidence. I am grateful to have been blessed with a brother like you.

Mary Jo DiNapoli

Thank you for being in our lives, but more importantly, thank you for being our "mom" when we needed one and couldn't imagine life without one. You filled in when you didn't have to, and for that, I am thankful. I'm sure the last few years have been lonely without your brothers and sisters, but despite how selfish this may sound, I'm happy that you stayed here with us and have been fighting the good fight for so many years. To my readers: No, my Aunt Mary never wrote such a horrifying letter to me; there is a great deal of fabrication to this novel. This woman, my Aunt Mary, has always loved me like a daughter.

Morgan Sue Eastman

Morgs, I love you, not at all like a stepdaughter. I love you like my real flesh, blood, and air. Ever since the day I met in you December of 1997, I knew that you were going to be a special and integral part of my life. I never knew how much of my heart you'd hold too. I'm so proud of the young woman you're growing and maturing into (finally). I have gotten to be a part of so many wonderful aspects of your life, moments that have brought tears to my eyes and warmth to my heart. Morgan, thank you for giving me a mother-daughter relationship, something that I longed to have for so many years. But, please remember, please accept that you have that elsewhere as well. Don't give up on her. Don't spend a lifetime with regret. Embrace what you have while you still have it. Trust me, our time with our loved ones is so fleeting and so fast; cherish it while you can. I know that I've been preaching these same words for years, but maybe this book, my pain, my regret will become more evident. Don't miss out. Find a way, you'll be glad you did in the end. (Am I ever wrong?)

Brock Anthony Eastman

You made me a "mommy," a title I feared I'd never have. When I look at you, I feel like a success. Everything about you is perfection at its finest; you're smart, sensitive, caring, giving, and athletic, the perfect package. But more importantly, when I look at you, I realize that dreams really do come true. You are what I wished for and dreamed about my entire life. I love you, Brojo.

Brevin Michael Eastman

I never realized that one person could bring such laughter and happiness to a family. It doesn't matter what kind of day I've had or how hard it's been, you brighten my days. You are the perfect mixture of your father and me. All of our creativity, craziness, and effervescence are balled up into one adorable, feisty, incorrigible, funny and loving little boy. My life wouldn't be as vibrant and complete without you. You never stop surprising me and making me laugh. I love you Brevie-Brev.

Emersyn Elisabeth Eastman

You terrify me. I spent my entire life praying for a baby girl, someone to dress up, take shopping, and talk "like friends" with. I got my wish; I got my baby girl. But all I can think about is the saying "be careful what you wish for." You are everything I ever dreamed of and wanted and so much more. But now, now, I have to do my part, and it terrifies me. Many women, adolescents and adults alike, blame their mothers for all that is wrong in their lives, for shattering their spirits and happiness. I never want you to feel that way. I never want to hurt you. Emersyn, I just hope that you always know how much I truly love you and that I'd do anything in the world for you. I pray that I get to be a part of every crucial moment in your life, witnessing it all. I'm so deeply afraid that someday my fate and heredity will be met, and you'll be left with such agony and loneliness, a void that cannot be filled. But Em, never forget that I love you and no matter what, I'm "always there."

My friends/my writing support

Jennifer Manion: You are my biggest fan and for that, I cannot thank you enough. You believed in me and my "talents" for years—even when I didn't believe in myself. I hope this novel found you back to your father in some way, reminding you of all that he was and how much you truly loved him. Jen that kind of love does and will go on. Your father is always there; nobody can or will ever take his place.

Tiffany Walker: It is no wonder that you are a cheerleading coach. You see the good, the brightness, the best in everything. Thank you for always being there for me, "cheering" me up when I felt down and defeated.

Lindsay Johnson: Thank you for taking an interest in reading again, so you could read my book and help find errors that I couldn't see. Thank you also for taking so many photographs of hands as we were on the quest for the perfect cover image. I appreciate all that you do for me. I'm so happy to get to watch as you learn the ups and downs of motherhood. I'm proud of the mother you already are. Believe me, it will be tough at times, but will definitely be the most magical moments of your life.

Lori Albright: Thank you for being so supportive and reading my book as quickly as you could. I know reading isn't necessarily "your thing," but I'm grateful that you'd go out of your way for me. I will love you like a sister forever. Additionally, thank you for always being my graphic designer and dealing with my nit-picking changes and corrections. Your images and creativity are truly art at its finest. For anyone interested in a graphic designer, then please feel free to contact Lori Albright at: albrightlori@hotmail.com

Kathryn Hunt: I am so sorry your loss had to be part of this book. I wish that you never had to experience such pain and suffering. Your daughter, Sofia Rose, should still be here with us today. It's unfair and wrong. Thank you for always being there for me and with me. Our coupled loss and grief has bound us forever. Let's just pray that my mom and your princess are together, baking cookies and filling in those missing roles for each other.

Megan Thompson: I'm glad you came into my life. Your kindness and compliments warm my heart. I am glad that you are now a part of my life. You are a defender of the innocent, fighting all that is evil and wrong in the world today. I've never met anyone like you. You're a feisty original.

Deloris Dehart: Thank you for reading my book and providing helpful feedback on the emotional side of the novel. Dee, love is a scary thing. It can sometimes be so hurtful and vindictive. But as you are learning and experiencing firsthand, it's truly the most fulfilling and rewarding part of life, nothing compares to it.

I'm so thankful that you've opened your heart and learned to "swoon like a schoolgirl again." Keith Poole, you're a true hero.

Mary Splittorf: All throughout the short time I had with my mother, I envied her hands. My mother had the most beautiful hands I've ever seen. When I decided what I wanted my cover to look like, I knew that I needed to search for the perfect hands to honor my mother. I set out on a quest to do her justice. Immediately, when I saw your hands, I knew that she would be pleased to have you "stand in" as her hand model. Thank you for allowing me to photograph your beautiful hands. You give literal meaning to "giving me a hand."

My cyber world friends and beta readers:

Joan Swan: If online therapy were a job, then you'd be the Bill Gates of the profession. Thank you for getting me through so many rough times with my writing and my personal life. I love your spunk and fire; it inspires me. (And scares me a little.) I love that friendships can occur miles and miles away through type strokes. Readers: You need to read Intimate Enemies, Fever, and Blaze, by none other than the spitfire, Joan Swan.

Michael Burhans: You truly are "the bomb," even though it's an outdated phrase. It fits you literally and figuratively. At a time when my mind was jumbled with hardships and heartache, your stories kept me entertained and sane. I could never thank you enough. Thank you for being a part of this journey for me.

Fred LeBaron: You are such a kind, sweet, and generous man. The entire cyber world adores you. Thank you for trying so hard to help me and for welcoming me into the writing world.

Denise Tung: Every time I wanted to give up and scrap the entire idea of this book, you held on and wouldn't let me even consider it. Thank you for making me delve deeper into those scary and sad parts of my life. I couldn't have finished this book without your kindness and encouragement.

Lisa Rutledge: You were the first person to ever make me feel like a "real author." You aren't just an "imaginary cyber friend," you're my real friend, always making me laugh and blush. Our conversations brighten many of my humdrum, monotonous days.

Angela McLaurin: I confided in you when I was too afraid to talk about the truth with anyone else. How could anyone hide her secrets from her Fairy Godmother? Thank you for always being so supportive and sincere, and especially for accepting my inability to use a computer in the 21st Century.

Janessa Osborne: You were my first fan, the first stranger to sing my praises. You made me feel important, when all I really felt was defeated. Thank you for lifting my spirits and advertising my work. I hope you enjoyed your namesake in the book.

Kim Box Person: You are my funny other half, the person who makes me guffaw at the craziest things. You are kind and helpful, but feisty and strong—wonderfully contrasting qualities. I'm lucky to be on your "good side." Don't let people destroy your spark, because you ignite joy in so many people.

Debra Celentano: You are a Godsend. To think that I had a whim, an idea to do a blog tour, and then WHAM, you took it all over and spent so much time and energy organizing an event for someone you'd never even met. You are truly a remarkably generous and thoughtful person. Thank you for all that you do and have done.

Jamie Marochino-Blair: James, you inspired me to write, to finally put the thoughts on paper. Thank you for being so passionate about writing. Without that passion, I wouldn't have done what I set out to do. Our friendship, our memories, and our stories will always remain close to my heart. True friendship can withstand anything.

The wonderful people of my first-ever Blog Tour:

**Please stop by these blogs and peruse the remarkable work and dedication these people put into promoting the work of many authors.

Kimberly Bower from Book Reader Chronicles

Michael Burhans from Vandeervecken Veritas

Debra Celentano from The Book Enthusiast

Kristi Foote Fortenberry from Reading Is My Time Out

Brandi Franklin from Sugar and Spice Book Reviews

Amber Gleisner from Up All Night Blog

Melissa Hardy from Smardy Pants Book Blog

Jessica Hurtado from The Little Black Book Blog

Holly Malgieri from I Love Indie Books

Becca Manuel from Becca the Bibliophile

Lyndsay Matteo from The Little Black Book Blog

Abby McCarthy from Up All Night Book Blog

Angela McLaurin from The Indie Bookshelf

Becky Nickulus from Reality Bites! Let's Get Lost!

Kim Box Person from Stick Girl Book Reviews

Dawn Robinson from Up All Night Book Blog

Lisa Rutledge from The Indie Bookshelf

Sandi from Book Boyfriend Reviews

Ashley Smith from Smardy Pants Book Blog

Stephanie from The Boyfriend Bookmark

Denise Tung from Flirty and Dirty Book Blog

Sherri Zee from Reading DelightZ

I would like to thank John Michael Montgomery, All-4-One, Atlantic Records, and the actual writers of the song, "I Can Love You Like That," Steve Diamond, Maribeth Derry, and Jennifer Kimball. The song truly helped me find my "Prince Charming." I couldn't be happier about taking "a chance" on him and spending the rest of my life with him.

The song "I Can Love You Like That" was published by: Windswept Pacific Entertainment Company d.b.a. Full Keel Music Company, Second Wave Music, Friends and Angels Music, Diamond Cuts Music & Criterion Music Corporation. All Rights Reserved

All-4-One. "I Can Love You Like That." And the Music Speaks. Atlantic Records. 17 June

1995. CD.

https://itunes.apple.com/us/album/i-can-love-you-like-that-single/id606041314

Montgomery, John-Michael. "I Can Love You Like That." John Michael Montgomery. Atlantic

Records. 27 Feb. 1995. CD

https://itunes.apple.com/us/album/love-songs/id434129654

A Final Heartfelt Notice of Gratitude:

Thank you to everyone who took a chance on an unknown "Indie" author and chose to read this book. Without avid readers, writers couldn't be heard and felt; their words would be lost. Thank you for reading my words and connecting to my life. I appreciate you.

Made in the USA
Lexington, KY
05 August 2013